"Good, I caught you in time. Another interesting development just came up."

Nature felt a coldness settle in. She sipped the warm coffee in an attempt to rid herself of it. It didn't help. She knew what he was going to say, what he was going to ask.

"The family became worried when they didn't hear from her and broke into her place. She wasn't inside. Her purse, ID, and car were there, but not her." Spangle cupped his hands around his coffee. He stared at it, avoiding eye contact. "We need to know if the same man was involved." He finally met her eyes, "Would you mind?"

The coldness knotted. She wanted to say no. She wanted to go home. Usually between sessions, she had some downtime, time to clear her thoughts, her nerves. Since coming to Florida, none had been allowed.

With a heavy heart, she said, "Of course."

Spangles face brightened. "Great. I'll give you the directions. Officer Stack of the Daytona area will meet you. I'll let him know you're coming." He rose to his feet, pulled a piece of paper out of his back pocket, and slid it across the table. "Thanks, Mrs. Kranderson. I'll keep in touch." He left before she could say anything else, or change her mind.

Web sat expressionless. He picked up the cup before him and sipped at its contents. A couple of sips later, he said, "I guess that means we aren't going home yet."

Nature pushed her plate away. She no longer had an appetite. "No...I guess not."

Web pulled the plate toward him. He picked up the fork and stabbed at a pile of eggs. With his mouth full, he repeated, "No...I guess not."

Praise for *Innocence Taken*

"Just wanted to let you know that the dust bunnies, laundry, and the kids' dinner will just have to wait...and it's all your fault. *Innocence Taken* is just too gripping to put down!!! Bravo!"

-Diane, author of *His Black Dahlia*
Featured in Horrotica, Issue 2

"*Innocence Taken* is one of the most compelling books I have ever read. This book grabbed me from the first page to the last; I couldn't put it down. An exciting, thrilling, and at the same time, horrifying ride through the mind of a clairvoyant and the madman that she is connecting to."

-Sharon, a reader

"*Innocence Taken* is very graphic and detailed, and so might not be suitable for every reader. It is a fascinating suspenseful novel though, and the characterization of Nature, the psychic protagonist, is well done and intriguing. The secondary characters are delineated well also. Many readers will be drawn to this story, despite the detailed violence of the murders. Janet Durbin will be an author to watch."

-Frost, reviewer from TwoLipsReviews.com

Readers should be forewarned that this book contains a considerable amount of graphic sexual violence. *Innocence Taken* is a seriously chilling tale following the chase for a sadistic killer that involves a lot of emotions, a great deal of suspense, and a heavy dose of horror.

...Nature and Web make for an appealing couple and their budding romance acts as a shining light in this often dark thriller.

-Jen H., reviewer from FallenAngelReviews.com

Innocence Taken

Janet Durbin

Whimsical Publications, LLC

Florida

Innocence Taken is a work of fiction. Names, characters, and incidents are the products of the author's imagination and are either fictitious or are used fictitiously. Any resemblance to actual events or persons, living or dead, is entirely coincidental.

If you purchased this book without a cover, you should be aware that this book may have been stolen property and reported as "unsold and destroyed" to the publisher. In such case, neither the publisher nor the author has received payment for this "stripped book."

To purchase the authorized electronic edition of *Innocence Taken*, visit Forbidden Publications.
www.forbiddenpublications.com

NOTE: This book contains graphic sexual content, violence and adult language. Intended for a mature audience.

Published in the United States by
Whimsical Publications, LLC
Florida

ISBN-10: 0-9787738-0-2
ISBN-13: 978-0-9787738-0-9

Printed in the United States of America

Acknowledgements

As I watched the evening news, a commentator talked about the latest kidnapping. Her body was tragically found a few days later. The more I watched, the more I pondered. The more I pondered, the more the idea for this book haunted me. I was going to have to write it. I knew it would be different, controversial, because of the graphic sexual material it contained. To calm the inner demons, and to test my skills as a writer, I wrote it anyway. It involved a serial killer.

Sharon and Gordon were my guinea pigs. They agreed to read the book as I wrote it and helped me stay on track. Month after month, they read, sometimes having to wait a couple of weeks before I got the next installment to them. How they did it, I'll never know. One thing is for certain, I'll be forever in their debt because they did.

Michele was another reader who kept me on track. After she finished going over it, she threw a tantrum about the ending. She said it didn't fit. I had to admit, she was right, it didn't. A rewrite solved the problem and all the parties involved were much happier with the results. Sadly, Michele passed away recently. I will miss her dearly.

Karen, the wonderful editor that she is, helped keep my grammar and punctuation as it should be. Without her astute eye for details, a few words would still be misspelled, and a stray sentence here and there would still be incorrect. Much thanks.

To all the people I work with, I thank each and every one of you for putting up with me rant about the book (along with all the other books I wrote.) Your feedback encouraged me to continue.

And to the readers. Without you, this book would merely be words on paper and nothing more. Thank you.

Also by
Janet Durbin

Journey of Twins Series
AFTER
*STOLEN**

*Coming soon from Whimsical Publications, LLC

———

Check out Forbidden Publications for the official electronic edition of *Innocence Taken*.

Available now at

www.forbiddenpublications.com

(Thanks, Rene, for giving the book a home in the electronic world. Furthermore, thank your staff: ML Benton for the ebook cover design and Ann King for the editing.)

Now,

without further ado,

I present...

the story.

ONE

A twig snapped behind her. Rew spun around. Before her was a man: dark and deadly. He moved with a speed she had never expected. A hand large enough to do the job well covered her mouth. An arm wrapped itself around her slender body, pinning it against the muscular chest. The man was naked.

She felt his hard penis against her clothed groin and whimpered. She knew what came next and dreaded it with every fiber of her body. She was a virgin.

The shortcut through the woods was the fastest way home from the high school. Not many kids used it because it was rumored to be haunted. Rew was late and knew her mother would be mad, so she took the chance. Now she regretted it horribly.

A thick piece of silver tape appeared in the man's hand. Where it came from, she had no idea. He placed it over her mouth, preventing her from calling for help. He forced her to move toward a clump of trees. Rope, hidden on one of the branches, hung there like a snake all coiled up. He yanked it free and tied it around her wrists and ankles. Her breasts were groped before she felt herself lifted off the ground and placed over a strong shoulder. She wanted to kick, to fight, to get away before he did the unspeakable. By the time the shock of the situation wore off, it was too late.

Deeper into the thick woods they went. Rew wished she would die. She did not want to go through this; she wanted to be home safe in her mother's arms. Her ass was pointing forward, her skirt hiked up to expose her white underwear. Her mother told her col-

ored underwear was a sign of loose girls. She knew without a doubt, she was going to find out what loose girls went through. His fingers squeezed her ass tight, keeping her from falling off. They burned into her flesh like hot embers left over from a fire.

The man stepped through an opening in the trees; a rundown shack stood before him. He walked up to the door, swung it open and closed it tight behind him. He moved to a cot with a thin stained mattress on it and laid her gently down. Light shined through tiny slits near the roof. There were two on each wall. They were the only source of light.

Rew saw his manhood was still erect. A smile creased his handsome face. If she had met him on the street, she would have thought him cute. Now all she saw was a very bad man.

The man straddled her, pinning her legs with his weight, and removed the rope from her ankles. He pulled one toward the wall and secured it with a strap hanging there. He pulled the other toward a post standing near the end of the cot. It was bolted to the floor to prevent it from moving. Her legs were now spread, making her most private area visible.

Rew started to cry as he spread her arms apart in the same fashion. She was completely defenseless, something she had never experienced in her eighteen years of life. She cried harder as he pulled a small shiny knife out from under the mattress and showed it to her. She tried to plead with him, but the tape made the words come out garbled. He simply smiled again.

The knife came toward her shirt. The sound of slicing echoed throughout the small room as it cut the fabric with ease. A white lace bra appeared. She had seen it in a store and, on a whim, bought it. It was one of the few things she had kept from her mother.

The man set the knife on the floor and pulled the shirt open. Her creamy flesh matched the whiteness of the bra. Her health class had taught her about skin cancer, and she avoided the sun when possible. He stroked the points of her breasts and watched as the nipples responded to his touch.

Rew tried to twist away; the straps around her extremities prevented it. He cupped each breast and pressed down on the nipples with his thumbs. She took in a breath through her nose, unable to stop herself. One hand slipped under the material and

caressed the smooth skin. The man had made no sound since Rew first saw him. It made the situation even eerier.

The knife appeared again; the bra flew open in response. Her erect nipples pointed upward. He bent over and ran his tongue over the tips before circling around, lightly touching the surrounding skin. Her breasts were a full C cup. She felt his teeth rake over the ends and heard sucking sounds as each was lifted with his mouth. She tried to blank out the noise and the feelings running through her body, without success.

She remembered feeling like this when Jared had tried to make a move on her. It was the day they had skipped school to go to the beach. Hidden in the dunes, he touched her in the same manner, rubbed her nipples just like now, and sucked on them just like now. Only she had not allowed him to go further. She was saving herself for the man of her dreams. He had been angry with her for weeks. She only laughed, playing him for a fool.

Now, she was the fool. She was the one being played with. A sharp pain brought her attention back to the present. The man pinched her nipples between his fingers, giving them a little twist. The tears flowed again. His other hand stroked his penis up and down. She saw a white milky liquid on the tip. His eyes were closed, his head tilted ever so slightly backwards. The smile looked like it was permanently etched on his face.

The hand on her breast moved to her stomach. The pointer finger circled her bellybutton several times before moving to the waistband of her skirt. She expected him to pull the elastic band down. Instead, he moved the pleated material upward, toward her stomach. The hand on his penis continued to stroke up and down.

She felt a finger run over the front of her underwear, toward her crotch. A wave of pleasure shook her body. She felt betrayed. She felt vulnerable. She felt she wanted more. The man flashed his exquisite white teeth in response to her shiver. He knew he had her now.

He felt the split of her lips and rubbed his finger over it. Moisture covered the fabric. He was thrilled at the prospects of entering this land of pleasure, but held back. He had to make sure this one was ready. The others had withered away when he pierced them; he wanted this flower to continue to bloom.

He pulled the waistband of her underwear down and felt the

patch of chestnut hair growing there. It was full, not shaven. He twirled it around his fingers, enjoying the silkiness of it. The girl looked frightened, but there was a hunger in her eyes, as well. A hunger he felt in his own body. He spread her vaginal lips and felt for the clitoris located at the center. The moment he touched it, she responded. He felt elated.

Rew felt his finger rub her clitoris. She sucked in a breath. A rush of tingling flowed through her body. It was not a bad feeling. It made her skin feel electrified. She wanted this man to stop, to allow her to go free, but at the same time, wanted him to touch her more and more. She did not know how to respond to the feelings. Was she a bad girl for liking it, or had her mother been wrong, wrong for telling her to wait.

She looked into his black eyes. They were wild with hunger. She felt afraid then, afraid of him touching her, of him hurting her, of him killing her. She closed her eyes and relaxed, waiting for him to rape her and let her go afterwards, hopefully.

The man felt the change in her body. It enraged him. Just when he thought he was so close to finding the One, she failed him. He would make her pay. He would bring back the eagerness for his touch.

He pulled his hand away and stood. Rew opened her eyes and watched as he moved to a box resting in a corner. It was the kind used to store wood, though no fireplace was anywhere in the room. He removed the lid and reached inside. She saw a metal rod with a tapered end emerge. The rod was nine inches in length and had the same circumference as a flashlight. He held it high for her to see, enjoying the look of horror emanating from her eyes. To him, the eyes were the voices of the soul. What one saw there was how the person was.

Returning to her side, he kneeled close to her crotch. He put the rod against the lips of her vagina and watched as she squirmed against it, trying to get away from it. He rubbed it gently, making her lips spread apart. The fabric of her underwear stretched to conform to her shape. He felt the warmth coming off her body. He knew her mind was fighting what her body wanted.

For the first time since he abducted her, he spoke. "Embrace the feeling. Give in to your body and enjoy."

Rew shook her head back and forth quickly. Tears welled in

the corners of her eyes. She pleaded with them for him to stop. He only shrugged his shoulders. A feeling of infinite sadness emanated from him.

"I had hoped you would be the One. But alas...."

Dread raced through her body with those words. She wondered what she had to do to become the 'one' he spoke of. If it would help her stay alive, she would do it. The man brought the rod to his lips. He kissed it then ran his tongue over the smooth surface like a kid with an ice cream cone. When he looked at Rew, she saw the full depth of his craziness.

The man brought the rod down onto the girl's thighs, hard. She flinched as far as the restraints would let her and screamed. The sound caused the man to hit her again and again until she stopped. She collapsed from the beating into a whimpering mess. The man reached up and stroked her hair, smoothing it back into place. He bent over and licked the tears from her face before kissing her taped mouth and straightening up.

Rew could not believe this was happening to her. What had she done to deserve this? Was it because she said no to Jared? Was this payment for being a bitch to him?

The light shining inside faded with the passing of time. Rew knew her parents would be looking for her. Would they look for her on her usual route? Would they even think of the path? Probably not. She never took the path. The only other time she had was on a dare. That was how she discovered the shorter way.

She felt rubbing between her legs and saw the rod was back. She watched as the man pulled her panties away from her skin and slid it against her. It was cold, almost as cold as the one holding it. She whimpered, but did not make any other sound. She did not want another beating.

The man left the rod resting where it was and picked up the knife again. He cut the panties off and dropped them on her chest, right under her chin. He wanted her to smell her love juices. The underwear was saturated with them. He returned the knife to the floor and picked up the rod once more. With one hand, he rubbed the tuft of hair covering the vagina. With the other, he guided the rod between her lips. He teased her, inserting just the tapered end then pulling it out again. He did this several times.

Rew wanted to tell the man to stop, to tell him she was a vir-

gin. At the same time, she wanted to tell him to continue. She was confused by the mixed emotions. The thought of being raped horrified her, especially after the recent beating. The more he teased her, though, the more her body tingled.

But, it was wrong, wasn't it? That's what she was always told. Now, with these sensations running through her, she wasn't so sure. When the tip was inserted, she tried to squeeze herself shut. It didn't work; it was too smooth. The brief contact made the tingling intensify. She moaned.

The man pulled the rod away and slammed it deep her vagina. This was something she had not expected. The smooth tapered end slid inside. It hurt. She tried to fight, to shift her hips away, but all it did was drive the rod deeper inside. He pulled it out and shoved it in again, regardless of the pain it caused. She tried not to, but couldn't help it. She screamed.

Suddenly, the man was lying on top of her. She opened her eyes and shut them immediately. Hands moved all over her body. He kissed her face and neck. She felt his hardness against her bruised legs. He had left the rod inside. His leg pushed against it, causing the pain to increase. She arched her back. It only drove her breasts into his chest, rubbing her tender nipples on his.

She felt his fingers spread the lips of her vagina. The metal rod disappeared, landing with a dull thud on the wooden floor next to the cot. The man's penis touched her. He shoved the swollen member in. She grabbed the straps holding her, bucked and screamed, and tried to get him off, to no avail. It only made him thrust harder. His grunting echoed in her brain. She wondered how she could have ever thought this man was cute.

He rode her like an untamed horse. With each thrust, he felt the pleasure of conquest filling him. She met his urgency with one of her own. That was what he imagined when she lifted her hips in response to his downward pushes. The screams went unnoticed. The room and everything inside vanished. All he knew was the pleasure. When his loins screamed at him for more, he pulled out of her vagina, lifted her legs as far as the restraints would go and drove into her anus. The tightness of her ass caused his penis to swell larger than before.

The girl under him was limp. She had passed out. The man, still lost in his pleasure, had not noticed. He shoved and grinded

his hips, and shoved some more. Her tight ass was his entire focus. An intense pain shot through his loins, causing him to arch back, teeth clenched tight. His penis released its juices deep inside. Wave after wave rippled through him. He thrust several more times before collapsing on the girl, panting.

He knew now she was special. She may not be the One, but she would do until he found her. No other had caused so much pleasure. He decided to take her far away. He knew the parents would be hunting for her and he did not want to give her back. She was his now.

Reluctantly, he pulled his penis out. A milky fluid ran out. It mixed in with the blood that ran from her vagina. The blood of a virgin no more. He smiled. The thought of him being her first love made him eager for more. He decided he had time. Stroking himself into a frenzy, he entered her anus and pumped, then pulled out and entered her swollen vagina again. He grunted with each thrust, bit at her nipples, and groaned when he ejaculated.

She was awake when he looked at her. Pain and fear filled her eyes. They were dry. He pulled out. She winched at the action. He smiled. Getting off her, he licked her vagina clean of the blood and semen covering it.

"You're mine now."

Her eyes remained dry. She tried not to think about what had just happened. She tried to think of green fields filled with flowers and butterflies flittering in the sky. She almost succeeded in disappearing into her fantasy world, but the man brought her back with his words and tongue.

A tingling sensation mingled with the pain. She felt ashamed. She had just been brutally raped and sodomized, yet her body craved for more of his touch. Now she knew she was lost. She would never be the same little mommy's girl again. The rest of the kids would look at her as if she was tainted. Maybe the boys would do the same thing as this man. That thought finally brought the tears to her eyes.

The man kissed her eyes and stroked her skin. She felt it burn where he touched. She pulled against her restraints, but they remained tight. He kept touching her, caressing her breasts, watching her.

After a minute, he rose to his feet, went to the same box he

had retrieved the rod from and pulled out some clothes. He dressed in a pair of jeans and a pullover shirt that hugged his muscular frame before returning to her. He loosened the restraints holding her feet and tied them together. He did the same to her arms. She gave him no resistance.

He lifted her off the cot and carried her outside. Dusk covered the area. The cool air caressed her bare skin, causing goose bumps to rise. She shivered. The man felt it and held her closer against his body.

A plain brown Ford van was parked among the trees, hidden from the road a short distance away. The color matched the bark of the surrounding trees. He opened the back, placed her inside, and gently touched her cheek before shutting the door. Rew felt her stomach roll. The man was taking her away. Her family would never find her now. She lay there, wondering what was going to happen next.

The man returned to the building. He picked up Rew's clothes, tossed them and the rod onto the cot, and rolled the thin mattress into a log. He used another bit of rope from the box to secure it. After spanning the interior a final time to make sure nothing else remained, he carried the mattress to the van and placed it next to the girl. He walked to the driver's door and got in. The keys dangled in the ignition. With a twist to the right, the engine purred to life. Pulling the gearshift into drive, he pressed on the gas pedal and rolled down the dirt road toward the main blacktop. Once there, he turned north.

All he thought about during the hours that passed was the wonderful feeling he had with the girl. She was his, now and forever. He would be able to have that feeling whenever he wanted it. That thought made him horny. He unzipped his pants and pulled his penis out. It was as hard as a rock. He looked down and admired it. The veins stuck out. He ran his fingers over them, feeling the tinge of excitement running through his body. It made him want her now.

Pulling off the road, he parked the van behind a clump of bushes, hiding it from any passersby. The darkness of night helped. He separated the curtain dividing the back from the front and saw the girl watching him. Fear filled her eyes. He loved those eyes. They were as blue as the sky. He crawled across the carpet

covering the floor. She cowered from him; he pulled her close. Flipping her over on her belly, he admired her ass.

It was small and tight. None of the cottage cheese look touched its beauty. He grabbed it with both hands and squeezed. The girl whimpered. He slapped her butt and held a finger to his lips. She quieted. Again, he swelled with pride. Feeling the ache of want, he lifted her hips and spread her ass. He played with the opening for her anus, circling it with first his finger, then his penis.

Rew watched with horror as the man came at her with his engorged penis. He lifted her hips and played with her ass. She felt it touch her anus and go in. She pulled her knees toward her belly, trying to reduce the pain. It didn't help. She remained silent throughout the assault, even though she wanted to scream.

The man leaned across her back and pushed harder. His breath huffed with each thrust. He reached for one of her breasts and milked it like he would a cow. She grunted when he pushed. He was elated. She was a gem. He wanted more. He straightened up on his knees, held on to her hips, and shoved his penis as far inside as it would go. He pulled out then shoved deep inside again. This time, she could not hold back. She screamed.

The man leaned over and slapped her across her head. He hit her over and over until she quieted down. He returned to his knees and pumped her unmercifully. When he had enough of her ass, he moved to her vagina. He wanted to drive his penis into her mouth, but knew it wasn't time for that yet. It would come. Thinking about her wet tongue moving over him caused his need to rise to an even higher level.

He pulled out and flipped her onto her back. He hoisted her knees up onto her belly and drove his aching penis home. The girl arched her head back, though she did not let out a sound. He lay on her legs and rocked his hips in an urgency driven wild by the need to release. Moments later, he did.

Rew felt every inch of her used body. Her anus throbbed and her vagina felt like it was ripped wide open. Yet, her body tingled with need. She felt the man's penis inside her, growing smaller. She felt him slide it out and get up. She felt the emptiness below, with its desire to be filled again. Did these feelings make her a slut? Her mind said yes, but her body said no. Which one would win? She had a feeling it was going to be her body.

The man slid into the driver seat and started the van. He backed out and returned to the road. The headlights shined bright in the dark. He knew he had about three more hours ahead of him before he reached his destination. He had a cabin in the Monongahela National Forest. When he built it from the local timber, alone, he took great steps to make sure no one knew of its existence.

No roads led to the cabin, he had to walk to it. It took just over five hours. A particularly dense patch of forest hid the van from eyes flying overhead, or those driving past on the road whenever he left it behind.

He had thought of everything.

Other girls were brought to it. He soon discovered they were not the One and buried them in the forest when he was through with them.

The sign he looked for lit up in the headlights in the predicted amount of time. It was a clump of holly bushes, the only one in the area. He had planted them himself. Turning the van, he disappeared through the opening and onto an overgrown trail wide enough for the vehicle. He drove slowly because the ground was soft and he did not want to leave tire tracks. He knew the tall grass would return to its upright position as soon as daylight hit it. He had watched on previous visits to make sure.

About three miles into the trees, a particularly thick growth of hanging vines seemed to block the way. He got out of the van and moved toward it. Pulling back a bunch, he exposed the hiding spot for the van. He returned, drove inside and replaced the vines. Dried dead leaves hung on the branches. It was late in the year. Snow would soon cover everything. He liked the snow. It was beautiful to watch as it fell. It made everything pure.

The man moved to the back of the van and opened the doors. The girl was asleep. She was beautiful, like the snow. His jeans shifted over the growing penis. He knew he had to wait, though. It would be daylight soon and he wanted to be as close to the cabin as possible before then. He was tired.

He grabbed a knapsack resting near the mattress and positioned it onto his back. It held a few things to hold him over until he reached the cabin. His cabin was well supplied, especially before winter when the snow made travel virtually impossible. He

wrapped a blanket around the girl before picking her up. She mumbled in her sleep, resting her head on his chest. He kissed her softly on the top of her head.

Turning to the northwest, he started through the undergrowth. It was not particularly thick this time of year. In spring, he would have a harder time of it because of the thorn bushes.

Halfway to his destination, he stopped to rest. He put the now awake girl down on the ground and removed the pack. Opening it, he pulled out a granola bar. It was his favorite kind: maple brown sugar. She looked at the bar with longing.

The man saw the look and pulled out a second. He handed it to her. She hesitated, but quickly grabbed it when he started to pull it back. Both enjoyed the maple taste, lightly doused with brown sugar. When they finished, the man took her wrapper and placed it inside the pack. It made him angry when he saw litter carelessly tossed into the forest. Positioning the knapsack on his back again, he replaced the tape and picked up the girl. He moved through the darkness with familiar ease.

Rew wondered how the man knew where he was walking. It was so dark. She was lucky to see the nose in front of her face. She knew she would be lost in a second if he decided to leave her alone. She snuggled deeper into the blanket, feeling the warmth of the man next to it. Her hands and feet were cold. The rope was not tight, but it prevented her from moving, thus reducing circulation.

The light of the coming dawn glowed red on the tops of the trees when the cabin came into view. Rew inhaled deep through her nose. It was rustic, yet beautiful in the way it blended with its surrounding. She felt a pang in her heart. She knew this was her new home, and that she would probably not see the ones she loved again. Her family and the police would never find her here.

The man remained silent. The only time she remembered him talking was the few sentences he said at the shed. The silence was deafening. She wanted to cry out, to have her voice echo into the valley below, but also knew it would mean the end of her short life. She wanted to live, to experience the joys of marriage, to see her parents again. To do that, she remained as quiet as a mouse.

The man hoisted her higher in his arms. He kissed her on the

forehead, and said, "Welcome home."

His voice had a deep, almost harmonizing quality to it. It broke the silence. Birds started singing, heralding the coming of dawn. Squirrels started barking out their calls, inviting others to join in. Both rustled through the branches, playing.

He moved to the door of the cabin and stepped inside.

Rew noticed it was as rustic as the outside. The furniture was carved out of wood, as was the bed. The bed stood in a corner near a fireplace. A metal ledge hung inside the fireplace for cooking. Electricity wasn't here. Neither was running water. Pans hung from hooks near the fireplace. Area rugs covered the floor for warmth and comfort. The place was neat and tidy.

The man carried Rew to the bed and laid her down. He opened the blanket to expose her tied limbs. That was when she noticed the straps. They were similar to the ones in the shack, but different. The ones for her arms were above, attached to the frame of the bed. The ones for her legs hung from the ceiling.

The man loosened her hands first. She squirmed; he slapped her across her face. The world swam in a sea of swirling mist as he pulled her arms up, securing them. He undid her legs and spread them apart, hanging them in the straps. Her swollen red vagina appeared; it excited him. He wanted to play with it, yet knew he had to warm the place up first. He couldn't let this wonderful gem get sick. That would end all his pleasure.

Reluctantly moving from her, he put some wood into the fireplace. He lit it with a match and watched as the fire grew. He grew along with it. The more he thought of the exposed vagina, the more he grew. As the warmth of the fire filled the room, he removed his clothes. He preferred to be naked. The feeling of synthetic material on his skin, even ones made of 100% cotton, made him cringe with displeasure. He preferred to be pleased.

Rew saw the clothes drop to the floor and watched as the man's penis jumped to attention. She stared as he began to stroke the member with love. Her body started to betray her. It wanted that member inside, even as her mind screamed no.

The man saw her. He refused to acknowledge her need and continued to play with his penis. He guided his fingers up one side of the shaft before moving down the other side. He spread his knees and played with his balls. Then he grabbed the shaft and

jerked the skin upward. He was not circumcised and the skin bunched up on the tip. He pulled it back down, exposing the moisture oozing from the tip.

He leaned his head back, watching the girl's reactions. She was becoming his more and more. He would bide his time, tease her, break down her defenses, her spirit, and forever turn her away from the life she knew. He liked to take them young. When they were young, he could mold them; make them more to his liking. When they no longer pleased him, when they no longer held a purpose, he disposed of them easily. That was his specialty. That was what he liked to do; and he was good at it.

He refused to take the tape off her mouth. He had tried that with the other girls; all they did was whine. He did not want to disturb the beautiful sounds of nature with that kind of pollution. That was also the reason he remained silent.

He turned to face the girl. She looked away for a brief moment then focused her eyes on his again. He could tell she was fascinated.

Rew's mind screamed no. She did not want this man to take her again. He hurt without care. Her body screamed yes, and her body was winning.

Her hips lifted off the bed and her nipples became peaks of hard flesh. She wished her hands were free so she could relieve the increasing pressure to her groin. She had never had sex before, but she knew how to please herself. She had played with her clitoris enough to make her cum. She always took a shower afterwards to hide the evidence from her mother.

The man smiled at her and jerked his penis harder. His face turned red from the effort. She thought he was going to explode right there. He moaned when a wad of sperm shot out, arching in her direction, landing on the wooden floor. It missed the carpet. With a sigh, he moved to a shelf, removed a cloth and walked to the mess. He squatted down with his legs open wide, displaying himself to her as he cleaned it up.

Rew watched in disbelief as his penis started to rise again. She wondered if he ever stayed down. The picture that popped into her head in response made her giggle. The man looked at her. He smiled, rose to his feet, and walked to the fire. He threw the cloth in. She giggled harder as his penis bounced while he walked. He

paused, stared into the dancing flames, before facing her. He moved toward her. Her eyes were glued on the bouncing penis. She failed to see the angry set of his jaw.

The man decided now was the time to fulfill another pleasure he wanted to do. He hated it when the girls laughed at him. He had to teach this one a lesson.

Ripping the tape off, he grabbed her lower jaw and lifted her face toward him, forcing her mouth open. She was so shocked by the maneuver she forgot to cry out. He crammed his penis between her soft lips. She tried to close her mouth. He yanked on her hair. When he felt her teeth rake the skin, he reached back and twisted her nipple. Each time she tried something unpleasant, he gave her pain. She finally relented and kept her mouth open.

He guided his penis in and out, causing her tongue to brush against the skin. He shoved it in, feeling the back of her throat. She gagged. He pulled it out. He slowly repeated the process. It felt as good as he had imagined. He indicated for her to suck on the penis. When she was too slow, he slapped her. Her lips closed; he felt the pressure of suction. It made him throb. He pulled his penis from her mouth and guided his balls close. She licked one, then the other. It sent a wave of pleasure up his spine. He shivered.

He stuck his penis back in her mouth. She sucked on it without him needing to indicate. He was in heaven. Only one thing would make this moment the best. He ejaculated in her mouth, deep in her throat. He held her head so she could not pull away, causing her to cough and sputter. He was pleased with her response. Maybe now she would not laugh. If she did, he knew he would enjoy punishing her again. He pulled his limp penis out of her mouth. Before she could spit out his cum, he replaced the tape over her lips.

The man could tell by the look in her eyes that she had never tasted cum before. Again, he was pleased to be her first. Stroking himself, he moved to her vagina. He kneeled on the end of the bed and sniffed her. The smell was sweet. He flicked out his tongue and tasted the juices within. They were as sweet as the girl. He knew they would be. Moving his tongue, he teased the little red clitoris. She raised her hips in response.

It was too easy for him. He liked pain and the reactions

caused by it. He got off the bed and moved to the shelf where some cloths sat. He grabbed some forceps resting next to them and brought them back to the bed. The girl looked first at the forceps, then at him. He saw fear. He was glad.

He opened the first one and pinched it on the right nipple. The girl drew in a breath. He opened the next one and pinched it to the left nipple. Again, the girl drew in a breath. No sound came from her other than the breath. When he clamped the third one to her clitoris, she finally screamed. He smiled.

He remembered the rod forgotten in the van. It was okay; he had another one, a bigger one; one acquired specifically for his pleasure. He left the girl crying and returned to the shelf. He removed the rod and held it high. The steel shaft glinted in the firelight. This rod made his huge shaft look small in comparison. He saw her eyes widen, tears streaming from their corners. He felt himself rise. This was exciting.

Rew pulled against her restraints. It only caused her legs to swing back and forth. The motion made his penis stand taller. It excited him. She tried to plead through the tape, but the only sound that came out was a garbled noise. The man frowned. He came at her, the rod held in front of him. She pleaded louder. The noise infuriated him. She knew it was useless, but she couldn't stop, she was so scared.

The man grabbed one of her swinging legs and yanked it away from the other. His fingers sank into the thigh, leaving deep indentations, causing the tender area there to announce its displeasure at such treatment. He was so angry. It was the first time she had seen him like this. She tried to shift her hips off to the side. The man held them in place, slipping his body between her wildly gyrating legs. He rammed the rod into her vagina, withdrew it, and rammed it in again. She couldn't believe the pain. It felt like she was being torn apart from the inside. She wanted to die at that moment. The man shoved and shoved and shoved.

Suddenly she felt lips on her face. The rod was gone. The forceps were gone. The tape was gone She had no idea when he had stopped. She felt his tongue caress hers. She responded. The touch was so soft. All she wanted to do was make this man happy. If she made him happy, he would not hurt her. She felt him cup her breasts. She felt him lay on top of her. She felt his

manhood enter her vagina. And she smiled. The nagging emptiness was filled.

The man moved his tongue over hers; she kissed him back.
He felt her resistance give. He rejoiced. He had her; she was his.
He entered her with the kind of joy he rarely felt and released his
seed with a roar of pleasure. He fell asleep on top of her, his penis
still inside her, his face nestled in the crook of her neck.

When the man woke, the sun was setting. He untied the girl
and took her outside to pee. She was naked. He liked her that
way. When they returned, he put a collar around her slim neck,
securing it with a small lock. A leather leash hooked on to the end
of the bed. He did not restrain her limbs. He knew her spirit was
gone. It showed in her eyes. He motioned with his hand what
would happen if she tried to escape. She nodded her head in re-
signed understanding. He was glad she knew how to be silent. It
allowed him to enjoy her better.

He put one of the pots on the fire and filled it with water from
a barrel. A drain ran into the wall from the outside and allowed
the water to run in. When the barrel was full, he blocked the
drain, preventing it from working. He put dried vegetables, along
with dried meat in the pot. The smell of stew filled the cabin.

Rew sat on the bed, watching. The collar chaffed. She knew
better than to touch it. That would infuriate the man and he would
hurt her. She wanted him to touch her in a kind manner, not the
hurtful way. She wondered what was so bad about sex that had
her mother telling her such lies about waiting to do it. She loved
the way her vagina seemed to ripple like a wave from the ocean
with his softer touches.

The man stood by the pot, stirring the contents. Rew rose to
her feet and moved next to him; the leash trailed behind her. She
reached around his waist and gently stroked his penis. It rose to
her touch. The man put the wooden spoon aside, reached for her,
and pulled her tight against his body. He grabbed her ass and
lifted her up. She wrapped her legs around him. He inserted his
penis into her and pumped her up and down. She arched her back
and met his thrust with her own.

Without any warning, he pulled out and threw her to the floor.
His lip curled. He grabbed the spoon and beat her already bruised
thighs, adding red whelps to the dark spots. She hissed in pain.

She didn't know what she had done to make him so mad.

A voice filled the room; it was his. "You will never take sex unless it is given. You will beg for it first—beg for it on your knees!"

He emphasized each word with a smack of the spoon. He wanted her to remember who the master was. He did not want her to take liberties that were not hers to take. Finally, he calmed. The spoon slowed.

She was crying silently. She took the punishment. She had been bad. All she wanted was to make him happy. Now he was mad.

The man held the spoon in front of his mouth and licked and sucked on it before returning it to the stew. He removed the stew from the fire. Rew cringed. She didn't know what he would do next. He extended a hand and helped her to her feet. She felt him lift her off the floor and indicated for her to wrap her slim legs around him. She did. He carried her to the bed and laid her on her back. She was surprised to see his penis limp.

He straddled her head and positioned his ass in front of her face. He indicated for her to lick his anus. She complied. She was afraid of what would happen if she didn't. Her pink tongue ran around his dark opening. He grabbed his cheeks and spread them. At the same time, he motioned for her to insert it inside. She pushed her tongue against the opening. The taste was retched. She wanted to stop, to throw up. The fear of punishment kept her going. She pushed it inside.

The man made her keep her tongue straight. He wiggled his ass and made her push it in and out. He enjoyed testing her devotion, her willingness to follow commands. It made him feel powerful, in complete control.

Rew closed her eyes. Her heart pounded. She was excited and grossed out at the same time. The things she was forced to do should never have been done by anyone barely eighteen years of age. Yet, here she was, doing things only whispered about during sleepovers with her girlfriends.

The man got off her. He ran his tongue over her face. She opened her mouth, accepting it. He moved down her body. She shivered. His tongue found her clitoris. She shivered again. He lay on her and pierced her mouth with his now hard penis. She

sucked it willingly. He pushed his member deep into her throat. She reached up and grabbed his ass, shoving it in deeper. He smiled and fulfilled her dreams. He pumped her so hard he couldn't believe she handled it. When he came in her mouth, she lapped it up like a puppy.

Time passed. Minutes became hours. Hours became days. Days became weeks. Rew ceased thinking about her parents, her home, her friends. The man was the only person important now, the man and his magical touch. The pain no longer mattered. The touch always followed. Sometimes she begged for the pain so she could get the touch.

The man tugged on the leash, pulling the girl outside. He did not need it anymore, but he liked it anyway. It gave him power. Lately, the girl was becoming too complacent. He bored easily. She didn't fight; she didn't show fear; she didn't pull against her restraints when he used them. She didn't even please him like before. It took the others months to reach this point. She achieved it in weeks. He knew she was not the One from the start, but had hoped she would change. The hope vanished with her lack of resistance.

He led her deeper into the woods. She had no idea what he was doing. She didn't know he was taking her to meet the other girls. He stopped when he reached a place covered with leaves, dropped from the trees draped over the clearing. He pulled the girl in front. He turned her toward him and kissed her sweet lips. He knew he would miss this one, but it was time to move on. He needed to be excited again.

He laid her back on the dry leaves and fondled her breasts. She smiled at the pleasure caused by his touch. She shifted her hips, opening her knees to allow him access. He reached down and played with the hair. His penis hardened. He knew this would be their last time together. He mounted her gently, something he had never done before. She groaned with joy. He moved in and out slowly, savoring their last dance.

Rew sensed something was wrong. He was too gentle. She opened her eyes. She looked into the black depths of his. They were void of feeling, of life, of anything. She kissed them, trying to bring something to them. They remained void. That was when she felt his hands on her throat. She arched her head back, think-

ing he wanted to feel the skin there. They tightened.

Breathing became difficult. She fought. She thrashed. She hit. The hands squeezed tighter. He pushed his penis in deeper. He closed his eyes and held on to her throat tight while he pumped her. She gasped for air. The man lost all sense of time. With a cry of release, he filled her with his sperm. When he opened his eyes, he saw hers staring into nothing. He never knew exactly when she had died.

Getting off her, he knelt at her side. He felt the tears as they rolled down his cheeks and dropped to his thighs. He silently cried—cried for the girl, cried for his loss, but most of all, he cried for the next girl he would meet.

When he finished, he buried the girl in a hole dug especially for her. She lay next to seven others. All of them his past loves. All of them young girls. All of them missed dearly by their families.

He covered the soil with some of the dry leaves, to hide the girl's resting place, and to keep her warm. He felt she deserved that much for all the pleasure she had given him. He returned to the cabin, dressed in the same clothes he had worn a little over three weeks ago, packed the knapsack, and pulled the door closed behind him when he left. A plain brown van pulled onto the blacktop five hours later.

TWO

Nature Kranderson bolted upright from her resting position. She looked around, bewildered. It took her a minute to get her bearings and to realize she was not in a wooded area, but in her own study. Four people sat in the room with her. Two were the people who hired her, one was her secretary and trusted friend, the last was the local sheriff. The sheriff did not look pleased.

"How long was I out?"

Sheriff Westerly retorted, "Six hours."

"Did you see anything?"

The woman asking the questions was in her mid forties. Gray streaks ran through her brunette hair. She was beautiful. The man next to her remained silent. He must have been a body builder at one time. His upper half still rippled but his waist rolled over his pants, probably from too much beer on football nights with the boys.

"Liz—give her a minute. She just came around."

"Our daughter may not have a minute!"

"It's been almost four weeks."

"What difference does that make? She could still be alive. I know she is—I can feel it." She stared at her husband, holding the front of his shirt tight in her clenched fists. "I can feel it!"

"Calm down, baby. Getting all upset doesn't make the situation any better."

Nature watched as Mark Mosby, her client, pulled his wife close. He looked at her with pleading eyes. Nature kept her expression blank. She knew what had happened to their daughter.

She had seen it in her vision, her gift, her nightmare. She was psychic.

She did not want to be the one to tell them but knew she must. They needed closure. She gripped the teddy bear tighter against her body. It had been the daughter's favorite toy. Even at eighteen, she still slept with it.

Someone moved toward her. A cup came into sight. A dark brown liquid filled it. The smell of tea wafted to her nose. She looked up to see her secretary standing there.

"Thought you might need this after such a long session."

Nature took the cup, wrapped her stiff fingers around it, and sipped at the contents. It helped warm the cold emptiness she felt inside.

"You always know how to take care of me, don't you."

"I have to. You don't seem to know how to do it by yourself. You need my help."

She tipped the cup at the young woman, "Help appreciated."

Sandy Nemoy was in her late twenties. She could have been a super model in New York, with her long slender legs, dynamite body, and flowing mane of blonde hair, but chose to be a secretary instead. Nature had asked her about it once. Sandy only laughed. She said she did not want to be stereotypical. Besides, she liked being a secretary, especially to Nature. It was exciting.

Sandy returned to her chair, crossed one leg over the other, and waited. Nature saw Sheriff Westerly eye those legs with appreciation. He noticed Nature looking at him and looked away, blushing. He may be in his fifties, but he was still a man after all.

The Mosbys shifted on the couch, bringing her attention back to the current situation. They were waiting for some word on their lost daughter. She had not come home from school and a missing person report was filed with the local police. Search parties combed the neighborhood and surrounding areas. They found nothing. After just over two weeks without any leads, the police moved on to other more pressing cases. Cases involving murder, shootings, and death. Unwilling to follow their example, they hounded the officers, friends, neighbors, and anyone they met, without results. That was why they were here now. Nature was their last option, their last hope.

Sandy had taken the desperate call on Wednesday. By Friday,

they had the money for the fee and the airfare to come to Montana. They were staying in the guest cottage on her property. It was the only building Nature refused to enter. The feelings emanating from it were too much for her to handle. Too much sadness, too much anger, too much loss.

"Mrs. Kranderson...?" Mark Mosby said.

Nature drew in a deep breath. She held it only a second before releasing it, the built up tension eased somewhat by it. This was going to be rough. She set the cup of tea on the end table.

"Mr. Mosby...Mrs. Mosby..." She nodded her head to each. "I'm afraid your daughter is dead."

"What?" Mrs. Mosby said, her face covered with disbelief, "That can't be right. I can feel her...she's alive....she's alive I tell you."

Mr. Mosby stared at Nature. He asked in a voice barely above a whisper, "Are you sure?"

"Yes." Nature looked at the wife, "She was late and didn't want you to get mad at her. She was taken from a shortcut through the woods behind the school."

Mrs. Mosby's mouth hung open, her hands clenched into fists before it, hiding it.

"Did you see who took her? Did she know who the person was?" Mr. Mosby asked all the questions. His wife was too stunned to speak.

"I couldn't see him. I could only feel the evil within. And your daughter didn't know him."

"Do you know where she is?"

"She's close to some mountains, somewhere not frequented by many, somewhere in a forest. I don't know which ones. But I do sense they are toward the east."

Mrs. Mosby bolted from her seat. She ran to Nature before anyone could stop her and grabbed her exposed hand. She pleaded, "You're wrong! You're wrong! Rew can't be dead, she can't be!"

Nature jerked her hand back, trying to free it. Liz wrapped her other hand around the wrist. Desperation and despair made the woman's grip strong, too strong to break free. She felt the woman's sorrow, her grief. She experienced her pain as if a knife had been plunged into her back. Her breath came in ragged

gasps. Her heart felt like it was going to rip out of her chest. Her world disappeared into a shroud of blackness. She started to scream.

"Liz! Let go, NOW!"

Suddenly, the hands holding her were gone, but the feeling from them remained. Nature heard Mr. Mosby shouting. She heard Sheriff Westerly, Web, shouting. She heard Mrs. Mosby crying. She kept her eyes closed tight. She was trying to work the horrible feelings out. Her body had had too much and wanted to withdraw. Finally, after what felt like an eternity, she was able to bring herself under control.

"Don't ever do that again," Westerly growled.

"She couldn't help it. Rew is our only child; the news hit her hard. How would you feel if you just found out your daughter was dead."

Nature opened her eyes and surveyed the situation. Sheriff Westerly stood in front of the couple, hands resting on his gun belt, legs shoulder-width apart, a cold look locked onto his face. The Mosby's were seated again. Mr. Mosby had his wife wrapped in his arms, rocking her back and forth. Sandy had remained in her chair. She knew the man with the gun could handle things. She had witnessed this kind of outburst before.

"I'm so sorry," Nature started, "You can stay in the cottage as long as you need." She rose to her feet, wobbled a bit, then grabbed onto the furniture as she made her way to the double doors that led to the rest of the house.

Sandy rose to her feet but did not help. Nature would not want it. She was very independent and would be insulted by the gesture. Westerly remained in front of the Mosby's, preventing them from following. The rest of the house was off-limits to outsiders.

Nature made it to the hall, shut the doors behind her, and leaned back against them. She closed her eyes, fighting back the tears. Every nerve was raw. She needed a scalding hot shower. She turned and stumbled her way up the stairs to the second floor.

Her house was located in a remote section of Montana. She had it specially built then sterilized before moving in. It could be considered a mansion to some, but she considered it home. She owned 375 acres, allowing her to be away from the crowds and

the unwanted feelings associated with them. Her property skirted the Charles M. Russell National Wildlife Refuge.

At the top of the stairs, a hall went right and left. To the right were the bedrooms. There were two in use at present. One was hers; Sandy used the other. Sandy was the only other person allowed on this level. The woman had great control over her emotions. Moreover, she touched as little as possible. To the left were more rooms, including her office. She loved her office. It was full of soft oversized chairs and a huge mahogany desk littered with her papers.

She turned right. Upon entering her room, she locked the door. She did not want company right now. Peeling off her clothes as she walked, she made her way to the large bathroom. A modern walk-in shower stood in one corner, an old-fashioned porcelain tub next to it. She slid the door open to the shower, reached in, and turned the hot water knob several times. The water rushed out. Gradually she mixed the cold water in, but only enough to keep from scalding her when she entered.

She moved to the built-in radio/CD player located on the wall near the doorway. Pushing play, the blaring sounds of *Nightwish* echoed throughout the room. She turned up the volume and returned to the shower. The infectious beat of an electric guitar caused her to dance into the hot water. It hit her skin, turning it beet red. Losing herself to the words about wishing to have an angel, she opened her arms wide and leaned back under the spray. She began to spin slowly. The hot water helped wash away the feelings of the girl, her mother, the tension.

Classical instruments blended with the sounds of heavy metal. She could feel the bass vibrate through the floor, the wall, her soul. As the music intensified, so did her dancing. She threw her mid length brown hair forward then back, like a major rocker during a concert. When the music changed to a melancholy one about a trail of tears, her own tears followed suit. The feelings washed away rushed back with a vengeance. She slid down the wet wall and curled into a small ball. The water pounded her. It hit and hit and hit, just like the rod. She threw her head back and screamed.

Downstairs, Sandy sat in her chair. She watched as the Sheriff and the Mosby's left through the side door. She heard the music

start afterwards. She felt the bass as it vibrated through the house. Now, sipping her coffee, she sat quietly as she listened to the screams.

The first time had scared the shit out of her. She remembered running up the stairs and pounding on the locked bedroom door. The screams continued. Sandy yelled to be let in. Nothing happened. The sound of running water continued. Just when she was about to smash the doorknob off with a hammer she had found in the garage, the door opened.

Nature stood in the entranceway, a towel wrapped around her medium sized body, wet hair in her face, dripping on the hardwood floor. Sandy had rushed forward to comfort her, but the other woman backed away. She remembered being asked to wait downstairs in the study. She remembered going down and waiting for what seemed like hours. When Nature appeared, she was calm. Her hair was still wet, but it lay neatly across her shoulders and back. The redness from crying was gone.

They talked far into the night about what was expected and how Sandy could help. Seven years and many sessions later, Sandy continued to do what was expected and help the woman who was not only her boss, but her friend as well.

Sandy decided to have a bite to eat. She had not eaten since before the session with the Mosbys and her stomach was growling at her. She left the study, making her way to the kitchen. All the fixings for a ham and cheese sandwich littered the counter when Nature finally joined her.

"Feeling better?" Sandy asked as she continued to spread the mayonnaise across the slice of whole wheat bread.

"Some."

"That was a bad one, wasn't it?"

A moments silence filled the room.

"Yes."

The word was barely above a whisper. Sandy paused, the knife hovering above the bread. She looked at her boss. Nature's head leaned forward, preventing the secretary from seeing her face. She knew this case was different. She also knew Nature would talk about it when she was ready. The knife resumed its back and forth motion. Upon completion, she handed the sandwich to Nature.

"I'm not hungry."

"If you don't eat, I'll have to shove a garden hose down your nose and feed you that way—you want that?"

Nature smiled. It was the only smile so far today. "Sandy, you are a blessing in disguise."

She took the offered sandwich and bit into it. The savory taste of smoked ham and yellow American cheese teased her palate. It was wonderful. It was the first thing she had eaten all day. Sandy plopped an open bag of Lays potato chips on the counter between them, pulled one out, and tossed it into her mouth.

"Why does something that's supposed to be so bad for you have to taste so heavenly?"

"It's only bad if you eat too much." Nature grabbed a chip and tossed it in with her partially chewed bite of sandwich. She smiled and her cheeks puffed out like a chipmunk.

Sandy couldn't help it; she did the same thing. Both women enjoyed playing with their food. It helped pass the time and made sure one was fed, regardless of whether she wanted to eat or not. When the sandwiches were gone, Sandy hooked her arm in Nature's, making sure not to touch any exposed skin, and led her into the other study.

This room had a fireplace, a set of comfortable easy chairs with high backs, and shelves loaded with books. Sandy led her boss to the chair on the right side of the warm fire before taking up residence in the left one. An oval shaped table sat between the chairs. A warmer with a pot of hot water sat in the middle. Nature grabbed the pot and poured each a cup of tea. She sipped at the liquid, dreading the next step—the debriefment of the session.

Sandy picked up a notepad and pen. She waited for Nature to start. Finally, after a few sips and a deep breath, Nature replayed what she had experienced.

"The man who took Rew is a mystery. For some reason—he stays cloaked."

Sandy raised an eyebrow. This was something never experienced before. The person was always able to be identified.

"Even when he stood naked, his face remained shrouded." Nature's shoulder shook. "The things he did to that girl... I wouldn't wish those horrors on my worst enemy."

Her secretary remained silent. She scribbled what Nature said,

making a log for the police, and for themselves. Nature did not seem to notice the action beside her. She was lost in the world of her vision.

"He drove a brown van. It was plain, nothing written on it, no bumper stickers, nothing that would help to identify it. The license plate was just as shrouded. It was as if he could block the important parts." Nature stared at the fire. "He enjoyed hurting her; in fact, he took great pleasure in it. He kept her naked, ready for use whenever his need filled him. And, he didn't just hurt her physically; he beat her down mentally too. When he became bored with her, when she no longer fought back, he took her to meet the others."

Those words caused the pen in Sandy's hand to hover above the paper. She looked at Nature, wanting to ask questions. She held back. She knew the answer would come soon enough.

"He's done this before. He's killed other young girls after becoming bored with them, after using them in unspeakable ways. Rew was the eighth one. Seven other graves were close to her. Seven..."

Nature looked at her secretary, "Oh Sandy...this man is a mass murderer...and he enjoys it. It makes him horny. He likes to turn young girls into his sex slaves." She leaned forward in her chair. "We have to tell Web. Can you call him and tell him to come back? Please?"

Sandy placed the pad on the table and rose to her feet. She moved quickly to the phone, picked up the handset, and dialed the sheriff's number. She did not need to look it up; she knew it by heart. They had worked together many times, on many cases. As she looked back toward Nature, she could see the cup in her hands shake, almost spilling its contents. She knew then that this was going to be like no other case they had dealt with before.

Sandy opened the door after the second knock. Sheriff Westerly stood there. He was an imposing sight with his broad shoulders, cowboy hat, muscular features, and blonde hair. She understood why Nature liked him; he presented himself well. Being sheriff had made him confident without being cocky.

"Good to see you again Web. What's it been...a few hours?"

"Funny."

"You coming in or just going to decorate the entrance."

Sandy moved to one side, allowing Web to enter. She led him to the same study where the session was held earlier that day. Nature sat on the couch, her legs pulled up. She looked worried.

"You have something." It was a statement, not a question.

"Yes."

"Is it bad?"

"I think you had better sit."

Web moved to the chair across from her. He put his hat on the table next to it and leaned forward, resting his elbows on his thighs. Sandy sat on the loveseat located next to the couch. She had the notepad in her hand.

"Web, this man that killed the Mosby girl...," Nature paused. "He's killed before. She wasn't his first."

"Are you positive?" Web knew it was a stupid question. He felt like he had to ask it though.

"I saw the place where he buried her. He talked about others." Nature got to her feet and started pacing. She stopped in front of him and said, "He's an evil one. He enjoys humiliating these girls then destroying them when he gets bored with them."

Web leaned back and blew out a breath. "This is bad. Wonder why nothing about this has come up?"

"I don't know. Maybe he takes them from different areas. Maybe no one has made the connection. There are so many missing persons." Nature sat down again.

"Were you able to see his face? Can you ID the killer?"

"No. It was shrouded. It never came in." Her shoulders sagged in defeat.

"I'll start researching and get back with you." Sheriff Westerly rose to his feet and moved to the exit. "Let me know if you get anything else." He left the room. The women heard the front door close.

Sandy glanced at Nature. "Glad he's with us. Remember how hard it was in the beginning?"

"It was rough trying to get law enforcement to listen. That big case involving the kidnapped son of a Senator made them stop and think." Nature snickered at the memory. "That was the first time we met Web."

"Yup. He's wonderful now. It wasn't always like that, though. I remember when he was a complete ass." Sandy made a face. "He thought he was god's gift to law enforcement. I guess mixing with us has brought him back to earth."

"We helped him solve a lot of cases and made him look good. He appreciates that."

"I think he appreciates you. I see the way he looks at you."

"Sandy!"

"Don't Sandy me...you like him too. Admit it. Why don't you just ask him out?"

Nature's mouth hung open in surprise. She snapped it shut. "Because we work with him. Going out would only complicate things."

"Only in your mind." Sandy rose to her feet. "I'm going to bed. I'll see you in the morning." She faced Nature before leaving, she added, "Brad's been gone for 14 years. It's time for you to live again."

Nature watched as her friend left. She remained on the couch, thinking. Maybe she was right, maybe it would do her good to go out again. But, should she ask Web? She wasn't sure about that. He was a working partner. To her mind that was more important than dating him. Besides, if something went wrong, she'd have to find another source for law enforcement. No, dating Web was out of the question.

Her thoughts wandered to the last night she and her husband Brad were together. They had made love on the couch, like teenagers, even though they were in their early thirties. Afterwards, Brad decided to drive to the local hamburger joint. Before he could reach it, a man driving an eighteen-wheeler was cut off. He lost control of the rig and it rolled onto their car, killing Brad instantly. When the police arrived and gave her the news, Nature fell into a deep state of shock.

Her post cognitive ability had developed after puberty but it had not always worked properly. The sudden death of her husband caused her ability to peak. She felt the feelings of each person who touched her. Their suffering, their happiness, their boredom...everything. She did not mind it at first. It was interesting to see how others lived their lives. After a while, being touched became a torture. The news people learned about her after she

helped with the Senator's kidnapping case. They hounded her. They made her life a bigger hell than the psychic ability did.

The police started coming to her for help, something that grated on the nerves of some, like Web. They brought items of the victims for her to touch, to find them. She was successful each time. Some were alive, able to be reunited with their families. Others were too late. Her reputation grew and families started contacting her on their own. She hired Sandy when she could no longer deal with the calls, with the people, and retain her sanity. She needed downtime.

Her husband's life insurance was substantial due to good planning. It allowed her to buy the land, build her house, and have plenty of money left over to live on. The most sophisticated security system guarded the surrounding area, helping to keep the news people away. They left her alone now.

Nature stretched out on the couch. She did not want to go upstairs. She was tired. Pulling the throw off the back, she covered herself. She fluffed one of the pillows and curled onto her side. That night she dreamed of her late husband...and of Sheriff Westerly.

Three

The man drove the van around the block. He had traveled far from the cabin. He was in Florida. Girls of all ages roamed the beach. They flaunted their bodies to the guys, teasing them, making them want them. He wanted them. He wanted one in particular. She walked with her friends. Her tiny bright yellow bathing suit barely covered her full breasts and crotch. Her long sun bleached hair covered her tanned back like a mane. He wanted to run his fingers through it.

He had driven to Florida because it was still warm here and the girls would still be wearing their bikinis. It also allowed him to shed most of his own clothes. He hated clothes. They made his skin crawl.

The blonde strolled past his van. She did not notice the man sitting behind the wheel. He felt his penis rise as he looked in his rear view mirror and watched her ass swing back and forth with each step. He could feel her breasts under his hands. He could feel his cock pushing into her tight ass. He knew she would be his. He would find a way to take her.

He watched as she went into a little café and came out with a drink. He watched as she separated from her friends and started toward a small red convertible sports car. He watched as she got in, started the ignition, then pulled out of the parking spot and drove down the road. Starting his own engine, he followed. He stayed a safe distance behind so she would not notice him. He wanted her. He wanted her badly, but would bide his time. This one might be the One. He hoped so.

He watched as she drove to another beach and parked. She got out and walked onto the sand, strutting her stuff in the tiny suit she wore the entire time. The man could tell this one liked to show off. He could tell he was going to have many pleasures with this one. He smiled at the thought. Parking the van, he got out and walked in the same direction, a discreet distance behind her.

He walked with a grace displayed only by one confident with himself. A tight black swimsuit showed off much of his muscular tanned body. Reflective sunglasses hid his black eyes. Girls watched him as he walked past. They admired his body and good looks. He smiled but remained focused on his intended love. He splashed at the waves with his bare feet.

The blonde was unaware of the man. She was too busy teasing a group of gawking boys. He angled his direction toward her while acting as if he was looking at the ocean and bumped into her, almost knocking her over.

"What the..."

"Oh...I'm sorry," he stammered. "I didn't see you. I was enjoying the waves."

Mindy was going to give this guy a severe tongue-lashing until she saw how handsome he was. She decided to have a little fun instead.

"Wow."

"Excuse me?"

"I might."

"Might what?"

"Excuse you."

"Oh. Like I said, sorry for bumping into you." The man started to move past her but she put a hand on his chest, stopping him.

"Not so fast. I think you owe me dinner."

The man played innocent, "I do?"

"Yea. You almost knocked me on my ass and I deserve dinner as payment for harm almost rendered." Mindy ran her fingers around his upper body as she circled him, admiring the view he gave from every angle.

"You do, huh? What if I decide not to? What then?" The man smiled to soften his words.

"Then I sue you for damages." Mindy brought her hand down and bumped into his penis.

"Then I guess I'll just have to take you to dinner. Where do you want to go? I don't know the area."

"How about my place? It's quiet and close."

"Your place it is. Lead the way."

The man wrapped his arm around her waist and they walked back to the parking area. Mindy was thrilled this one had accepted. Most of the men here were old or immature. She could tell this one was different. She led him to her car and gave him a peck on the lips.

"Follow me lover boy."

She got in, pulled out of the parking spot, and waited. The man returned to his van. He drove behind her to a small bungalow located about four blocks from the beach. He parked next to her. She got out, went up to him, grabbed his hand, and pulled him toward the one with the number five on it.

"This is my place. It's small, but cozy. That, plus it's not attached to another building...gives us privacy." She smiled slyly.

The man saw the distance between the buildings. He noticed their shutters were closed, blocking out the intense rays of light. He heard the hum of air conditioning and knew the windows were shut. He smiled.

Mindy guided him to the door. Letting go of his hand, she bent over, making sure her ass faced the man standing next to her, taunting him, and reached under a flowerpot sitting next to the small patio. A key lay hidden there. She unlocked the door and returned the key to its hiding spot. She pushed the door open wide.

"Come on it."

The man walked past her, the side of his arm brushed against one of her breasts, and entered. The room was filled with white wicker furniture like the kind found at a Pier One store. He saw the tiny kitchen, no dining room table, because there wasn't any place to put one, and the quaint little twin bed tucked into the corner.

"What do you think?" Mindy had come up behind him, standing close enough to whisper in his ear.

He took off his sunglasses, "It's cozy alright."

Before he could say another word, Mindy came around and planted her lips on his. Her hands groped his body. He grabbed

her arms, pulling them away. He did not want to seem too easy.

"Hey...what do you think you're doing?"

"I want you." Her voice was husky with need.

"You're too young for me."

"I'm legal. I'm eighteen."

"Eighteen huh...prove it. I'm not going to jail because of some under aged little girl." He could see she was getting mad. Good. He liked a little fight with his sex.

Mindy pouted before she moved to a small table next to the bed. He followed. She picked up a purse and flipped it open. She pulled out her driver's license and held it up for him to see.

"Okay, you're eighteen."

The man did not have to pretend any longer. He grabbed her, smothering her with his lips. One hand moved to her breast while the other reached for the string to her top. He pulled the cord and the tiny bit of material fell to the floor. He bent over and sucked on her perky tits. Mindy didn't wait. She tossed the license and wallet aside and reached for his crotch. It was bulging.

"My, what a big cock you have," she whispered.

"The better to dip you with, my dear."

He hesitated, wanting to ask her something. She sensed it. "What do you want?"

"Do you like it kinky?"

"Depends on how kinky." She had tried a lot at her young age.

"Like ropes and tape."

"Oh...you're one of those kinds."

The man's heart almost stopped. He thought she was going to kick him out and that was not going to happen. He had her here, alone, and she was not getting away.

"There's some in the top drawer in the kitchen. I'll wait for you here. Mindy crawled onto the bed and lay down, arching her back so her breasts stood out. She smiled. She had been right about this one. He was different. She was in for an exciting time.

The man walked to the kitchen. Mindy watched his ass, liking what she saw. She couldn't wait to get her hands on it again. He found the items and returned. She allowed him to tie her arms to the bedpost then one of her legs. He left the other loose. She blew him a kiss before he put the tape across her lips. She had no idea how deadly this man was. She was about to find out.

He fondled each breast lovingly before moving toward her crotch. She wiggled, enjoying his gentle touch. He ran his hand under the material and slid a finger between her vaginal lips. She lifted her hips, forcing the finger to go inside her. She gyrated her hips, moaned, and pleaded with her eyes for him to take her. He became infuriated with her. He was supposed to lead the sex...not her.

Getting to his feet, he returned to the small kitchen. From one of the drawers, he grabbed a small wire whisk he had spotted earlier. He returned to the bed and pulled the rest of her swimsuit out of the way. He spread her legs. Mindy watched him, curious. When she realized what he was going to do with the whisk, she tried to fight. He backhanded her. She fought harder. He backhanded her again. He was smiling. He was loving this.

The man guided the whisk toward her vagina. Gripping it tight, he worked the many wire strands inside. Mindy screamed. She tried to kick the man. He pinned her leg against his body. He twisted the whisk back and forth like a mixer. He watched the lips curl one way then the other. He felt his penis stiffen. Leaving the whisk where it was, he got to his feet and removed his swimsuit. His penis touched his abdomen. He stroked it.

Mindy's eyes were filled with pain and fear. She saw the maniac look in his and knew she was in trouble. She wondered about her decision to allow this man to tie her up. She wondered about her loose behavior. Now she knew she was going to pay for it. She whimpered when he lifted her free leg, exposing her ass.

He fingered it, shoved the whisk deeper into her vagina, and fingered her ass again. He grabbed his penis and guided it toward her. Mindy tried to shift her hips away, but the tied leg wouldn't allow it. He was holding the other tight against his body. He shoved his swollen member in without the aid of lubricant. It hurt. It wasn't like the other times. Those guys had used lubricant.

He squirmed his hips in a circular motion, bumping into the whisk in the process. It shoved in deeper. She cried out. Then she moaned. The feeling running through her body was wonderful. She realized she loved it. He pushed in and out as hard as he could. His entire shaft disappeared into her anus. She arched her back, helping it go in. She gripped the ropes holding her arms and pumped him.

She never realized the tape was gone until his penis was crammed into her mouth. She ran her tongue over it like an ice cream treat, teasing the tip. The man had his eyes closed. He savored every touch. She felt it hit the back of her throat. She arched her head back, taking it all. She felt the whisk twirl again. It hit her clitoris. It excited her.

Suddenly, her mouth was filled with his sweet cum. She felt the shaft ripple as it released its load. She drank every drop, sucking the member until nothing more came out. When he pulled out, she expected him to untie her. He didn't. Instead, he covered her mouth with the tape again. She questioned him with her eyes. He only smiled.

He padded to the kitchen and opened the refrigerator door. He bent over, looked in, and pulled out a can of Pepsi. He was glad it wasn't diet. Popping the pull-tab, he took a long drink. The can was emptied in three swallows. He reached in for another.

Moving to a chair, he sat down, opened his legs and played with himself. He was trying to decide when he was going to sample her again and how he was going to get her to his van unnoticed. He knew he would have to wait until dark. He also knew he was going to enjoy the long drive back to the cabin. He knew this one wasn't the One, but he was going to make the most of her company anyway. As with the others, he would bide his time until he became bored, then hunt again.

Nature sat up on the couch, gasping. She had been dreaming, dreaming about the man, the one who loved to torture. She clutched at her throat. She could still feel his hands there. Sweat covered her brow. Swinging her legs over the side, she got up and went through the dark house to the kitchen. When she opened the door to the refrigerator, the bright light caused her to turn away and blink several times. She fumbled inside, grabbed a bottled water, then pushed the door shut, blocking out the painful light. She twisted the cap and took a long drink. The cold moisture wet her parched throat. She pulled out a stool from the breakfast bar and sat down. She moved the bottle to her forehead. It helped reduce the heat coming off it as well.

What was it about this case that bothered her? None of the

others had even crossed her mind. Why was this one different?

"Couldn't sleep either?"

The sound of Sandy's voice nearly caused her to jump out of her skin. Nature turned to see her secretary leaning against the doorframe, wrapped in an oversized white terrycloth robe, her arms crossed before her.

"Don't DO that. You nearly caused me to have a heart attack. Out in the middle of nowhere...that would not be good."

Ignoring the comment, Sandy went to the fridge, grabbed another bottle of water, and moved to the other barstool next to Nature. She took a drink before setting it on the counter. Reaching over, she flicked on a small florescent light over the bar. It was shielded, preventing the glow from hurting their eyes.

"I heard you calling out. I listened for a while. When the noise stopped, I knew you were awake. That's when I heard the stool slide across the floor. I decided to join you."

Nature gripped the bottle with both hands. She stared at it. "I was dreaming about that girl...and the man who did those terrible things. I tried to see him, but he remained hidden. He laughed at me."

"I heard you moan several times."

Nature remained silent. She remembered the touch of the man's hands on the girl. She remembered the touch of her husband on her own body. She missed it. She missed him. She was lonely.

"What do you think it means?" Sandy asked.

"I think it means I want to solve this case so badly that I'm subconsciously responding to it. I want him caught before he kills again."

"You'll catch him."

"But will it be in time?"

"I hope so."

Both women sat at the bar talking until the rays of daylight broke over the horizon. They moved to the patio located to the rear of the house and watched in silence as the reddish orange colors of sunrise washed over everything. When they became too tired to stay awake, they went inside. Both retired to their rooms in an attempt to get more sleep. The sun was high in the sky before either did.

Heavy pounding on the front door jerked them awake. Nature heard Sandy's bare feet trot down the stairs. The front door opened and voices echoed in the hall. Silence followed. Then she heard footsteps come up the stairs. She sat up as Sandy entered. Her look was blank.

"Sheriff Westerly is downstairs. He's not alone. Another man is with him. I think he's another cop."

"What happened?"

"I don't know. They wouldn't say."

"Take them into the study. I'll be down in a few."

Nature threw the covers back. She walked to the dresser, pulled out a comfortable long sleeved pullover shirt and put it on. Jeans hung on hangers in the closet. She grabbed a dark pair and put them on. Once dressed, she went into the bathroom and ran a comb through her hair. She was glad of the fact that she didn't need makeup. To her, it was a bother to put all that stuff on. Satisfied with the look, she went downstairs to meet the men.

Web stood by the side exit, looking out at the many panes of glass. Another man with a cowboy hat hanging from his hands sat on the loveseat. He stood when she entered the room. Nature was thankful that Sandy had not let anyone sit on her preferred spot, the couch. She walked to it and indicated for both men to have a seat before she sat. The stranger returned to his previous position. Web moved to the chair.

""Web...what brings you here?"

The sheriff looked first at her, then at the other man. When he spoke, her heart fell. "There's been another kidnapping."

"When?"

"Two days ago."

"Where?"

"Florida." He turned to the man on the loveseat, "This is Officer Spangle. He's from the Orlando area."

"Brevard County, ma'am."

His voice was soft, but it carried across the room. Nature liked the sound of it.

"A girl disappeared. The family found her gone and searched but couldn't find anything. They called us. However, like them, we found nothing. I remembered reading about you and was hoping you'd come help us locate her."

"Are you sure she didn't run away?" Nature asked.

"No ma'am, she didn't. She loved her family, they're a close lot."

She looked at Web, "Do you think this is tied in with the other case?"

"It might be. That's why I brought Spangle here."

"I see."

Sandy came into the room and stood behind Nature. The older woman looked over her shoulder at her and smiled. She turned back to the officers. "I'll come—but under certain circumstances. First I want Sheriff Westerly to go with me." Sandy started to speak but Nature held up a hand. "Sandy...I want you to stay here. If I need information, I want you to be the one to look it up."

"But Nature..."

"Sandy, you're the only one I trust, the only one I allow to stay here. Please follow my request."

"Okay...but I don't like it." Sandy showed her displeasure with her stance. This was the first time they had not traveled together, and she didn't like it, not one bit.

"Second, I need as few people there as possible. And third, I need something that was special to the girl, something not touched by half the county."

"You got it...all of it." Officer Spangle stood. "When do we leave?"

"You will fly back as soon as possible to get things ready. I will meet you there."

"You're not flying with me?" The man looked surprised.

"She doesn't fly...too many people...too close. They might touch her and that would not be pretty," Sandy said.

"But won't that waste precious time?"

"Not with two of us taking turns at driving."

"I'm not sure if I can be away that long," Web said. "I was elected to be sheriff...not a taxi driver."

"Do you want to catch this killer?" Nature spat at Web. "I think you do. Why else would you bring this man to me?"

"Because I know you can find her," he shouted. Web got out of the chair and moved to the outside door, staring at the open plains beyond. "And because I want her found alive."

Nature looked at Spangle, "I have a camper. I can be on the road in one hour. Web, can I count on you?"

He kept his back to her. After staring out the glass a second longer, he said, "Yea. Can I use your phone? I'll have to make arrangements." He turned around. "And I need to get some clothes."

"I have some. They aren't uniforms, but they'll fit." Nature did not tell him they belonged to her late husband. He didn't need to know.

Sandy took the sheriff to the kitchen. When she returned, she led Officer Spangle to the garage where she told him to wait in the SUV parked there. She would take him to the airport since Westerly would be on the road with Nature.

Upon coming back to the study, she said, "I think leaving me behind is a mistake. We've worked many a case together and I know how you operate."

"Sandy...if this guy finds out about me, I want you out of the way. You're my best friend. I don't want him to focus on you."

"I can handle myself."

"I don't need that kind of distraction—or worry. I want to catch this jackass quickly."

Before Sandy could respond, Sheriff Westerly returned to the room. "Everything's all set. Deputy Frewerson will watch out while I'm gone. I told him I'd be away for about a week on a case." He noticed the tension in the room. "Is everything okay here?"

"It's fine." Nature hugged Sandy close. Sandy didn't say anything. She remained stiff.

Nature left the room and went upstairs to pack. Sandy exited out the side door, heading toward the garage where Deputy Spangle waited. The engine for the SUV roared to life. Westerly heard gravel hit the garage as it flew out from under the spinning tires. The sound faded as the vehicle left the area, taking Spangle back to the airport. Westerly shook his head. He knew this was going to be a long ride. He only hoped it would be worthwhile and a killer found before it was too late for another girl.

Half an hour later, Nature entered the study with a bundle of men's clothes in her arms. Sheriff Westerly halted his pacing and moved to take them from her. She turned away.

"Please don't touch me."

"Just wanted to help. I forgot about the touching thing." He backed off.

Nature set the clothes on the loveseat. "There are some shirts, pants, and socks here. We can get the other things you need on the road." She stepped back, allowing him to come closer.

Westerly picked up a shirt and held it against his body. "Looks like it will fit. Where did you get these things?"

A look of sorrow washed across her face. It was gone a second later. Westerly almost didn't see it, it was erased so quickly. He did not know much about Nature's past. Both she and her secretary did not talk about it. He took the silence as a cue and changed the subject.

"Are we going by way of 94?"

"Yes. We'll take I-94 to I-39 then go south."

"I'll drive first." Westerly folded the shirt and put it on top of the rest. "What can I put these in?"

Nature didn't argue with Web about the driving. She was exhausted from her restless night. She moved into the hall and brought a suitcase through the door. She placed it beside the stack of clothes on the loveseat before stepping away.

"Thanks."

The sheriff kept out a pair of jeans and a stripped button up shirt. "I'm going to change before we leave." He paused and looked at Nature. "You mind stepping out?"

"I'll wait for you in the hall."

Nature closed the door behind her. She knew when she took out Brad's old clothes; it was going to hurt. She did not realize how much until she saw the shirt in front of Web. It brought all her memories back in a rush. She hoped she was not making a mistake by letting the sheriff use them. She was pulling on a pair of soft tan leather gloves when the door opened.

Sheriff Westerly stepped into the hall with his suitcase. He took her breath away. He looked so much like Brad. She turned toward her own suitcase in the hopes of hiding her reaction. Picking it up, she moved toward the front door.

"Let's hit the road."

Westerly gripped the handle of his suitcase tighter and followed Nature. When she didn't lock the door, he paused. "You going to lock up?"

"No one will bother the place."

"You sure about that?"

Nature faced the sheriff. "Sheriff Westerly—do you want to waste time bickering about locking the door—or do you want to get on the road before dark." She spun around on her heels and continued toward the garage.

Westerly frowned. He did not like the idea of leaving the place unsecured. He set the suitcase down, grabbed the door, opened it, turned the lock, and closed it again. He gave the knob a twist to confirm it was locked before picking up the suitcase and moving toward the garage. Nature was already in the cab, in the passenger seat. The camper was one of those with a truck front and a camper back. He went to the back and put the luggage inside. Returning to the front, he got in the driver's seat.

"Happy?"

"Quite—you?" Westerly responded, a smile covering his face.

Nature looked out the window without responding. Web turned the ignition key and started down the same road Sandy took earlier. He drove toward the town of Jordan where they would get on I-94 East. Silence filled the camper as the miles disappeared behind them.

Four

Mindy felt each and every bump the van drove over. She had been in the back of the van since last night. The man driving had taken her from her home in Florida and now she had no idea where she was. Her arms were tied behind her. They had fallen asleep some time ago. Each of her legs hung from a rope secured to the roof. They swayed with the movement, causing the rug under her to rub her bare skin raw.

The rest of her felt just as raw. The man had used her in every way conceivable. She had never had so much sex before. Now she hated it, hated it with every fiber of her body. When she found a way to hurt him in return, she would.

The van pulled over. She watched the curtain pull back and the man crawl toward her. He moved between her swinging legs, placing an arm on either side of her body. He hadn't spoken during the entire drive for which she was glad. She hated the sound of his voice almost as much as she hated him.

He lowered himself on to her body. She felt him kiss her taped mouth. She felt his hands on her breasts. She felt him spread her ass with his legs. Then she felt his engorged penis brush against her skin. She wondered if this man ever stayed down. He never seemed to be satisfied for long. She waited with a clenched jaw for the inevitable, but it never came. Instead, he got off her and moved toward an object lying partway under a blanket. When he pulled it out, she saw it was a riding crop, one of the kind used by jockeys.

The man watched as the angry glare in the girl's eyes turned

to fear. When he first saw her, he knew she was going to be a pleasure to work on, but he had not realized how much until he saw her level of defiance. He had pulled over more times than he cared to admit to sample her. She was such a joy to ride. Now he wanted to whip this mount into shape.

He brought the whip up and held it high, loving the way she looked at it, then at him. He brought it down across the backs of her legs. By the time he stopped, whelps covered each leg and trickles of blood ran from them. He was as hard as the whip. With a need driven wild by her pain, and her defiance, he shoved the end of it into her anus. She screamed. It met resistance as she squeezed her ass shut. When he attempted to shove it in again, she bent her knees and twisted away.

Her resistance only excited him more. He knelt between her legs and forced them to remain apart. He lifted her ass and brought the anus into sight. The girl was almost bent in half. She shifted her shoulder to one side, causing him to lose his grip. He grabbed the hair covering her vagina and lifted, glaring at her. She remained still. Tears ran from her eyes.

The man guided the whip to her anus again. His body and arm held her legs apart like a vice, preventing her from turning. This time, he crammed the whip into the opening and yanked it back. He did this so many times that his arm grew tired from the effort. Finally, when he could take no more, he fell onto her body and rammed his penis into her vagina.

He rode her like a wild man, his urgency so great. His screams mingled with hers as he twisted and grinded. When he didn't think he could take any more pleasure, he released his sperm deep inside. He collapsed onto the girl's body, his sweat mingling with her tears. He lay there, kissing her face, eyes, and taped mouth. He felt so much pleasure that he could not wait to get her to the cabin. There he would not have to worry about anyone finding her and taking her away.

He left the riding crop in her. He wanted her to remember who was in charge here and what he had done to her during the journey. He had seen the tears flowing from her eyes, but he had also seen the defiance behind them. He was in heaven. He realized now that the last girl had been too easy. This one was a gift, a gift he planned on unwrapping for some time to come.

Putting the van into drive, he merged in with some big trucks rolling on I-95 toward their destinations. He loved the sight of the big rigs with their many lights. They reminded him of his favorite holiday, Christmas. He smiled as he slid behind a small convoy, humming holiday melodies as he drove.

Fast food wrappers covered the dash of the camper as they continued across the states. They were close to Eau Claire, though Nature knew they were not going to make it there tonight. It had been close to noon by the time they left her house. It was just past midnight now. Westerly was tired. He didn't admit it, but she could see it. A sign glowed in the headlights as they drove past. It was one of the green ones that showed how far it was to whatever lay ahead.

"A rest stop is just up the road. Why don't we pull in for a couple of hours? We both need some sleep."

"I can make it a bit farther."

"Web...you're tired. I'm tired. After some rest, we can make it to Atlanta before we have to stop again. Please?"

The last word was the one that sunk in. "Okay...we'll stop for a short time. But not for long. We need to get there before the trail gets cold." He glanced at Nature. She nodded her head in agreement.

Westerly put the right turn light on when the off ramp appeared. He exited from the highway, slowing as they neared to parking area. Pulling into a spot made for larger vehicles, he turned the camper off. The clicking from the cooling engine and the roar of trucks as they passed by were the only things to break the silence that filled the cab.

Nature opened her door and got out. She stretched her tired muscles and said, "There's room for two in the back. I have a bed over the cab if you want to use it."

"I'll stretch out here."

"Are you sure? You'll rest better in the back."

"I'll be fine." Westerly pulled his long legs from under the steering wheel and stretched them out on the recently vacated seat.

"If you change your mind, the offer stands."

The sound of snoring was his response to her words. She saw Westerly's chin was resting on his chest, his arms crossed in front of him. She smiled as she made her way to the back. Returning with a blanket, she draped it onto his sleeping form. He mumbled something in his sleep as he changed positions. She could not make it out. She shrugged her shoulders.

The air was cool once the sun dipped below the horizon. She shivered as she made her way to the back of the camper. Once inside, she moved to a bench seat located behind the table. She transformed the area into a bed and was sleeping soon thereafter.

It seemed as if she had just shut her eyes when a hand shook her awake. She opened them to see Westerly standing there. He had a cup of vending machine coffee in his hand.

"It's strong and black. For machine coffee, it tastes okay."

"What time is it?"

"Almost two in the morning."

"Already?"

"Come on sleepy head. We need to get moving. We have a long way to go." He set the coffee on a counter beside her and exited.

She groaned as she sat up. Every joint ached from sitting too long. Picking up the coffee, she took a sip. It tasted awful. She set it down again. The urge to pee motivated her to get up more than the lousy coffee did. Or Westerly for that matter. Flipping back the covers, she got up and moved to the closet sized bathroom. After completing her mission, she picked up the stuff she referred to as mud and exited the back.

Westerly was leaning against the driver's door. His cowboy hat sat forward on his head, a similar cup of mud was in his hand. She watched as he guided it to his lips, grimaced at the taste, and lowered it again.

"Tastes okay huh? Boy was that an overstatement."

"Hey, what can I say? At least it wakes you up."

"You want me to drive?"

"No."

Web turned around and grabbed the door handle. He opened it and sat down before she could object. Shrugging her shoulder, she moved to the other side and got in.

"You're not one of those chauvinistic types are you?" She

asked as she buckled her seatbelt.

"Not to my knowledge."

"But you won't let me drive."

"Nope."

"Why?"

"Because I was raised to treat women right."

"Even if treating them right means being unfair and chauvinistic?"

"Yes ma'am."

Nature looked out the window. She shook her head at Web's logic. It was nice to be treated like a lady, yet irritating to be treated like an invalid. The engine started. She watched the big rigs parked with their lights on as they drove past. A few seconds later, the camper merged smoothly onto I-94.

Not many vehicles were on the road at this time of night. Nature leaned her head back against the headrest. She wondered about Web. She also wondered about the killer. What would be waiting for her in Florida? What kind of nightmares would she have from this session? Would the kidnapper be the man...or would it be someone else? She hoped the girl was all right.

"What do you know about the girl?"

"Not much," Webb answered. "I know she had just turned eighteen, but that's about all."

"Why did Officer Spangler come to me?"

"Because he heard about your successes and hoped this would be one also. You're pretty much famous among the police community, you know."

"No...I didn't"

Nature did not like the idea of being considered famous. All she wanted to do was help the victims and their families, whether it was by uniting them or helping them find closure for their loss. Silence filled the cab once again as she closed her eyes to think.

She woke with a start some time later, a scream locked in her throat. She did not know how long she had been asleep. The dream was still fresh in her mind. Westerly faced forward, his eyes fixed on the road, his arm resting on the window ledge. Sweat covered her brow. She wiped it off with the sleeve of her shirt then rolled down the window to get some fresh air.

"Where are we?" Light reflected off the road, making it look

like water.

"About three hours out of Nashville." He glanced at her. "Do you have those nightmares often?"

She sat up, unable to look at him. He had seen her vulnerable side. She had forgotten about that when she made her decision to leave Sandy. Now it was exposed.

"Yes." The word was almost lost in the rush of air flowing into the open window.

He frowned. The five o'clock shadow covering his face shifted. His eyes remained glued to the road. Nature was grateful that he did not look at her.

"You hungry?" he asked.

"Starved."

A blue highway sign indicated that a McDonalds was one of the eateries located ahead. Web veered onto the exit ramp. At the stop sign, he turned the camper to the right. A gas station was next to the hamburger place. He pulled into it first.

"I'll place our order. Meet me there."

Westerly nodded his head as he removed the gas cap. Nature strolled to the McDonalds and went inside. Before she moved to the counter, she beelined it for the restroom. She emerged a few minutes later, her bladder empty, her stomach as well.

It was almost eleven o'clock. Lunch was going on, for which she was glad. She wasn't much of a breakfast person. She let several other patrons go ahead of her. She was waiting for Westerly.

The door opened and Westerly entered. He was a striking figure with his hat, boots, and muscular body. Brads clothes looked good on him. Two teen girls sitting in a booth watched as he walked over to Nature. They leaned close and whispered, glancing in his direction several times. He was oblivious. He was looking at the menu.

"You ordered yet?"

"No, I was waiting for you."

Nature smiled. She watched the girls fan themselves as if hot before breaking down into giggles. They continued to watch as he walked across to the counter. He ordered his food, waited for Nature to order hers, then paid for everything. Chivalry was in action again.

While they waited for the food to be delivered, Nature thought about where they were going and what awaited their arrival. The girls, with their innocence, reminded her of Rew. She couldn't help it; they were so like her. A rush of sadness flooded her heart. She had to get outside; she had to get away from the girls; she had to get away from everything.

"I'll be outside."

"You okay?" There was concern in his eyes.

Nature ignored the question. She had to get out now, before she lost control. The gloves on her hands protected her from the feelings of others but they did not help against what was within herself. She shoved the door open and practically ran to the camper. Getting into the passenger side, she leaned her head back and closed her eyes. Her heart was racing, her breath matching its speed.

Westerly opened his door and got in. He set the food down between them, the drink carrying tray next to it. He looked at Nature. She refused to look at him. She had to get herself under control before she did that. If she looked now, she would lose what little grasp she had.

"You going to be okay?" His voice was gentle, soothing.

She nodded her head yes, her eyes remained closed.

He continued to look at her, one arm thrown over the steering wheel. He knew so little about the woman sitting next to him. He knew only about her ability because she had used it to help solve many of his cases. As if sensing his eyes upon her, she opened hers and looked at him. She quickly looked at the floorboard, unable to maintain contact.

"It there anything I can do to help?"

"Nothing."

"Do you want to talk about it?"

"No."

"Nature...I want to help. The one thing I have discovered over the years is that it helps to talk it out."

"Web...please...let it alone for now. I need time."

"Would it help if you called Sandy?"

Nature was forever grateful for those words. They showed that he understood, that he would not demand she talk to him. "No, that's not necessary. I'll be fine." She opened the bag, grabbed

one of the French fries and popped it into her mouth, allowing the end to stick out like an antenna.

The girls were leaving as Westerly backed the camper out of the parking space. They smiled at him before they turned toward the local town. Nature watched them disappear down the sidewalk. She hoped that they would remain safe, that they would grow up to be wonderful mothers and wives, that they would not be another statistic—like Rew.

The miles flew past as they made their way to Florida. Westerly hung his arm out the open window after his meal was finished. Nature wasn't hungry anymore, but ate to keep Web off her back. He was so much like Sandy. Maybe that was why she was drawn to him. Maybe that was the reason she insisted on his being here, instead of Sandy.

"Web, why did you agree to come with me?"

"Because you asked me to."

"Web...really, why?"

He didn't answer immediately. He stared at the road ahead.

"Web?"

"Because I want to see that bastard caught as much as you do. I want to see that son of a bitch castrated and hung for what he did." He looked at Nature. She saw the fire in his eyes. "I want other families to not have to go through what the Mosbys had to go through."

"What if this girl is dead?"

"Then we work harder. We find him before he kills again."

Nature saw him return his gaze to the road ahead. She turned hers forward also. A sign for Savannah showed they were about two hours away from the city. She looked back at Westerly. He was bleary from driving for so long with only short rest breaks in between. She watched as he shook his head to clear it.

"Web, you've been driving for almost 18 hours. Pull over and let me drive. You need to get some sleep."

"I can make it."

"To what? An early death?" She was angry at his stubbornness.

"We have to get there. We have to save the missing girl from that monster."

Everything fell into place. She understood what drove him to

get there in such a reckless manner. "Web...pull over. I'll make sure we get there quickly." She reached over, resting her gloved hand on his shoulder.

He flinched at the touch. He knew she was right, though. He was exhausted. The camper slowed. It pulled off onto the grass. He put it into park once it stopped, got out, and walked to the passenger side. His legs were wobbly. Nature slid across the seat to the driver's side. Westerly got in, crossed his arms and waited.

"Well...we're not going to get there quickly unless you start moving," he snarled.

Nature ignored the harsh words. She knew why they were there. She felt the same way. Checking the side mirrors to make sure it was safe; she put the camper in gear and pulled back onto the highway. They had almost eleven hours before they reached their destination. It would be too late to check in with the police when they arrived. Nature wanted to get there, but, then again, she didn't. She never looked forward to the sessions. They caused her to die a little bit each time, just like the victims. She hoped this time would be different. This time, she hoped the outcome was good. This time, she hoped the girl was found alive and returned to her loving family. Snoring was her only companion during the long hours that followed.

Five

The holly bush came into view. It was just before sunset. The man was tired. He had driven throughout the day, stopping only to sample the girl when his need overwhelmed him. He pulled the van off the blacktop and onto the overgrown drive. He parked it behind the vines, as he had before, with the other girls. He got out and went to the back, opening the doors.

The girl lay on her back, legs hanging spread apart, arms tied behind her back, naked. She glared at him with hatred. He reveled in the look. It made him want her now. He knew he had to wait. He had to get to the cabin. A sense of urgency filled him. He did not know where it came from, or why. All he knew was he had to move.

He crawled in beside her. She moved as far away as her restraints allowed. He reached up and unbuckled one of the restraints, letting the freed leg fall. It landed with a resounding thud. He turned his attention to the other leg. It also fell with a thud. The girl winched with pain. He smiled. He held a finger up, wagging it, indicating she'd better behave when he moved her. She nodded her head slightly.

The man shifted to the back of the van, helped the girl into a sitting position and jumped out. He grabbed her arms and pulled her backwards. When she reached the edge, he lifted her to her feet. Her legs buckled from long periods of inactivity. He held her until he was certain she could stand on her own. She shivered when the cold air hit her bare skin. He wrapped a light blanket over her shoulders. He slammed the doors to the van shut and

pulled the girl to the trail leading up into the mountains. He allowed her to walk in front of him because he was too tired to carry her.

The trail lay invisible in the growing darkness. The girl stumbled several times, forcing him to take the lead after she scraped her leg on a branch. He knew the way. He knew what was in the way. He groped her breasts and crotch before he untied her arms from behind and retied them in front. He wanted her badly. His penis was as hard as the nearby trees. He had to wait. He had to get her to the cabin first, where he could make her his without the chance of interruption.

Three hours into the walk, he decided he couldn't wait any longer. He had to have her. He tugged on her arms, causing her to fall on her hands and knees. Unzipping his jeans, his penis leaped to freedom. He did not wear underwear. Kneeling behind her, he grabbed her hips and shoved his penis deep into her anus. He liked the anus best. It was tight and rubbed him better than the vagina ever could. He pumped and pumped. Mindy cried out. He didn't care. No one was close; no one would hear her. He lifted her hips higher and pushed as hard as he could. It wasn't enough; his need filled him too much. He couldn't ejaculate. He had waited too long.

In frustration, he withdrew. He looked around in the darkness for something, anything he could use to excite himself further. While he was distracted, Mindy rose to her feet. His back faced her. She moved quietly away from him, her eyes glued on his shadowy form.

She stepped on a twig. It snapped. The man spun around, seeing her. He became enraged. He charged at her. She fell to one knee, making it seem as if she was giving up. He hesitated, almost on top of her. She planted the heel of her foot firmly into his groin. His penis felt hard under her foot. The man fell over, his hands clutching his wounded part. She leaped to her feet and ran, ran as if her life depended on it, because it did.

Mindy crashed through the undergrowth. The darkness of night made it difficult to see beyond arms length. Leaves covered the ground, hiding tree roots and other obstacles. She fell down many times. Her hands remained tied; she did not have time to free them. The ground started to slope downward. She flew with

it. Her breath was ragged. She had not exerted herself this much in a long time. She ripped the tape off and stopped to catch her breath. A crashing noise sounded behind her, deep in the shadows. She ran on.

She thought several times about stopping and hiding. Each time, the thought was dashed by the sounds of close pursuit. The man after her wasn't trying to be quiet. He wanted her to know he was there. He was probably going to use her in even more horrible ways before he killed her. She wasn't going to let that happen. She had to get away, to warn the police. She had to stop the maniac from hurting another girl.

Mindy had her head down, trying to put distance between her and the man chasing her. When the trees cleared before her, she was in a full out run and could not stop. She flew over the edge. Her screams echoed throughout the valley below. It bounced in tempo each time she hit an outcrop of rock or tree. It stopped when she did, at the bottom of the cliff.

The man leaned over the edge. He had heard the screams and slowed his forward progress, thus preventing himself from following her. He couldn't see anything. The dark covered everything, including the girl. The thought of her twisted dead body lying speared by a tree or bloody across the ground excited him. His penis grew. He gripped himself and began to pump. He jerked harder and harder, faster and faster, until he finally found the release he sought. With a moan of pleasure, he ejaculated over the edge, hoping it hit the body of the girl below.

Anger replaced the joy caused by his release when he thought about the loss of the girl and the pleasure associated with her. A frown formed as he put his limp penis back inside his jeans. Now he would have to hunt again, hunt for the One. He would have to return to Florida, where it was still warm. Maybe he would go to the Keys, or maybe Miami. He would make up his mind along the way. Still angry about the loss, he stormed back the way he came until he reached the trail leading to the van.

He had calmed down completely by the time he pulled onto the road, heading south with the hopes of finally locating the one he sought. He hoped to find her and bring her back to the cabin before the winter snows set in. A smile creased his face. The fact that he had not rested was forgotten. He was on the hunt again.

The tires sang on the road as the miles passed. Nature hummed to herself, harmonizing with their music. She kicked herself for not bringing some of her favorites CD's. She'd forgotten them in the rush to pack and get moving. She thought about turning the radio on, but vetoed it. Web needed sleep, not heavy metal with a twist of orchestra, or the twang of country, or anything else for that matter. The snoring beside her had gone on for close to nine hours.

"Nice singing, ever consider it full time?" The words came out from under the tilted hat.

"No. Too much work and travel. I like quiet in between blasts of loud."

Web straightened up. He yawned and stretched his tall frame as far as he could in the cab.

"Feel better? Not quite so grouchy?"

"Sorry about that. I guess I didn't realize how tired I was." He looked out the window. He didn't like to admit when he was wrong. It made him feel inadequate, less of a man.

"I made you a ham and cheese sandwich. I had to stop to go to the bathroom and decided to eat too. It's beside you in the plastic bag. A bottle of water is in the holder."

Westerly looked beside him. As promised, the sandwich sat next to him. "Wheat bread huh. I prefer white." He took it out of the bag and bit a large chunk off, chewing it slowly.

Nature glanced at him and started to laugh. He looked like a chipmunk with a huge stash in his cheek. He was oblivious to his appearance.

"Whut?" His word was muffled by the food.

Nature only laughed harder. Tears flowed from her eyes, making it difficult to see in the dark. She finally gave in and pulled to the side of the road. She let go of the wheel and held her belly instead. The tears of laughter running down her face changed to tears of sorrow. The transition was so subtle; Westerly did not notice it at first. When she rocked back and forth, sobbing, he spit the food out the window. He moved over next to her and hugged her close.

"Shhh, it's okay, it's okay. Let it out," he said softly as he

smoothed her hair.

Westerly began to see what he thought was a cold, hard woman in another light. She was wonderful; she was caring; she was vulnerable. He had to protect her. He held her close, feeling the sobs wrack her body. When they subsided, he continued to hold her.

"Please let me go. I can't take it right now."

"Nature…"

"Please…not now."

He let her go and moved back to his side of the cab. He was angry. He was disappointed, both in himself and in her. Nature raised her head. She kept her gaze forward. She knew Westerly was mad at her, mad at her rejection. But, she wasn't ready, wasn't ready for what he wanted. She had felt it in his touch. She was still too raw from the last session. And, she missed Brad dearly. After wiping the tears from her face, she pulled the gear lever down into drive and merged back onto I-95.

Daytona was just over an hour away. According to the card given to Westerly by Officer Spangle, they had to go beyond it to Brevard County, to a city called Cocoa. That meant they would arrive in Cocoa at around eleven o'clock at night. Too late to check in with the police. The headlights of the camper lit the yellow reflectors in the center of the road. She started to count them silently to herself. It passed the time. Web kept his face pointed toward the window. He didn't finish the sandwich. When the silence was too much, she broke it.

"Web, I'm sorry."

"Don't worry about it," he said more to the window than to her.

"Web, really…I'm sorry."

"I said don't worry about it."

That was her cue to drop it. He didn't want to discuss it. Just like when he did not push her earlier, she was not going to push him now. They rode the rest of the way in silence.

The highway sign for SR 520 glowed in the brightness of the headlights. It indicated the turnoff was coming up. As predicted, their arrival time was ten minutes after eleven. She drove down the ramp and turned left. A motel was ahead on the right. She was tired. Deciding it was the best place to stop for the night, she

pulled into the parking area. They would contact Spangle in the morning.

Westerly was out of the camper as soon as it stopped. He had yet to say anything since her break down and rejection of his comforts. At the moment, she was too tired to care. All she wanted was the warm comfort of a soft bed. He walked into to the lobby and checked in. When he came out, he indicated for Nature to drive around to the back. She pulled into the parking spot in front of their room and turned the engine off. Before Nature could get her door open, Web got out and moved to the back of the camper. He had both suitcases in hand when he walked toward the stairs. They were on the second floor.

She stood up with a sigh. After making sure the camper was locked, even though she knew Web would not leave it unlocked, she followed him upstairs. The door to their room stood open. He was putting his suitcase on the bed closest to the door; hers was already on the farther bed. He reached inside and grabbed his toothbrush and paste. Pajamas followed, draped over his forearm when he moved to the bathroom and closed the door behind him. Nature sighed again. Closing the door behind her, she walked over to her suitcase. She opened it, removed her own pajamas and hygiene items then sat on the bed to wait.

Web opened the door and stepped into the main area. Nature gazed at him then quickly dropped her eyes. She rose to her feet, keeping her gaze locked on the floor. She knew the pajamas he wore. She knew them intimately. She moved past him toward the bathroom. When she passed, they brushed against each other. Even though she did not have contact with skin, she felt the electricity coming off him. Her heart pounded. She practically ran into the bathroom, shutting the door quickly. Leaning against it, she tried to get herself under control.

She hated the fact that they worked together. She hated herself for giving Westerly Brad's clothes. She hated the fact that he looked so good in them. It made her regret leaving Sandy at home. At least with Sandy, she felt calm, in control. With Web, nothing inside was calm. Everything remained in constant turmoil.

The sink stood in front of her. She removed her gloves and grabbed the hot and cold knobs. The zing of Web ran through her. She had forgotten he had touched it prior to her. She held them

lightly, allowing his feelings to run through her. She felt his concern, his fears, his loss. Letting go, she rubbed her hands together. She wondered what it was that he had lost. Picking up a folded washcloth, she opened it and used it to touch anything else in the room. Once she finished with the toilet, brushed her teeth, and changed, she opened the door.

Westerly was lying under the covers on his side. His back faced her. He didn't move or acknowledge her as she pulled her own covers down and slid under them. She threw an arm above her head after she fell back onto the pillow. Staring up at the ceiling, she tried to figure out what he had lost. Eventually, sleep overcame her. Though it was not filled with the rest she had hoped for.

The man reached the beach at nine in the morning. He loved Florida in October. The weather was great and the girls clad in almost nothing. He cruised up A1A, watching the people walk along the sidewalk. He had settled on Cocoa Beach because it was the home of *I Dream of Jeannie* and *The Cape,* both shows he used to watch, both no longer shown, unless in reruns.

He knew most of the young ones would be in school. He thought about them sitting at their desks and wished he could sit with them. He wished he could take one under the bleachers and show her his pleasures. The more he thought about it, the more frustrated he became. The last one had died before he could get the full pleasure out of her that he had wanted. The loss was okay though, she had not been the One. He was hunting for her now. He was sure he would find her this time.

He was at a traffic light, waiting for it to turn green. A group of older women, their silver hair shining bright in the sunlight, crossed the street in front of him. They looked like they had just come from the beach, probably walking to stay in shape. From the way some of them looked, he knew they needed to walk more.

Since his arrival, he had not seen anyone who might be the One. He was about to give up and head south, toward Miami, when a sweet young thing sped past the older ones. He watched as she stopped, turned back, and waved at her parents. They were in front of a nearby real estate business. She ran toward a

park located down the road. He watched as she disappeared over the boardwalk onto the beach. She looked about eighteen or nineteen.

She's the One...I know she is. She is, she is, she is. He sang the catchy tune in his mind, even after the light turned green.

He merged into the left turn lane and entered the park. Pulling the van into a parking spot close to the exit, he got out and placed a magnetic sign of the side of the van before he started after the girl. On the boardwalk, he saw her walking south, kicking the waves, her shoes swinging in her hand. She was wonderful with her half shirt and short shorts. Her long brunette hair was pulled back into a ponytail. He knew she would eventually return this way. He would bide his time, no matter how long.

The girl turned north, heading toward the boardwalk. She was returning. The man reminded himself to breath normally. He waited. When she was close, he smiled. She smiled back. It was a sweet smile, full of beautiful innocence.

"New to the area?" he asked.

"We will be."

"We?"

"Me and my parents."

"Welcome. Where are you from?"

"Texas."

"What brought you all the way from Texas?"

"My dad got a job at the space center."

He leaned back against the railing for the steps. "Wow, that's cool." Straightening, he asked, "Hey—can you help me with something?"

"Depends on what it is."

"I have to move a heavy trash can out of my vehicle and my helpers deserted me for breakfast. I could really use your help."

She looked around the parking lot. "Which one is it?"

He pointed to his van. The magnetic sign he had placed on its side before following her indicated he worked for the city trash service.

"You work here?"

"I confess...I do."

She looked at his pullover shirt and shorts, lifting an eyebrow in doubt. "Is this a uniform?"

"It is when you work in Florida." He knew she had no idea what the workers wore. She was new to the area.

After a quick glance across the street, toward the real estate place, she answered, "Okay."

He was elated. He led her to the back of the van and opened the doors. A large beat up oil drum was inside. He got in and attempted to move it. It wouldn't budge. He waved for her come in to assist. Again, she hesitated, but decided it was okay. Besides, it was broad daylight. No one would do anything at this time, not with other people walking by. She got in.

When she moved next to him, the man grabbed her hair and slammed her head into the drum. She slumped to the floor, unconscious. The man covered her with a blanket before dragging the barrel out of the van. He left it close to another. Getting behind the wheel, he reached out and removed the sign. Moments after the girl entered the vehicle, it was driving toward I-95, toward the cabin.

He knew he had to get out of the area quickly. The parents would be looking for her soon. He turned left onto SR 520. He drove past a hospital, a Wal-mart, a mall, and a Best Western. He merged onto the highway, heading north. Before long, he knew he would stop and show the girl his pleasures. For now, he needed to put miles between him and the ones who threatened to take his prize away.

Six

Nature heard the phone as it was set down on the cradle. She rolled over and saw Westerly sitting on the edge of the bed, dressed in jeans and a light blue pullover. He had a card in his hand.

"Did you call Spangle?"

"Yea."

"Is he going to meet us somewhere?"

"The Denny's."

"Did he give you directions?" She knew it was a stupid question. She didn't care.

"Yea."

"I don't usually do breakfast before a session."

"I do."

Westerly pulled up his pant leg and strapped a small revolver to his calf. Nature understood. No cop, no matter how far they were from home, went anywhere without a weapon of some kind. It was second nature to them, especially if they were on the job as long as Web was. It was the same with her, she never went anywhere without at least two pairs of gloves.

She flipped back the covers, picked out some clothes, and got ready faster than usual. Once the dirty clothes were put away, she moved to open the door leading outside. Westerly was there first. He opened it, standing off to the side to allow her to pass. She smiled. He remained aloof, professional. He made sure not to touch her. Her smile faded.

Nature went down the stairs to the camper. To show her defi-

ance at his behavior, and hide the hurt, she opened her own door and got in before he could reach it. He shrugged his shoulders, walked to the driver's side, and sat down behind the wheel. He stuck his hand out for the keys held forgotten in her gloved hand. She gave them to him. The engine purred to life. He backed the camper out and exited onto SR 520, heading toward the beaches.

They stopped for the red light at the intersection of SR520 and SR 3. The Denny's was just up the road on the right. The camper was in the center lane of a three-lane roadway. Both had their attention focused on getting into the right lane as soon as the light changed. They ignored the oncoming traffic. If they had been looking, they would have seen a plain brown van drive past, a lone occupant sitting inside.

Westerly cut the driver of a BMW convertible off immediately after the light changed. A well-manicured finger rose to meet the occasion. Nature smiled. It had been a long time since she'd received such a gesture. The last time was with Brad.

He turned the camper into the entrance of the diner and parked next to a deputy's car. The car was unoccupied. They went inside. The waitress came up to them, reaching for menus.

"Two?"

"Actually, we're meeting someone."

Deputy Spangler raised a hand in greeting, waving them over. The waitress glanced over her shoulder, toward where they looked. She faced them again. "I see your party is already here. This way please." She led them to the booth, placed menus in front of them, and took their beverage orders. Spangle had waited for them. She returned with their coffee, promising to return when they were ready to order the rest.

When she was gone, Spangle said, "You made good time."

"We pretty much drove straight through," Westerly said.

"When do you want to get started?"

"Whenever you're ready." Westerly picked up his cup and sipped. He grimaced. Setting it down, he added three packets of sugar, stirred it, sipped again and decided it needed more.

"After we eat," Spangle said, picking up the menu. "I know I asked you to start right away but, with this job, one never knows what will happen next, or when the next meal will be. A good breakfast is the best way to start the day"

Nature remained quiet. She dreaded what was coming. The sessions always took a lot out of her. Leaving the menu on the table, not interested on what lay inside, she sipped her coffee. She drank it black.

The waitress returned with a wave from Spangle and took their orders. After dropping the orders off with the cook, she refilled their cups.

Nature watched her walk away before turning her attention to the officer across the table, at Spangle. "Have you found anything more?"

"I'm afraid not. I do have what you requested in my car. I left it there to reduce the risk of others handling it."

"Thank you."

The waitress appeared a short time later with two complete breakfast bowls in hand, meat lovers style. She set them in front of the men. Nature tried not to smell the food; it made her sick. She tried not to listen to the noise in the diner. She tried not to dwell on the feelings running through the cup. Feelings from the waitress: her loves, her concerns about her child, her worries about paying her bills, everything about her. Even though gloves protected her hands, her lips still touched the cup when she drank.

"Nature, you okay?"

Nature opened her eyes at the calling of her name. She saw empty dishes on the table. She must have phased out, for how long she was uncertain. Westerly watched her, his eyes filled with concern. Spangle glanced in her direction. He did not maintain contact. He did not know what to think of the situation. Nature knew he would feel that way again, soon.

Her knuckles were blanched from holding the cup too tight. She relaxed them. "I'm fine. I just want to get this over with, that's all."

She rose to her feet, picked up the bill that had been delivered without her realizing it, and paid it. The men followed. Westerly was not pleased with her paying, but she was certain he'd get over it. She walked to the police car and waited. Spangle fished his keys out of his pocket and opened the trunk. A brown paper bag lay tucked among the items stored in its depths. He brought it out and handed it to Nature. She looked inside. She smiled. A Chi-

Chihuahua looked back.

"Her mother gave that to me. She said it was the one thing she loved best."

The smile vanished. Spangle shuffled his feet. Westerly watched traffic flow past the Denny's. Nature knew it was time, time to go to the house.

"Can you take me there, now? To where the girl was last seen?"

"Do you want to ride in my car?"

"No!" The word was venomous. She could not bear the thought of riding in a car where criminals rode. Seeing Spangles face, she regretted her tone. "Sorry, I didn't mean it like that."

Spangle nodded his head in understanding. "Hey, it gets to the best of us sometimes." He shut the trunk and walked around the vehicle. He stopped next to the door and said, "Follow me," and got in.

Nature crumpled the bag closed. She wasn't ready, not until she got to their destination. Westerly held her door open then moved to his once she was settled in her seat. They followed the police car north, toward Titusville. A small airport with several small planes soaring above it was off to the left when the police car put on its turn signal.

Hidden in a group of trees was a quaint little house. It looked like it was built in the sixties. The walls were white, the trim a soft blue. Flowers bloomed in pots on either side of the porch. It looked cozy. Spangle pulled his car to the right of the dirt drive-way, allowing the camper to pull straight in. All three got out and walked to the front door. Spangle knocked. No one answered. He tried the door. It opened. He knew it would. While driving to the house, he had used his cell phone and instructed the family to leave before they arrived. He had also told them to leave the door unlocked. He stepped back, indicating for Nature to go in first.

She walked in. The smell of potpourri filled it, causing her to imagine a field of wildflowers. The house was spotless. She waited for Deputy Spangle to show her where to go. He guided her to the back right corner of the house. The room was small. Posters of Johnny Depp and Orlando Bloom covered the walls. The covers on the bed had pictures of *The Lord of the Rings* on it. It reminded her of a child's room, not that of a young adult. She looked ques-

tioningly at the officer.

"She was mentally challenged. Her age may have been twenty, but her thought process was that of a seven year old."

She returned her attention to the room. She was glad the parents were gone. If the news was bad, she didn't want a repeat of Mrs. Mosby's actions. She removed her gloves and put them in a pocket. Stepping to the bed, she sat down. Westerly had the bag. He opened it for her. She reached in and removed the toy. She held it close.

The girl washed through her. "Her mother called her Sunshine, even though her name was Alice, because her face lit up when she smiled." Natured stretched out. She closed her eyes. She lost herself in the girl, lost herself to whatever happened the last day she was seen.

Alice was up early. She liked to get up before anyone else; it allowed her to feel like a big girl. She delighted in watching the birds through the back door during the quiet time. Today, a blue jay sat on a branch, twisting its head all around. Alice imitated it, the smile her mother loved so much covering her face. She heard a noise behind her. She saw it was her mother.

"Sunshine, I have to go to the store. Want to come?"

"Nope. I want to watch the pretty birds." She pointed out the window to the blue jay.

"I don't really want to leave you here alone."

"But Mo-o-o-m-m-m. Please? I'm a big girl now. You said so. I can take care of myself."

"Yes, you are a big girl now. If I leave you here, will you promise to stay in the house and not open the door to strangers?"

Alice nodded her head up and down rapidly. She returned her attention to the window, nose pushed up against the glass.

The mother smiled. She picked up her keys and purse. She would not be gone long. The store was right up the road. And, it was too early for anyone to stop by. She'd be home before then. As she moved toward the front door, she said, "Remember...don't open the door to strangers."

Alice ignored her. Her whole attention was on the feathery creatures outside. Opening the door, mom locked it and shut it

tight behind her. Almost immediately, the sound of the car was lost with the rest of the morning traffic. Sunshine stayed where she was. A matter of minutes later, a loud knock on the door caused her to look away. She walked toward the front and peeked out one of the side windows. A man stood there. She smiled. She opened the door. The man wasn't a stranger.

"Hi Alice. Is your mom here?"

"Nope. She went to the store."

"Whatcha doing?"

"Looking at the birds, wanna see?" She grabbed the big hand and pulled the man to the back window. When she looked out, the birds were gone. "Awww, no more birds."

The man wasn't looking out the window; he was looking at Alice. "I know where they went. Want me to take you there?" He licked his lips.

"Yea!"

This time, the man took Alice's hand and led her to his car. He drove to a wildlife park a few miles away. It wasn't visited much. He knew this. It was perfect. He drove down the winding dirt road to a secluded site. He got out. He opened the girl's door and led her deeper into the woods. She followed willingly. She wasn't afraid, this wasn't a stranger.

Alice's attention was focused upward. She was trying to see the birds she heard behind the many leaves. She didn't pay attention to where they were going. He stopped and looked up with her. He moved next to her. He reached out and wrapped an arm around her waist.

"This is a great spot, isn't it?"

"I don't see any birds." She turned her body in all directions, trying to see everywhere at the same time.

"Maybe we should sit down. Maybe that will bring them out." He sat down on a log. He patted his thigh, showing her where to sit.

She glanced up one more time before she sat down, pouting. "Stupid birds."

I have a worm we can show them. Want to see it?"

"Yea. They like to eat worms." She smiled.

The man got up and unbuckled his pants. He pulled them down. A large ugly thing that looked like a worm popped out. She

gawked at it; it was huge. She had never seen a worm that big before. She thought it was strange that it was attached to his skin. It looked like it was growing out of his body.

"Wow."

The man smiled. "Have you ever tasted a worm Alice?"

She shook her head no, never taking her eyes off it.

"You can. You can make sure it is clean for the birds."

He guided her in front of him, making her kneel. He pulled her mouth to the worm. He grabbed her hair, tugging her head close to his body, then back. She gagged on the worm. It was too big. It went down her throat. It tasted nasty. She tried to pull away. He prevented it. He forced the nasty thing down her throat again and again. She started to cry.

Suddenly, he stopped and knelt in front of her. He hugged her close, soothing her. He kissed her face all over. His hands moved to her breasts. He squeezed them. She didn't understand. Why was he doing this? All she wanted to do was watch birds, not play with worms. He laid her on the ground. She felt her skirt hike up. She felt him reach into her underwear. She felt his fingers rub her. She grabbed his hand to make him stop. He continued. He no longer smiled.

She whimpered. He slapped her. She cried out. He slapped her again. He ripped her underwear off and threw them into the trees. He lay on top of her, forcing her legs apart. He moved the worm close to her pee-pee and shoved it inside. She cried out in pain. He covered her mouth with his hand.

She had never felt pain like this. Tears ran from her eyes. She wished he would take his worm out. All he did was ram it in over and over. He grunted with each push. She hurt with each push. She wanted her mommy. She wanted the see the birds in her backyard. She did not want to see another worm again for the rest of her life.

In an instant, her world flipped over. She found herself face-first on the ground. The man put all his weight on her. She couldn't breathe. Every time she tried, dirt filled her mouth and nose. She felt her legs separate and his worm enter her pee-pee spot again. It hurt worse than before. She struggled. He was too heavy. He pressed on her head, keeping her toward the ground, preventing her from screaming. The grunting resumed. Breathing

grew impossible to do. He didn't notice. He was lost in his thrusts. Her last thoughts were of her mother...and the birds.

When the man finished, he realized Alice was dead. He hadn't meant to kill her, it just happened. Scared, he dug a shallow pit and placed her body in it. He covered it with some leaves and twigs. He returned to his car and drove away, never telling the mother he had visited. He pretended to be shocked when told of the girl's disappearance. He convinced them. They never suspected him. He thought he was scot-free.

Nature found herself lying on the floor when she came around. She did not know how or when she got there. She was curled into a tight ball. Tears streamed down her cheeks. The floor was wet with them. She had been crying for some time. She was hugging the Chihuahua toy close to her body. She heard movement in the room. She opened her eyes.

Westerly was getting to his feet. He squatted beside her when he realized she was awake. "It's not good, is it?"

Nature sat up, wiping the moisture off with the back of her hand. Westerly reached out to help her, she shrugged him off. She did not want anyone to lay hands on her, not right now. The session was too fresh. She was too raw. He stood up, his face resuming a professional appearance instead of the concerned one it had a moment ago. Spangle remained by the door. His arms were crossed in front of him. He did not look happy.

"She's dead," she said.

"Did you see who did it?" Spangles hands moved to his gun belt. He gripped either side of the buckle firmly, his knuckles turning white.

She bowed her head. She wished he had been a stranger. Someone the girl had not known. Someone she would not have opened the door for. Instead, the man was a family member. He wasn't the one they sought, the one who had killed Rew.

"It was her uncle."

The faces of both men darkened. One because of who it was, the other because of who it wasn't.

"You're sure?" Westerly asked.

"I saw him. I saw what he did to her. He took her to a nearby

wildlife park. He tricked her and used her horribly. He didn't mean to kill her." She paused to take in a deep breath. She exhaled it between pursed lips. "He buried her in the park."

"Can you take me to it?" Deputy Spangle straightened.

"Yes...it's not far."

This time, the camper led the way. Westerly followed her directions to the dirt road. He drove to where she saw the uncle stop. Spangle stopped behind them. She got out but refused to enter the woods. She pointed to where the men needed to go.

"Down that trail. You'll see her underwear close to a pile of fresh leaves. She's there." Nature moved to the back of the camper. She opened the door. Unable to look at the men, she added, "I'll be here when you return." She closed the door behind her.

Hours later, after the forensic people had gone, after the news people interviewed whoever would talk to them, after Spangle had departed, Westerly opened the camper and got in. Nature was lying on the bench, curled under a blanket.

"We found her where you said. She's been taken to the morgue." He sat on the edge of the bench. "Spangle told me they arrested the uncle. He confessed. He may not have been the man we were after, but at least he won't be able to hurt another girl again.

Nature listened. She heard his words, yet they did not help. What she needed was a scalding hot shower. She missed her home. She missed Sandy. She missed Brad. She felt her resolve give. The tears flooded from her. She reached up, causing the blanket to fall away. She pressed her clenched fists into her eyes. Westerly glanced over his shoulder. He saw her tears. He felt his heart rend. Ignoring caution, he scooped her up into his arms and hugged her close.

He didn't try to kiss her, he only held her tight. She didn't resist. She clutched his shirt, pinching the skin underneath. He said nothing. She sobbed like she hadn't done in a long time, not since Brad's death. Finally, after she had no more tears to shed, she calmed.

"Can we go home now?"

"Yes. If Spangle needs more information, he knows how to get hold of us."

"Can we stop at a music store?"

"Of course, anything you want." He brushed her hair away from her face. "We have to go by the motel before we hit the road. We left our stuff there."

Pulling away, she rose to her feet. She stepped into the open air, its gentle breeze caressing her skin. Stretching her arms wide, she began to spin. Westerly leaned against the camper, arms folded, and watched. He saw her face relax. She had returned to herself once the spinning was complete. He opened her door and shut it after she sat. He got in and drove the camper toward the motel. He looked forward to going home. He missed Montana with its wide-open spaces. He missed his quiet life.

When they pulled into the Best Western, they were surprised to see a police car. Spangle got out after they parked. He came up to the driver's side. He leaned onto the window frame. They could tell by the look on his face, he was not in a good mood. They never expected what he said.

"The police from Cocoa Beach just reported a missing person. A family was at a real estate agency, looking for a house. Their eighteen-year-old daughter became bored so she went to the beach. Several eyewitnesses remembered seeing her a short while later with a man. They don't remember seeing her after that."

"How does that involve us?" Westerly questioned.

"They don't remember what the man looked like, but they do remember seeing a plain brown van drive away."

Three words in his statement made both occupants sit up promptly. They looked first at each other, then at the man leaning against the camper. Those three words, words said after a previous session, were...plain brown van.

Seven

"Shit"

The man saw the sign over the highway. It was the sign used in Florida for amber alerts. It told people about someone missing. Right now, it told of a missing girl. It also told of a plain brown van. He knew it was talking about his van. He had been careless in his venture to get the One.

He had to get back to the cabin in a hurry so he could find out if she truly was the one he sought. Deep inside, he knew this girl was the One. He saw it in her eyes, or at least thought he had when they were last opened. They remained closed. In his enthusiasm to get her, he had hit her head against an oil drum. She was still unconscious.

He was close to the state line. He hoped that once he crossed it, he would be okay, that he would not have to ditch the van. He liked it. It suited his purpose well. Twenty minutes later, he passed the Georgia state line. He relaxed a little, but not much. He still had a long way to go. He decided to take the other route home, the one he traveled on less frequently. It would take him longer, though he did not think the people on the lookout for him would find him as easily.

He merged onto Highway 16 before entering Savannah. The more time passed, the more miles he put away, the more he relaxed. The girl was his. He was not about to give her up. He was surprised that he had not wanted to sample her yet. She was sweet and she was young. Two qualities he liked in his women. He pulled into a rest area, before taking the detour, to restrain her

and to remove her clothes. He did not want the synthetic material spoiling his pleasure. This time, he put a rag in her mouth before taping it shut. He hated the idea of taping her beautiful mouth, but it was necessary until he arrived at the cabin.

A state trooper drove past on the other side of the highway. He tensed. He watched it in the mirror. He maintained his speed. The car did not pull a sudden u-turn; it did not turn on its lights; it did nothing out of the ordinary. It kept going down the road, oblivious to his presence. He smiled. He started to think about home, about how he would gain untold pleasure from the girl, about how she was The One he had sought for so long. He glanced down at his lap. He saw he was hard. Making sure no one could see what he did; he pulled his penis out and began to stroke it. The more he stroked, the more he thought of the girl. The more he thought of the girl, the more he smiled. He continued to smile for many miles.

Nature stood on the boardwalk, looking at the ocean beyond. Westerly was beside her. He did not touch her. He remained professional. She grabbed the railing with her gloved hands. She watched as a cruise ship made its way across the water. She wished she was on it, but knew she would not be able to take so many people, no matter what size the ship was. Deputy Spangle walked up to her. He stopped a respectful distance away. He too would not touch her. Another man was with him.

"Mrs. Kranderson, this is Officer Myristate. He's with the local police department. He's the one who took the report."

The officer tipped his hat, "Ma'am."

Nature glanced at him. He looked like he should be still in high school with his boyish appearance. She nodded acknowledgement before returning her gaze to the water.

"How old was she?" She asked.

"Excuse me?" Myristate asked.

'How old was she?"

"Eighteen."

Nature closed her eyes. She wished the visions coming to her mind would disappear. The ideas of what that monster had planned for this girl were something that no child should ever

have to endure; she faced the officers.

"Did the person who abducted her touch anything?"

"I'm not sure of all the places," Myristate said. "But the witnesses do remember him touching some stuff."

"Can you show me all the places where he stood?"

"Right here for one."

Nature looked at the railing. Nothing but wood was visible. She saw Westerly stand back and took a deep sigh. She did not like it, but she was going to have to follow through. She removed her gloves and grabbed the rail. Feelings of happiness flowed through her, along with feelings of wonder, joy, love, and delight. Nothing resembled the feeling of the man here.

"Where else?'

"This way."

Myristate moved toward the parking lot. She followed. Westerly was behind her. Spangle brought up the rear. The officer stopped at an old rusted oil drum. It sat next to another one with trash in it.

"The witnesses said there was one trash bin here earlier. They noticed two after he left. They thought he must have worked with the sanitation department and didn't think much of it at the time."

Again, Nature inhaled deep. She released the breath before touching the drum. With her eyes closed, she gripped the rim and immediately felt a zing shoot through her body. She recognized it. She saw the man as he loaded it in his vehicle. He remained shrouded like the last time. She felt his lust. She felt his need to hunt. She felt sick. She let go with a shudder. Moving her hand around the drum, she tried to detect the girl. She found it half way down on one side. It was a small trace. She could see her smile, her lovely face, her innocence.

She turned away from the drum. Her legs were wobbly. She felt hands hold her. They guided her to a bench and forced her to sit. She heard someone retching. She realized it was herself.

"It was him, wasn't it?"

Westerly was kneeling in front of her. When she was finally able to look into them, she saw his eyes were once more filled with concern. She nodded her head yes, unable to bring words past her constricted throat. His face became grim. Standing, he turned to the officers.

"You need to fingerprint the drum. The man who kidnapped the girl touched it."

Officer Myristate stared at Nature, "Are you sure?"

Westerly answered for her. "Yes, she's positive."

"I don't know."

Myristate was skeptical. He did not know who this woman was. He did not want to base an entire manhunt on her say so, just because she touched an oil drum supposedly touched by the kidnapper. If the information were wrong, his superiors would have his ass. Not to mention the lawsuits that would arise.

"What's taking you so long...move!" Westerly took a step closer to the officer. He was angry.

Deputy Spangle moved in front of Westerly. He faced the hesitant officer. "Can I see you for a minute?"

Both men moved away. Westerly remained where he was. He watched as they talked. He saw the beach officer cross his arms in front of his chest. He saw the deputy wave his arms toward the north. He saw the officer frown. The deputy frowned. After a few minutes of heated discussion, the officer moved toward his car. He reached in, removed the mike, and spoke into it. Spangle walked their way.

"I convinced him to do as you asked."

"What was his major malfunction?"

"He doesn't know about Mrs. Kranderson, about her reputation. I filled him in."

Movement caught Westerly's attention. He watched as a vehicle pulled into the lot. Another officer got out, a fingerprint kit in his hand. He moved to the drum, completed his task quickly, and returned to his vehicle. The drum was placed in the back of a pickup. It followed the previous vehicle.

Nature remained where she was. She had not watched anything. Her thoughts were on the man, and the girl in his possession. What was it that made him impossible to see? Was it the evil she felt? Was it the need driving him? What? She felt a hand on her shoulder and looked up.

"Let's get something to eat."

She was not hungry but knew Westerly was right. She had to eat, whether she liked it or not. The image of Sandy nagging her came to mind. Her secretary constantly reminded her of the fact

that she would be of no help to anyone if she starved herself to death. She missed Sandy and again wondered about her decision to leave the woman behind. She would call her when they returned to the motel.

Westerly guided her to the camper. He tucked her inside before he got in. Starting the engine, he asked, "What you want?"

"I don't care...whatever you want."

"I saw a Steak 'N Shake on the way here."

"Sounds good. We can go there if you want." Her voice sounded so drained.

He put the camper into drive and pulled onto the road. Spangle stayed at the scene to coordinate things with Officer Myristate. This was not Westerly's territory. He did not have jurisdiction here. He glanced at the woman next to him. She was focused on the scenery as it passed. He returned his attention to the road. It was getting late but the traffic had not thinned. In fact, it was heavier due to people going out to eat or party, whichever, he didn't care. All he wanted was food and sleep.

They picked up drive thru and continued on to the Best Western. Nature did not want to have to deal with so many people, especially after having to deal with the feelings of the hidden killer. The smell of the food caused her stomach to grumble. She was not sure if it was because of hunger or nausea. She cracked her window to get some fresh air.

"Are you okay?"

"I will be. I just need to take a shower." She thought about having him stop at a music shop to get a CD but decided against it. She needed the shower more than she needed the music. She stared out the window at the lights of the businesses.

They parked in the closest spot to the room, got out, and made their way upstairs. Nature was tired. She stumbled a couple of times. Westerly tried to help her but she shrugged his hands off. She did not want anyone touching her, not even Web.

Once in the room, Westerly sat in a chair near the small table. He turned on the television and pulled out his portion of the food. He ignored her as he started to eat. Nature knew he was mad, but she could not help it. She needed a scalding hot shower immediately. She needed to feel fresh again, not tainted. Her food remained on the table, untouched.

She made it to the bathroom and shut the door behind her. Leaving the lid down, she moved to the toilet and eased herself onto it. Hiding her face with her hands, she cried quietly for several minutes. When she recovered enough, she got up and turned the water on. She had to pull her hand back when the water became too hot to keep it there. She adjusted the temperature slightly before shedding her clothes. She stepped under the water. It turned her skin red. She ignored the feeling. She immersed herself under the strong stream coming from the showerhead.

The emotions that Alice experienced: the innocence, the joy, the loss, the fear, and especially, the pain, flooded through her. Those, and the feeling of the evil consuming the man they sought, so soon after the Alice session, caused her to crumple into a heap. The water hit her. It felt like a thousand tiny needles. She tried to block the emotions, to get them to go away. She couldn't. They filled her every fiber. They threatened to consume her completely. She threw her head back and screamed.

Web bolted to the bathroom when the screams started. He tried to open the door, but it was locked. He pounded on it. The screams continued. He yelled. He threw his shoulder at the door several times. It held. The screams continued. Finally, he stood back and kicked the door. It flew open, slamming into the wall. Before it had a chance to bounce back, he was inside the room.

The shower curtain was shut. The screams echoed in the tiny space behind it. He yanked it open. Nature lay curled into a tight ball. Her skin was beet red from the scalding water hitting it. His entrance went unnoticed.

He stepped into the shower, blocking her from the hot water. He grabbed her, pulling her against his body. He sat down, ignoring how wet he was getting. He wrapped his arms around her. He whispered soothing words. He kissed her wet hair. He held her tight.

Nature felt the arms wrap around her but she was lost, lost in the feelings of Alice. She heard the words. She struggled to regain control. She turned her thoughts to Brad. She used his love to help her as she had so many times before. She felt Alice's grip on her loosen. She relaxed into the arms holding her.

Westerly felt Nature relax. He watched as she looked up at him. He saw her brown eyes. He realized he loved those eyes:

their depth, their color, everything about them. He bent over and kissed her. She responded, kissing him back. He did not realize she was lost in the rapture of her lost husband, that she did not really see him.

He kissed her lips, her face, her neck. He moved his lips to her breasts. She sighed with pleasure. He sucked on them. She moaned. He moved his lips back to hers. They kissed with a hunger both had not felt in a long time.

He rose to his feet and picked her up in his arms. She wrapped hers around his neck. He carried her to the bed. She gripped the material of his shirt tight. The feelings of Brad ran through her. She knew deep inside that he was dead, but he was so alive right now. She did not want that feeling to leave. She felt the bed under her. She felt the lips on her body. She knew to whom they belonged. She knew they were not Brad's. She didn't care.

Westerly threw his wet clothes onto the floor. He knew it was wrong to do this, that they were working partners, but the feelings running through him overpowered any rational thought. He lay on her. He guided his hard penis toward her. He felt her legs spread. When he entered her, he felt her stiffen.

Nature experienced an unexpected jolt when Web entered her. She felt his love. She also felt the loss he had experienced, the loss of his child. She could not handle it, not with everything else that had happened today. She struggled. She pushed against his chest. She tried to get him off her, out from inside her.

Westerly felt her struggles. He wanted to stay where he was, but knew it was impossible. She was rejecting him. He withdrew. Sitting up on the side of the bed, he leaned forward, resting his elbows on his knees. He stood, moved to the suitcase, and grabbed some dry clothes before moving to the bathroom. He shut the door quietly.

Nature rolled onto her side. She covered her nakedness with the sheet. The feeling of Web was still there. The feeling of his hardness inside, his joy, his letdown, his sorrow, still ran through her. She understood now what she had felt earlier, about his loss. She wished she could comfort him. Maybe after she got her emotions under control, she would try. She only hoped he would allow her to talk with him. She cared for him, she finally admitted it, but

she was not ready for a relationship yet.

The bathroom door opened. She glanced at Web. He did not look at her. His eyes were focused of the floor. "I'm going out. I'll be back soon."

"Web...I'm sorry."

He held up a hand, "Don't. I knew it was wrong from the beginning. We work together. That's where it should stay." He walked across the room and left, locking the door behind him.

Nature stayed in the bed a few minutes longer then sat up on the edge. She looked at the pile of wet clothes. Kneeling down, she scooped them up. They were cold. She hugged them close to her body. Brad flowed into her. She saw his smile and his boyish good looks. Another image superimposed over him. She saw how similar the smiles were. She was surprised. Because of her decision about not becoming involved with someone she worked with, she had missed it entirely.

She brought the phone to the floor. Picking up the receiver, she dialed for the operator. She did not have a calling card. She never needed one. Instead, she called collect. Sandy would accept the charges.

"Hello?'

The voice sounded sleepy. The clock on the table glared at her. She realized how late it was and regretted calling. Biting her lower lip, she said, "Sandy?"

"Nature? Is that you?"

"I'm sorry about calling so late. I didn't realize what time it was."

"Who cares? Are you okay? You sound down."

"I'm okay. I miss your company, that's all."

"I can come out."

"No, that's not necessary. I just wanted to talk."

"Is Westerly giving you a hard time?"

"No." Her words were almost too soft to be heard. "Sandy...I want to ask you something."

""Shoot."

"Why were you so interested in pushing Westerly into a relationship with me?"

"Because you need someone beside me. You have hidden yourself from the rest of the world for far too long. You need to

experience life again. And not with one of the girls."

"But why Westerly?"

"Because you two were made for each other. Saw it right off." Sandy paused. "And because he needs someone too. Who else better to be with than you?"

Nature heard Sandy's faint laughter. "Sandy...it wasn't because he's similar to Brad?"

"Heavens no! Are you kidding? He doesn't look one bit like him."

Nature relaxed her tense shoulders. She could tell from Sandy's tone, she was telling her the truth. "Can you do me a favor? Please let me decide who I should date and when."

"Aww but...." Her tone sounded playfully hurt.

"Sandy..."

"Yes mother. I'll behave." Sandy changed the subject. "How's it going with the case?"

Nature filled her secretary in on all the details. After she finished, Sandy blew out a breath of air. "That must have been intense. Are you sure you're okay? I don't mind coming out so I can help you."

"Westerly's doing fine. He's catching on quickly about what to do and not do." That statement brought a sad smile to her face.

"Nature, please call me if you want me there. Don't try to carry the world on your shoulders alone."

"What? This from the one who said I was a recluse from the world?"

"You know what I mean." The concern in Sandy's voice was heartening.

"I know. I will call if I need you. I promise. Go back to sleep. I'll talk with you later."

Nature set the receiver in the cradle. She remembered the wet clothes on her lap. She shivered because of their coldness and because of the memories emanating from them. Picking the wad up, she carried them to the bathroom and draped them over the shower curtain. She rubbed the fabric on her face before getting a nightgown out of her suitcase. Putting it on, she crawled under the cover. The feeling of Web was strong. She moved to the farthest side, the side they had not used. Fluffing her pillow, she set her head down and tried to sleep. It eluded her for a long time.

Eight

The man pulled into a gas station outside Knoxville to fill up the van. He wanted to make sure he had a full tank before finishing the last leg to the cabin. The girl was awake. She watched him with her dark brown eyes. He was pleased with those eyes. They were enchanting.

He still had not taken her. It was an unusual thing for him; he liked to right away. For some reason, this one was different. She pulled away from his touch when he groped her breasts, but did not cringe. She held still when he rubbed the hair between her legs, as if any movement would invite him in. Again, she did not cringe. He liked that. He smiled at her before getting out of the van.

He thought about her the entire time he pumped the gas. He was so distracted that he did not notice the police car as it pulled into the station. It parked next to the building. The officer got out and went inside. The man put the nozzle back in its holder and turned around. He froze, but only for a second. Continuing into the building, he walked up to the counter and pulled out his wallet. He placed several bills in the clerk's hand. Hearing someone walk up behind him, he glanced back. The cop stood there.

"Afternoon." He nodded his head slightly in greeting.

"Afternoon. Great day to be out isn't it?"

"Gonna get cooler later. You have much longer to work today?"

"Just started," The officer said.

"Well, good luck tonight. Try to stay warm." The man started

to the door.

"You too."

The man kept his step casual as he returned to the van. He started the motor and pulled onto the main road. He merged back onto I-75. He glanced into his mirror often. He allowed himself to relax only after he was past Knoxville. He was still safe. The girl was still his. He decided that when he reached the Virginia state line he would pull over and finally get a taste of the girl. He was not going to last until the cabin, as he had planned. He passed the miles thinking about the many pleasures he would have with her.

Patricia thought about how she had been so naive, naive into thinking that nothing would happen in broad daylight. She wished she were able to kick herself, but the ropes holding her legs apart prevented it. Her arms were restrained in the same manner. She felt like a side of beef. Her extremities swayed with the motion of the van. The man driving stopped only once. He groped her in several places and rubbed his own growing hardness at the same time. He returned to the driver seat without doing anything else. She was surprised when he had not raped her. She knew that was not going to last.

When she was a little girl, her father had coached her on how to respond if she were ever abducted. She laughed because she knew it would never happen. She was too careful. Now look at her. She remained calm. She followed his advice. She didn't fight. She assumed that was the reason why she remained unsoiled. Maybe the streak of luck would continue. She hoped so.

The thought of her father brought the faces of both her parents to mind. She missed them severely. She knew they would be searching for her. As time passed, she wasn't sure if they would find her. If she did not fight, if she let this man have his way, maybe he would let her go. That thought sustained her during the hours that seemed to drag on forever.

The gentle rocking motion lessened. At first, she thought it was her imagination. When the van stopped, she knew it was true. The curtain dividing the front from the back opened. She saw the hunger behind his eyes. She knew the time had finally come. She would not be able to stop him. He was going to take her.

Sex was not a new thing to her. She dated Randy for two

years. They were friends to start. Their relationship blossomed after the first year. She thought they were going to get married. They would have, but her dad took the new job in Florida and the family moved. Randy said he would call as often as he could, once they settled into a place. They were at the real estate business, trying to do just that, when she was kidnapped. She missed Randy dearly. If he were here, he would take this son of a bitch on and knock his lights out.

The man inched his way to her. He stopped next to her butt. He smiled as he ran his hand over the smooth skin. The girl twitched. His touch tickled. He played with the anus and the vagina. She watched him. Her eyes filled with dread but not fear. He was ecstatic. Maybe this was the One. She met all the requirements so far. He only had to sample her to find out if she fulfilled the rest.

He lowered his face to her crotch. He touched her lips with his nose. He rubbed her clitoris with its tip. He flicked his tongue up and down. He inserted it and withdrew it. She never moved. He became bored. He decided to liven things up a bit.

He shuffled to her head and yanked the tape off. The girl drew in a quick breath from the pain. He smiled. He covered her mouth when she tried to speak. He held a pointer finger to his lips, indicating for her to be quiet. She nodded her head. He released her mouth and removed the rag inside. He moved his hands to his belt and zipper. He slid out of his pants. He straddled her face and lowered himself onto her gently. He guided his penis toward her mouth. She turned her head away. He tightened his legs against either side of her head, forcing her to look straight. Her expression was blank.

A warm sensation filled him as he slid his penis into her mouth. The tongue felt silky smooth. She curled it around him. He lifted himself then lowered again. He felt the back of her throat. It teased the tip. He slid the penis in and out, slowly at first, then with more urgency. The girl gagged. He loved it. It made her throat all the more enticing. He forced her to take all of him, whether she could do so or not. He heard her choking. He heard her attempting to speak. He shoved harder. The annoying sound of communication stopped. He crammed his penis in until nothing remained outside. He heard her throw up.

He allowed her to turn her head aside, to clean out the mouth, before resuming his thrusts. She never cried. She remained calm. He pumped with all his might. She took it all. He ejaculated deep in her throat, staying there until no more cum rippled out. She swallowed every drop. He kissed her groin, her vagina, her ass.

He got off her and circled around to her other side. He took out the rod from the toolbox he kept in case of emergencies. It was the same rod he had used on Rew. He slid it between her ass cheeks. He teased her anus before he shoved it in. She squeezed in response; she did not make a sound. He pushed it in until the end was the only part showing. The girl had her lower lip between her teeth, biting it.

He adored her. He loved her quietness. He loved her calm. He loved everything about her. To him, she was better than anything else in the world. He lay on her again and put his now hard shaft between her vaginal lips. He pierced her with all the love he felt. He kissed each breast. They responded to his touch. He needed more.

Getting off her, he pulled the rod out. He slipped it into her vagina. Laying on her again, he worked his own rod in next to the metal one. This time the girl hissed with pain. He matched both rods in motion. They slid together, rough as first, then more easily as her love juices flowed. He was in heaven. He felt his heart race, his breath quicken, his world disappear. He began to grind his hips.

Patricia wanted to scream, to fight, to hurt this man. She didn't. She knew if she made a sound, he would kill her. She lay there, taking both his and the metal rod together. The pain was excruciating. She hoped he would finish soon. She did not know how much more she could take before she had to scream.

Suddenly, she felt his penis in her mouth again. He shoved it as far back as he could. He wiggled his hips. He moved the metal rod around in a circular motion. She wasn't sure which was worse, the pain from the metal one or the agony of the real one. She tried not to gag. The man seemed to enjoy it when she did. She was unsuccessful. She felt the metal rod disappear as it was removed. It reappeared once again in her ass. In all the times she had sex with Randy, he had never done this. He thought it was gross. Now she knew with certainty, he was right, it was.

The circular motion resumed, stretching her anus farther than she could ever have imagined. His tongue worked its way into her vagina. She was being violated in every conceivable way. She had secretly watched videos with her girlfriends, videos like this, but to actually experience it was another thing. It hurt. For the first time since the man started, she cried.

The man felt the wetness on his balls. He heard the sniffles. His heart shattered like a crystal vase that was dropped. He was so close, so close to finding the One. This girl, with her tears, showed him that she was not it. He shoved his penis in harder and harder. He needed to find the pleasure he had moments ago, before the tears. He shoved the rod back and forth, twirled it between his fingers. He sucked on her vagina. No matter how hard he tried, the feeling of elation would not resurface.

He finally loosened his load in her mouth. He did not feel any joy. He felt sadness. He was a few hours away from the hiding spot for the van. He decided to continue toward it. He knew he was going to kill the girl. He had to. He could not let her go. She would bring the police and he needed to be free, free to hunt once more. He removed the rod and cleaned it off with a cloth before putting it away. He put the tape across her lips. He did not bother with the wad of material. It didn't matter. He would not have to stop again.

Pulling his pants on, he got into the drivers seat. The van crept onto the road, merging with the other traffic. The man behind the wheel had a look of infinite sadness across his face. He was getting tired of looking. He wanted to find the One and settle down. He wanted to rest. Hopefully, this time, he would find her. Behind the curtains, the girl continued to cry.

Nature opened her eyes and looked at the bed next to hers. It was empty. Light glowed between the closed curtains. It was morning. She got up and changed her clothes. Nothing in the room indicated Westerly had come back last night. She wondered where he might be. Maybe last night was too much for him. Maybe he decided to leave, to return to Montana. The keys to the camper were missing. She rummaged through the suitcases, all the furniture, and the bathroom. They were definitely gone. She

remembered her thought about Westerly leaving. She bolted from the room and ran toward the parking lot.

The camper remained where it had been parked yesterday. Nothing looked out of place. Grabbing the handle to the cab, she tried to open it. It was locked. Blocking the light, she peered inside. The cab was empty. She continued around the vehicle until she stood before the back door. The handle turned with ease.

Westerly lay sprawled on the floor. She clambered in as fast as she could, given the narrow space. She felt a strong pulse at his wrist. Moving her hand to his neck, again, there was a strong pulse. She pulled back when he snorted awake. He lifted his head and glared at her, his eyes bloodshot from too much drinking.

"Yes?"

He flopped his head down on the floor. The thud sounded painful. She winced in sympathy.

"What time did you get in?"

Westerly rolled over with a groan. He threw an arm over his eyes. The bright light shining in the open door hurt almost as bad as his head. "Don't know...late."

Nature leaned her back against the wall. She pulled one leg close to her body and wrapped her arms around it. "You should have come to the room. The bed's more comfortable than this floor."

He peeked out from under his arm. "I don't think I would have trusted myself."

She grimaced. "I'm sorry..."

"Nature...stop saying that. It was wrong. We both know that. We work together. Getting involved like that would only mess things up." *There...I said it.* He thought. *Even though I'm not sure I mean it.*

He lowered the arm onto his eyes so that she could not see them. His true feelings would have been obvious, even to a blind man. He bent a leg, keeping the other straight. Suddenly, he was on the move. The drinking binge from last night indicated it wanted freedom. It no longer wanted to remain in a dark warm stomach. It wanted to see the world.

Nature heard Web throw up several times. A few dry heaves followed before quiet settled in. She stayed where she was. She did not want to embarrass him. Instead, she pondered what he

had said. It was a carbon copy of what she thought. She liked Web but respected his decision of keeping their relationship on neutral ground. It helped make the job less of a hassle. Especially a job as hard as this one.

The door to the bathroom opened. Web held onto the frame with one hand, and his stomach with the other. He looked like a Mack truck had run him over. When he was sure it was safe to leave the sanctuary, he worked his way to the couch.

"Feeling better?"

"Give me a minute to think about it." He sat down, placed his palms on either temple, and pressed. After he relaxed, he said, "No."

"Want something to eat?" A smile crept onto her face. She knew the answer, but could not help getting a jab in.

The mention of food caused Westerly to turn greener than he already was. He puffed out his cheeks and ran into the bathroom again.

Nature shook her head. She got to her feet and moved to the back door. Before she exited, she turned around. "Web...I'll be in the dining area having breakfast. When you can, come join me." The smile broadened when the sound of heaving was her only reply.

It was almost an hour later when Web made it to the dining area. He still looked a little peaked but at least he was not green.

"Doing better now?"

"A little." He smiled sheepishly as he sat down.

"Are you able to eat yet?"

The waitress came to the table while they spoke. He grimaced at the thought of food. He ordered coffee alone.

"I guess that answers my question." She speared another batch of eggs and shoved them into her mouth. She smiled at the look on his face as he watched her.

He thanked the waitress when she brought his coffee. After taking a sip, he asked, "What do you want to do now?"

"I want to go home. I don't think there is anything else we can do here. Maybe this time we can get out before something else comes up."

"Let's hope so."

Almost as if on cue, Deputy Spangle walked in the door. He waved when he caught sight of the pair at the table. He moved in their direction with determination. Nature groaned. Westerly glanced over his shoulder and groaned along with her. They were under control by the time Spangle reached them.

"Good, I caught you in time. Another interesting development just came up." He sat next to Westerly and indicated to the waitress for a cup of coffee. She nodded her head and brought it over to him. Once she was gone, he continued. "A girl north of here disappeared close to a week ago. Witnesses remember seeing a plain brown van outside her bungalow shortly before then."

Nature felt a coldness settle in. She sipped the warm coffee in an attempt to rid herself of it. It didn't help. She knew what he was going to say, what he was going to ask.

"The family became worried when they didn't hear from her and broke into her place. She wasn't inside. Her purse, ID, and car were there, but not her." Spangle cupped his hands around his coffee. He stared at it, avoiding eye contact. "We need to know if the same man was involved." He finally met her eyes, "Would you mind?"

The coldness knotted. She wanted to say no. She wanted to go home. Usually between sessions, she had some downtime, time to clear her thoughts, her nerves. Since coming to Florida, none had been allowed.

With a heavy heart, she said, "Of course."

Spangles face brightened. "Great. I'll give you the directions. Officer Stack of the Daytona area will meet you. I'll let him know you're coming." He rose to his feet, pulled a piece of paper out of his back pocket, and slid it across the table. "Thanks, Mrs. Kranderson. I'll keep in touch." He left before she could say anything else, or change her mind.

Web sat expressionless. He picked up the cup before him and sipped at its contents. A couple of sips later, he said, "I guess that means we aren't going home yet."

Nature pushed her plate away. She no longer had an appetite. "No...I guess not."

Web pulled the plate toward him. He picked up the fork and stabbed at a pile of eggs. With his mouth full, he repeated, "No...I

guess not."

Nine

Nature sat in the passenger seat watching the scenery as it went by. The directions took them past the beach. The ocean was gentle at the moment, which was more than what she could say about herself. She was in complete turmoil.

Spangle had mentioned the brown van again. Those words brought the feeling of the kidnapper to the forefront. She dreaded having to sense him again. The first time with Rew was bad. The second time with the Texas girl had also been bad. At least with those sessions, she had had time to recoup. This one was the day after one, which was the day after another. Not enough downtime in between. She hoped her frayed nerves could take it.

Westerly pulled into a parking area in front of a group of small bungalows. A police car sat in front of the one with the number five on it. They parked next to it. He got out. She remained in the camper. He walked to the front of the vehicle and waited. She shivered. He faced the building, giving her time to collect herself. She silently thanked him before grabbing the handle to open the door. With a heavy sigh, she got out. They moved to the door together. Before they reached it, it opened.

"Mrs. Kranderson?"

She nodded her head yes.

"Deputy Spangle notified me that you were coming. Thank you. I'm Officer Stack."

She saw from the expression on the officer's face and the shine in his eyes that he was sincere in his statement. She was grateful. The coming event was stressful enough. To have another

strong negative emotion nearby only added to the situation and she needed all her strength, especially if the missing girl was actually taken by the mysterious man.

The officer reached out a hand to shake hers. She hesitated, then grabbed it, giving it a firm shake. When he saw the gloves, he realized what he had done and blushed. He let go quickly.

"It's okay. I get this often." She smiled to soften the man's embarrassment.

"Sorry....I forgot..."

"Can we go inside?" A small crowd was gathering. They whispered and pointed in her direction.

"Oh," He glanced around, "Yea." He stepped back and made room for the pair to enter.

The inside was as quaint as the outside. Everything was tidy except for the soda cans sitting on the small table and the area around the bed. Nature saw the restraints hanging from the bed frame. She saw the clothes piled on the floor. She saw the small wire whisk lying next to them. She froze with dread. There was no doubt in her mind. This was the work of the man.

Westerly came up behind Nature. He ignored the room. His eyes were on her. "Is it him?"

Instead of answering, she moved deeper into the room. She took a glove off and picked up one of the cans. She immediately dropped it, spilling soda on the floor. She rubbed her fingers on her pants trying to get the sensation of slime off them. The room seemed to grow smaller. She was having some difficulty catching her breath. She hated the thought of touching the clothes but knew she had to.

Her legs were weak as she made her way to the bed. She hesitated once she stood next to it. In a fluid motion, she stooped and picked up the girls swimsuit. Again, the sensation of slime filled her. Unlike with the can, it filled her to her soul. She saw the girl tied to the bed. She saw the haziness that was the man as he did so many horrible things to her. She felt the hunger that consumed him. She stared at the wall but did not really see it. She was lost in the acts performed here.

Westerly matched strides with her, moving when she did. He saw her pick up the suit. He saw her gasp. It looked as if she was lost, lost in the vision, like before. When the gasping continued,

causing her lips to turn blue, he knew she was in trouble. He grabbed the clothes from her hands and threw them to the side. Nature was unaware. She was trapped. He held her and slapped her across the face several times. Finally, she took a deep raspy breath.

Westerly picked her up in his arms and started for the door leading outside. The officer followed.

"Do you want me to call an ambulance?"

"No."

"But she looks bad."

"I said no!"

He kicked the door open and carried Nature into the fresh air. She had passed out, something he considered a blessing. He hated to see her suffer during those damned episodes. It ate at his heart. The back of the camper appeared before him. He did not remember the walk to it. He yanked the door open. He entered with Nature slung over a shoulder. He gently laid her on the couch. After making sure she was able to breathe on her own, he returned to the back and exited. The officer was waiting for him.

"Stack, you need to put out an all points bulletin for a plain brown van. It will be driven by a single occupant."

"Do you have a description of the driver?"

"Unfortunately...no."

"What about a tag number?"

"I don't have one." Westerly remembered what Nature had said in Montana about the vehicle and the lack of anything else.

The officer looked skeptical. Westerly had to give him credit; he listened. Taking out a notepad, he jotted down the pertinent information before going to his car. He spoke into the mike for a minute before he returned to Web.

"The info is out. It's a bit thin but I hope it helps."

"I hope it is enough to save the life of the girl...or girls...in his possession." Web remembered the girl recently taken from the beach. Now the killer possibly had two in his possession. Deep in his heart, he thought the first girl was already dead. He didn't say so to the fellow officer before him.

Stack nodded his head. He glanced at the camper. "She okay?"

"She just needs rest."

"You going to stay in the area?"

"I think we're both ready to go home."

"Give it another day. I'll know by then if I need you or not."

He glared at the man as if he had just asked him to take a flying leap off the Golden Gate Bridge. He was tired. Nature was tired. He needed to get back to his job. So many things were drawing them back. Yet, they had to stay, stay to assist with the hunt for a killer. He sighed.

"One more day. After that, we go home."

He decided to leave the camper where it was rather than drive around and have Nature wake up to a moving vehicle. If she woke up disoriented, she might hurt herself. That was something he would not allow. He cared too deeply. Since he hadn't a snowballs chance in hell of being with her, the least he could do was protect her.

He returned to the back, got in, and made sure Nature was still okay before he pulled out a drink from the small fridge. He sat in a chair and looked out the window. Traffic flowed past at a steady rate. The sounds of their engines were almost rhythmic, stop for the light down the road, go again...stop...go...stop...go.

The next thing he knew, the light outside was graying with the coming of night. He jerked around and looked at the couch. Nature was gone. He flew outside. He did not see her. She was not in the cab. His heart raced. Where could she be? Was she okay? He had to find her.

Suddenly, he saw her. She stood under a tree, arms crossed in front of her. She was staring at the sky. White fluffy clouds floated gently past. They were turning pink with the coming sunset. Her long brown hair waved with the slight breeze. He rushed to her side.

"Nature...what do you think you're doing running off like that."

She continued to watch the clouds. "I didn't run. I walked."

"You know what I mean."

"Yes...I do."

Her voice was so soft. He had a hard time hearing it above the drone of the nearby traffic. He moved in front of her. Dark circles surrounded her eyes. She looked exhausted.

"Come back inside. You need to rest."

"Rest..."

He steered her toward the camper. Before they could reach it, a van pulled into the area. It had one of those camera things mounted on its roof. Westerly groaned. The press had found out about them. Now there would be no peace. Now there would only be hassles.

A tall good-looking man jumped out. He had a piece of paper in one hand, a mike in the other. He ran over, shouting questions before he reached them. A man carrying a camera was hot on his heels.

"Mrs. Kranderson! Mrs. Kranderson! Can I ask you some questions?"

Westerly urged her to move faster.

The reporter blocked the way. "What do you know about the recent kidnappings in our area?"

Nature flung her arms up to ward off the mike shoved in her face. Westerly stepped between the woman and the reporter. The camera operator swung his camera back and forth. Total pandemonium broke out.

"Is it true you can sense the killer through objects belonging to the girls? Are they still alive?" The reporter shot out questions in rapid-fire fashion.

"Leave her alone! Get outta here!"

Westerly forced the man out of the way. He wrapped an arm protectively around Nature and dragged her into the camper, slamming the door in the reporters and camera operator's faces. The reporter wasn't giving up so easily. He banged on the door, shouting more questions. Nature covered her ears. She squeezed her eyes shut as tight as they would go. She spun around to face the door.

"Go away! Go away!"

Westerly hugged her against his body to quiet her down. The last thing they needed to do was feed into the man outside. He whispered nonsense words. He brushed her hair back. He guided her to the couch and forced her to sit. When she stayed there, he went back to the doorway and peeked out the curtain covering the window.

The reporter stood with his back to the camper. He was speaking into the mike. The camera pointed toward the vehicle then back at the man. When they were finished, they returned to

their van. They stayed. They did not leave as he hoped they would. If he wanted to move the camper, he had to face them again. That wasn't going to be pretty. He might go to jail for kicking the shit out of a reporter. That would not be good. He had to protect Nature.

The man decided not to go to the cabin. He decided to go hunting instead. The girl was still with him, something he usually never did. He had kept her so that when the pent up pressure inside became too much, he could release it on her. She had ceased to be a person. She was now only a means to an end. He had used her in unimaginable ways. She no longer responded, even when he knew she was in pain.

He drove to a bar and parked in the rear. He wanted something to drink, something other than water or soda. It had been a long time since he wanted alcohol. Tonight, it just seemed right. He needed to wash away the sadness that engulfed him.

Walking into the gloomy interior, he went to the farthest corner of the bar. He pulled out a stool and sat. The bartender came over, took his order and left. He returned shortly with the drink. The man sipped at the bourbon. It burned his throat all the way down. It felt good. He glanced up at the television. The local news was on. The mouths of the commentators were moving but nothing came out. The volume was too low.

He saw pictures of farm equipment, local fairs, and the news on the soldiers in Iraq. He didn't envy their lifestyle. They had no say as to what happened to them. Other local news flashed across the screen. He, for the most part, ignored it.

The bourbon was finished and he was getting up when a picture appeared on the television. It was a picture of the girl in the van. The difference was in this picture she was smiling, like in a school photo. He froze. He saw the girls name across the bottom. He saw the parents hugging each other He saw a police officer talking into a mike before his face.

The picture changed. It focused on a camper. He saw a woman being hustled past the reporter. He was mesmerized. She was beautiful. Her brown hair flowed like silk, her figure was average, even a tiny bit on the chunky side, but that wasn't what mat-

tered. It was her eyes that had him glued. He only saw them for a second, but it was enough. He now understood why he could not find the One. He was looking for someone too young. Excitement filled him. He felt himself rise to the occasion. He had to leave. He had to get on the road. He stayed long enough to find out where she was before heading out the door and around the building.

Patricia heard the man get in. She no longer cared. She knew what came next. She heard the curtains part, then slide shut. She saw the man come toward her, felt his hands all over her body. In a short amount of time, she had felt those hands a lot. She hated his touch. She hated the feel of the rods, his and the metal one, as they were shoved into any opening in her body. She hated herself. Since she did not believe she was going to survive this journey, she decided it was time to fade into her imaginary world, a world where she was free to run, where her parents waited for her with open arms, where Randy knelt and proposed to her.

She never knew when he finished and got off. She had no idea when the van started rolling down the road. She was in her world, a wonderful world. A world where it wasn't a nightmare to have sex, where she no longer hurt. She knew it was time, time to remain. A faint smile came to her lips, lips that were no longer taped. It never faded, even when the man stopped to use her in ways that no one should ever have to endure during the long drive back.

After getting a quickie from the girl, he started toward Florida. He backtracked on highway 75 until he was outside Atlanta. That was where the police reminded him about his choice of vehicles. The man watched as one trailed him. He remained calm. The lights were off. The officer was just following. He saw a sign for a mall and exited. The cop also exited. He frowned. He went several miles down the road and entered the parking area. The cop followed. He parked in a spot close to the building. The cop drove past. He glanced out the window as the brake lights came on and faded with release. While other cars made their way through the lot, blocking the officer's view, the man left the van and moved toward the mall entrance.

He watched as the police car disappeared around the building. He hesitated, not sure what he should do. Should he return to the van or continue the direction he was going. When the police car

reappeared, his decision was finalized. He made it into the store without incident. He spun around at the sound of a car traveling at a high rate of speed. The tires squealed when the driver slammed on the brakes, causing the car to turn slightly. The officer flung his door open and crouched behind it, gun extended beyond the safety of the vehicle, pointed at the van.

People in the store congregated toward the windows. Their expressions varied. Some were fascinated by the actions taking place while others snickered and poked fun at the police. The man blended in with them, showing the same fascinated appearance. He stayed behind a group of older women. Their constant chittering grated on his nerves. To alleviate the irritation, he pictured a group of geese in a children's cartoon honking back and forth. Even though he laughed inside, he kept the proper look on his face. He did not smile.

Another police car screamed into the area, siren blaring, lights shining. It was followed by another and another and another. When the screeching stopped, the man would have bet money that over half the police department surrounded the van. Someone by the door opened it a little bit. A voice echoed into the store.

"Driver, get out of the vehicle." Hesitation. "Driver...get out of the vehicle!"

That statement told the man that the cop who went around the building had missed his departure from the van. He was thankful for his good luck. He hoped it continued.

The crowd watched as one of the cops moved from around his car. He hunched over and ran up to the van. Slowly, with both hands holding his weapon, he inched along the side. Once he reached the drivers window, the cop threw the door open and pointed his weapon inside. He lowered it when no one sat there.

Another officer ran to the van. He stayed near the back, weapon held ready. The first cop joined him. After a brief exchange of nods, one grabbed the handle and threw the door open while the other pointed his gun toward the interior. Both officers paled. They straightened. Their mouths hung open.

The girl before them was naked. Her long brown hair was a tangled mess. Her brown eyes stared at them; they could tell she did not see them. A slight smile creased her lips. She was lost,

lost in a world of her own making.

One of the cops recovered from his shock, put away his gun, and crawled in. Her limbs swayed with the motion of the van. Ropes attached to the roof wrapped around the wrists and ankles. The skin was raw and bleeding. Bruises covered her everywhere. She never responded.

"Call for an ambulance," the officer said as he unfastened the ropes.

The other officer stared.

"Gerald! Call for an ambulance NOW!"

The shout caused the frozen officer to come alive. He grabbed the radio mike attached to his shirt and spoke into it. A response from the dispatcher indicated the requested ambulance was on the way. He called out for a blanket. One of the many officers popped the trunk of her car. She brought one over. She gasped at the sight of the girl, but recovered quickly. Getting in, she covered the battered body before moving to her head. She cradled it in her lap, whispering nothing words while smoothing the tangled hair away from her young face. The brown eyes remained empty, unresponsive.

The man watched. He regretted the loss of the girl. He should have killed her after he learned she wasn't the One. Now he had to hope she was not able to give the police a description. On the last stop, she never responded to his pleasures, to his everhungry needs. She only smiled. Maybe she was too far gone, too far to come back. That would be a blessing. He departed from the window and entered the main part of the mall.

The rest of the mall was oblivious as to what was transpiring outside. They talked, laughed, and shopped like usual. They ignored the man walking among them. An odor wafted in the air. He sniffed deep. Following the scent, he walked to a food stand where pretzels and such were sold. He bought one, along with a small bottled water. He sat on one of the benches located a short distance from the stand. While munching on the pretzel, he watched the crowd.

He was thinking of how to get another vehicle for the trip south when the sound of laughter echoed from behind him. It was coming his way. He did not turn around. A woman and her daughter strolled past, bags from various stores hung from their arms.

He felt his crotch begin to swell. He crossed his legs and bit into the salty food, savoring the taste. They moved away. He chewed, swallowed, and rose to his feet. He threw the rest of the pretzel in the trash bin. He opened the water bottle and drank until his thirst felt quenched. It found the trash bin also. Strolling at a casual pace, he watched their asses swing with each step, teasing him as he followed. He smiled.

The females left the mall on the opposite side from the police action. They were talking about what they had bought, unaware of the man behind them. The mother pulled out her keys from her purse. She walked to the trunk and inserted one into the lock. The daughter was too young to drive yet. She looked to be about fifteen. The man saw his chance. No one was near. When the mother was bent over the open trunk, placing the bags inside, he ran up behind her and shoved her hard. Arms went in all directions. The woman tried to catch herself but the man prevented it. She fell in. He slammed the trunk shut.

The daughter gawked at the man. She was too startled to cry out. Before she could recover, he covered her mouth. The man pulled her close and removed the keys from the trunk. Dragging her to the driver's door, he unlocked it. He threw her in. He sat down beside her, hugging her against his body. It was an older model with a full seat. Something he missed in the newer cars.

Pounding echoed throughout the interior of the car. Muffled shouting followed it. The mother called out the girl's name repeatedly. The man turned over the engine. It purred to life, drowning out the offensive noise. Fortunately, it was an automatic. It allowed him to keep an arm over the girls shoulder. He put it in gear and drove out the nearest exit. Within minutes, he was back on the highway, making his way toward Florida and the woman he felt was the One.

Ten

The man saw the sign for Daytona. It indicated the city was still many miles ahead. He sighed. He almost regretted killing the girl. Her breasts were too small and she had been too young for him. Her body was in the trunk along with the mother.

He still had the mother. He kept her because she was older, like the one on the television. When he thought of the woman, he felt his penis harden. He rubbed his pants, exciting himself further. He exited the highway. At the stop sign, he turned right onto a two-lane road. He headed north. If the woman were gone from where the TV said she was last, he would find her. She was too important.

A dirt road was on the left. The man saw it coming and slowed. He turned onto it. It led into an overgrown area near a lake. He smiled. He liked lakes. They reflected the sunlight the way a crystal glass did when hit by the bright light. The rainbow colors were a joy to watch. He parked the car near a clump of cattails. He sat on the hood for several minutes, feeling the warmth from the metal heat up his bottom. He enjoyed the twinkling on the water. With a content sigh, he got off and started toward the trunk.

Mrs. Murray, Nellie, felt the car stop. She held her dead daughter close. She was in shock. One minute they were laughing and shopping, the next, Maria was gone. She had cried for a long time, unable to believe what was happening.

The trunk opened. She raised a hand to block the bright light shining in her eyes. She felt Maria shift. She tried to grab her

daughter; a hand slapped her. She whimpered. Her daughter disappeared. The trunk slammed shut again. Darkness consumed her. She hit the trunk. She screamed for Maria. She cried out as the pain of loss wracked through her again.

The man removed the girl from the trunk. He had no need for a dead body. He was going to leave her in the lake. As he picked her up, he caught a flash of her vagina. It, in turn, caused him to bulge. Even in death, he had standards. She was still too young for him.

He placed the girl on the ground, stepped back so he could view the forbidden pleasure better, and unzipped his pants. The penis leaped out. He wrapped his fingers around it and pumped and pumped until the pent up need exploded from the tip.

Many hours later, he was back on the road. The mother remained in the trunk. The daughter was not with her. He had left her floating in the lake, a morsel for the alligators located there. Since he was getting close to his destination, he tied ropes around the woman's extremities and secured them to the frame. He did not want her to bang against the metal, thus alerting others of her presence. A gag covered her mouth. He had future plans for her.

Thinking about the mother passed the time while he drove the rest of the way toward the woman of his dreams. He grew more certain with the passing of time that she was the One, the one to complete him, the one he would spend hours upon hours sharing his many ways of pleasure with.

Nature was bored. They remained in the camper to avoid the obnoxious reporter outside. She had slept for almost twelve hours. It was much needed rest. She felt like a human again. She stood by the little stove. A frying pan with two hamburgers in it sat on top. They sizzled and popped as they cooked. It was early afternoon.

"That smells good."

"It's my own special recipe."

"A special recipe for hamburgers...what will they think up next." Web shook his head. He smiled to show he was teasing.

Nature grabbed a hand towel. She spun it tight in her hands and popped it at the man standing near the window. It hit his

butt. He yelped with pain. She tossed the towel down and picked up the spatula again. She assumed an innocent look.

"What was that for?"

"Just because."

Web rubbed the spot where the towel hit. He returned his attention to the window. The van remained parked across the way. It had not moved since its arrival. He frowned. "I thought they'd get bored by now and leave. I guess you're big news."

The mention of the reporter caused Nature to sigh. She was frustrated at being cooped up. Any time she tried to go out, a man jumped out of the van and started her way, mike in hand. She ducked back inside to avoid him. That was a day and a half ago. She was sick of it.

"Maybe we should make a dash for it. Get to the cab and head for the interstate. I want to go home." She flipped one of the burgers. "The police obviously don't need us. They haven't returned."

"Officer Stack asked us to wait."

Nature slammed the spatula onto the counter. She spun around to face Web. "I don't care! I'm tired of this place! I want to go home!"

Before Web could say anything, she was out the door heading toward the van. The reporter got out. He started toward her. He stopped and waited when he saw she was coming his way. He held the mike ready. The camera operator was setting the camera on his shoulder. She reached them as Westerly was getting out of the camper.

"Mrs. Kranderson, what do you know..."

Suddenly, the reporter was spinning toward the ground, his sentence incomplete. The mike flew into the air. It landed with a thud. The camera operator gawked.

Nature stood over the downed man, her fist held ready to deliver another punch. She was furious. "Why can't you just leave me alone? Go make someone else's life a living hell!"

The reporter rubbed his jaw. He made no attempt to get up. He glanced at the camera to see if it was rolling. It was. He looked back at the angry woman. "I only wanted to get your side of the story."

"You don't need it. Get it from the cops if you want it that badly...or make it up. That's what you're good at."

"But Mrs. Kranderson...I want to report the facts."

"Facts....I'll give you facts!"

She lunged toward the cringing man but arms grabbed her from behind, preventing her from reaching him. Westerly dragged her back to the camper. She fought. She shouted. Once inside the vehicle, she cried in frustration. Westerly remained by the door to keep her from leaving again. He moved the curtain and watched the reporter get to his feet. The man smiled after talking to the camera operator. He picked up the lost mike. Straightening, he started talking into the camera. Web groaned. He knew what he was reporting. He didn't like it.

Something bounced off his back. Westerly turned to see a spatula hit the floor. A very angry woman stood with a pot in her hand. She cocked her arm and launched it at him. He ducked.

"What did you do that for?" he shouted.

"You should ask!"

"I tried to stop you from making a complete ass of yourself but...too late." He gestured toward the window. "That reporter is having a field day right now. He has footage that makes you look like a crazed lunatic. If a national network gets hold of that...there goes your reputation."

"I don't care about my reputation!"

"What about helping those girls! Do you care about that?"

The two stood glaring at each other. Nature broke the staring contest. She flopped onto the bench.

"I do care. I want to find that sicko as badly as you do. It's just that my nerves are raw. I haven't had my usual down time between sessions. I haven't had any time to recover." She leaned forward, resting her elbows on her knees, hiding her face with her hands.

"Neither have those girls. They went through hell before they died. Remember that whenever you decide to be an ass again."

He turned away from her and returned his attention to the window. He was tired. Tired of being here, tired of idiot people, tired of death. He had been with law enforcement for more years than he cared to count. In that time, he saw so much death...including that of his family. A revengeful maniac had followed him home. He came back after Web left for work and killed his daughter. He almost killed his wife. After she got out of the

hospital, she filed for a divorce. That was 15 years ago. He still wasn't over it.

Arms wrapped around his waist. He felt Nature hug his back. He reached up and placed his hand over hers. He forgot that her gloves were off.

She felt his pain and loss surge through her. She wanted to pull away. The fact that he was someone she cared about prevented it. She wanted to help. The vision of Web finding his murdered daughter and his stabbed wife wracked her insides. The vision of him falling to his knees trying to shake Megan awake, the vision of his hands covered with her blood, and the vision of him throwing his head back, screaming long and loud, caused her to shudder. The death of her husband had been hard. This was a sheer nightmare.

The vision changed from the house to one at the hospital. She saw Web sitting at his wife's bedside. She saw the wife wake and him reach for her hand. She pulled it away. She turned her head, refusing to look at him. Web reached for it again. She put her hand under the covers. His face fell. It wasn't enough that he had lost his child, now; his love was lost to him too. The killer's revenge was complete. He had lost everything, including himself for a while.

Nature felt the tears run down her cheeks. The man in her arms turned to face her. She felt his lips on hers, gentle at first, then with more urgency. He pulled her close. She felt his hands move over her body. She felt him lift her shirt. She didn't resist. She wanted him as much as he wanted her. She no longer cared that they worked together. They had something in common, something that would reduce any chance of messing up their working relationship. They shared the pain of loss, loss of loved ones.

Web kissed Nature. He reached under her shirt and felt her smooth skin. Her nipples rose to his touch. He pulled her shirt off. He bent over and kissed each breast. She bent back; she didn't stiffen like before.

What he was doing was wrong. He knew it. It could mess up everything they had accomplished, but it had been so long since he had been with anyone. So long since he allowed himself to feel this way. He was finally able to admit it, admit that he loved Na-

ture. He was finally able to break free of the grief and open the door to his heart.

He picked her up and carried her into the space in front of the table. He laid her on the floor, stretching out beside her. He looked for any sign of rejection in her eyes. He saw none. Smiling, he bent over and kissed her again, soft, and gentle. She reached her arms over his neck. She curled his hair with its splashes of gray around her fingers. He rubbed her breasts, squeezing them, feeling the erect tips in his palm.

Nature grabbed his hand and guided it lower. He took the hint and unsnapped her pants. The zipper echoed across the camper. They smiled. He stood to pull on a pant leg. She arched her back to make it easier for him to remove the clothing. His disappeared after she was naked. She lay there admiring the firm body standing above her. She knew he was in his fifties; he still looked good.

He closed his eyes and took in a deep breath, releasing it slowly. He was afraid she would stop him like the last time. He wasn't sure he could take it if she did. When he felt her hands brush against his erect penis, his heart raced. He leaned his head back as he felt her soft lips surround the swollen skin. He experienced untold joy when the lips sucked him deep then withdrew, repeating the process again and again. He grabbed the cabinets on either side to prevent his knees from buckling. He moaned when he felt her fingers teasing his balls.

Web could not believe his luck. A short two days ago, he was smashed from drinking away her rejection, her sudden panic at their making love. Now, she filled him with a love he had only felt once before in his life.

Nature saw his head lean back. She saw his legs quiver with excitement. She wanted him now. Releasing his penis, she worked her mouth up his body. When she reached his nipples, she circled each one with the tip of her tongue. She loved the sensation of his body against her tongue. It was something she had not done for 11 years, not since the death of her husband. It felt almost weird, but, at the same time, it felt right.

She placed her hands on Web's head and pulled his lips toward hers. They touched. Their tongues snaked around each other. They both were hungry, hungry for something neither had had for some time. Web broke the kiss and buried his face into

her neck, wrapped his arms around her, and guided her to the floor. He lay on her, kissing her again, like a man who had found water after crossing the desert without any.

Nature opened her legs, wrapping them around his. She brushed against his hard penis. She wiggled her hips, helping it find its mark. When she felt the tip against her opening, she grabbed his ass and pulled. Web followed her lead. He pushed gently. When the tingling of ecstasy filled his every fiber, the gentle rocking of his hips took on a new motion. He started pumping harder and faster. The woman beneath him stiffened.

A new aura flowed through Nature when Web entered her. She felt the blend of several men. She felt her husband with his love for her, she felt Web with his love and pain, and she felt the man. The memory of what the man had put those girls through, the suffering and torture, filled her. In her heart, she knew the man was not here...that Web would not cause her to endure the same pain. That thought, and the feelings emanating from the one in her arms, allowed her to block out the bad and accept the good.

Web knew she was going to reject him again. He could feel it in the stiffness of her body. If she did, he would leave. He was not able to handle the emotional roller coaster ride any longer. He cared about Nature too much. He would not be able to stay around her if he could not have her. He closed his eyes and waited for the inevitable struggle to begin. When it didn't, he opened them. She was looking into his with those beautiful brown eyes of hers. Love and acceptance filled them. He was overjoyed. It showed in his passionate lovemaking.

Their lovemaking continued long into the night. On the stove, a pan with cold hamburgers, sitting in a pool of white grease, was on a back burner, forgotten. Outside, two men sat in a van. Wrappers of takeout food covered the dash. They were cold and they missed their families.

"How much longer do we have to do this?" The man who operated the camera asked.

"As long as it takes," the reporter said. "The upper echelons think this one will be a huge story."

"At the moment, I think it is a huge pain in my ass. I need a shower and my wife."

"All you think about is sex."

"You're one to talk. I heard you moaning out last night." He assumed a dramatic pose, "Oh...oh...Monica...Monica...oh baby...take it baby...take it."

The reporter smiled. "Jealous."

"You know it."

Both men settled into their seats. They spoke of their families, the couple in the camper, and about the missing girls. After a while, the only noise inside the van was the sound of snoring.

Nature caressed her fingers across Web's shoulder. A sense of completeness ebbed through her. She didn't realize how much she had missed it. It was nice. Her light caress woke the sleeping man. He glanced at her, his eyes thick with sleep. He smiled.

"Morning sunshine," he muttered.

"Morning to you bright eyes."

"Did you sleep well?"

"Not an ounce." She lied.

She kissed him. He responded with renewed passion. They made love again. The rising sun heralded their release with its rays of pink and yellow. Afterwards, they showered in the small stall, laughing and giggling like kids.

Nature glanced out the window when she finished dressing. There was no movement in the van. "Web...do you see anything going on over there?"

He moved to her side, "No."

"Wanna make a break for it?"

"To the cab?"

"Yea."

"And go where?" He knew the answer. It was the same one he wanted.

"Home." She dropped the curtain back in place. When she faced Web, she encircled him with her arms. "I miss my ranch. I miss Sandy. I miss the quiet."

He wrapped his arms around her, "Me too. Besides, I need to get back. Deputy Frewerson is probably going crazy by now."

She gave him a peck on the lips before letting go. "Since you drive like a cop," she walked to the counter and picked up the

keys, "you get to go first."

He took the keys from her outreached hand. Once he stood by the door, he spun around on his heels, holding the keys in the air like a gun, and said, "Ready deputy?"

Holding her fist up, the pointer extended like the barrel of a gun, she said, "Ready Freddie."

Web flung the door open and leaped to the ground at a run. Nature was hot on his heels. They separated and went to either side of the cab. Web unlocked his door and leaped in. He quickly leaned over and pulled the handle, unlocking the passenger door. Nature hopped it. As she was shutting her door, a shout echoed across the parking lot. It came from the van.

The reporter and camera operator were flinging their doors open. They were too slow. Web fired up the engine, threw the gear lever into reverse, and stomped on the gas pedal. The camper responded immediately. Smoke rose from where the tires spun before getting traction. He slammed on the brakes and pulled the lever into drive. He saw black marks in the mirror when the camper shot forward. The men from the van were leaping back into their vehicle. He watched it start after them.

The camper flew down Madison Ave. At the next intersection, Web turned sharply to the left onto Nova Rd and headed south. The camper rocked back and forth but Web brought it under control quickly. He looked back. The van was trapped by traffic. With any luck, it would stay that way until they got out of sight. He saw a sign for Morris Blvd and turned right. They drove past the Daytona Beach International Airport. Web considered turning into it and hiding but the camper was too obvious. It would stand out. He glanced at Nature. She was hanging on to the seat with one hand while the other had a death grip on the door handle. She noticed him looking at her. He held up a thumbs-up gesture. She smiled, refusing to release her grip.

Web returned his attention to the road and saw a sign for I-95 up ahead. On Beville Rd, he turned right and mashed the gas pedal. The news van had disappeared several blocks back. He didn't reduce his speed. It might catch up any second now and he wanted to make it to the highway before that happened. He relaxed a little only after the camper merged in with the I-95 traffic. As they passed over a bridge, he and Nature saw the van sitting

off on the side of the road. They had apparently taken a wrong turn and went around the airport instead. He honked the horn and waved. Nature also waved. She was having as much fun as he was.

It felt good to be heading home. Home. It was a word that had meaning again. As if sensing his thoughts, even though she wasn't touching him, Nature glanced sideways at him. She snuggled against his body when he raised his arm, placing it over her shoulder. They rode that way for a long time, both glad to finally be on the road heading north.

Eleven

The man entered the Daytona area just after two. He drove down several streets trying to locate the one the news people had focused on. He saw a sign for a local airport. He ignored it. He had no use for planes. They just made a lot of noise and polluted the environment. He decided to stop and ask directions.

He pulled into a gas station and filled the tank. The trunk remained quiet. He noticed a van parked in a spot outside the door. It had one of those camera mounts on top of it. He wondered if it was the same film crew. If it was, he knew it would be a sign, a sign that he was on the trail of the One. He went inside to pay.

Two men hung out by the coffee machine. One wore a suit. They seemed nervous. He moved closer to the glass coolers with the drinks inside. They stood just off to the side of where the men were. He listened to their conversation.

"What do you think will happen?"

"It wasn't our fault. We did the best we could under the circumstances. If they would have sent us some relief, we would have been ready instead of being so damned tired," the guy in the suit said.

"Do you think they will can us?"

"Nah. If they did, then they'd have to do our job."

That made the guy in the jeans chuckle. "Yea, I could just see Veronica sleeping in the van."

"I'd like to see Veronica sleep in the van." The suit lifted his eyebrows a couple of times.

"I bet you would, you sex craved maniac. Don't you ever get

enough?"

"Not when it involves a good looking thing like her."

"Speaking of women, what did you think about the one in the camper? What was her name?"

The man was getting bored with their conversation. He was about to lose hope on getting anything useful when the sudden mention of the camper caused him to pay closer attention. Maybe they would give him some information that would help him in his search after all. He glanced at the drinks, listening, making it appear as if he was having a hard time deciding.

The suit pulled out a notepad. He glanced at some words on the page. "Nature. Nature Kranderson. She was okay. I wouldn't mind exploring what she had."

The man seethed. If she was the One, then this kind of talk was inappropriate. He held his tongue though.

"I bet that guy with her got a taste of her." The man in the jeans poured some coffee into a cup. He put a lid on it before continuing. "They slept in that camper all night. Can't imagine that happening without a bit of hanky panky."

"Now who's the sex craved maniac." The suit moved away with the man in jeans. They paid for their coffee and returned to the van.

After he recovered from his initial anger, the man stood before the drinks, frozen. Realization hit him. Did he actually hear what he thought he heard? Did he actually have a name to go with the face? Could his luck be that good? Could she truly be the one he sought for so long?

"Hey buddy. You gonna stand there and let all the cold air out or are you gonna grab something.'

The man was jolted out of his reverie. He grabbed a bottle of Pepsi and shut the door. Walking up to the counter, he said, "Sorry about that."

"Just don't let it happen again."

"I won't." He pulled out his money. "I owe for this and a tank of gas."

The clerk looked out the window. "That yours?" He indicated the older model Ford sitting at pump six.

"Yeah."

"Nice car."

"Thanks."

"That will be $31.75."

The man handed over two twenties. He took the eight dollars and folded it with the other bills. He dropped the quarter into one of those fundraiser things that sat on the counter. Picking up the soda, the man whistled a catchy little tune he remembered from somewhere as he pushed the door open. He had no clue what the name of the song was. He just liked it.

He patted the trunk as he went past. The thought of the woman inside caused him to think of the woman on the TV. He got in and twisted the lid off the bottle. He took a long drink before starting the engine. He had no idea which way to go. The men from the van gave no indication as to which direction the One had escaped. It didn't matter. He had something that was of far greater importance. He had a name. With a name, one could find out any information one wanted on the internet, even an address and phone number. And with a name like Nature, the list would not likely be long.

He smiled as he pulled back onto the street and started in the direction indicated by the sign for the nearby university. At the university, there would be computers. Where there were computers, there was access. Where there was access, there was information. He looked forward to seeing what he could find out about a woman named Nature Kranderson.

The deer stood in the trees ahead, grazing on some bits of grass. The hunter had followed it for the last few miles, careful not to alert it of his presence. It felt good to be away from the office. It felt good to be out in fresh air. The last time Mark had gone hunting was about this time last year. His wife nagged him to take the boys but he needed to be alone. Besides, his boys were more interested in video games and their computers, than they were about roughing it in the woods with their dear old dad. If he had brought them, the entire vacation would have been a waste.

He crept quietly up the trail, making sure to place his feet on nothing to draw attention to him. He saw the buck, a twelve pointer, just ahead. He raised his gun. He took aim. He shifted forward slightly. A noise sounded beneath his foot. The buck's

head rose abruptly. It looked in his direction. It bolted for the cover of the trees. He swore. Looking down, the hunter saw a rock. It had moved when he leaned forward, causing a twig part-way under it to snap. Mark picked it up and hefted it into the trees. A dull thud echoed back to him. It sounded weird. Since the buck was long gone, he decided to investigate.

He worked his way closer to the cliff wall. As he drew near, a stench hit his nose. It smelled sicky sweet. It smelled like when the trash was not taken to the curb and the meat inside rotted. He pulled his shirt over his nose to reduce the intensity. Something lay at the base of a large boulder. It was partially covered with leaves. Mark could not tell what it was. He inched forward. The stench increased. It caused his stomach to roll, to toss a bit of acid up into the back of his throat. He swallowed hard, feeling the burning that remained. He almost turned back, but curiosity had him now. He had to see what it was.

He leaned over and brushed some of the leaves out of the way. He fell back, away from what lay underneath. He turned around and threw up. When he finished, he leaned a shoulder against a tree. He glanced over at the body.

The girl lay sprawled at an awkward angle. Her outstretched arms were tied together. Her belly and part of a leg were gone, eaten by wildlife. Part of her face was chewed and one breast was missing. Blonde hair lay tangled around her head. He could tell she was young. The hunter was glad his boys were not with him. This was something they did not need to see. He wished he hadn't. Working his way back to his truck, he got in and picked up his cell phone. He had purposely left it in the vehicle so no one could bother him. He was glad he brought it now. He dialed 911.

Within an hour, the area surrounding the body was a hive of activity. The hunter was questioned and his name and phone number written down before he was allowed to leave. Mark got into his truck. He drove down the dirt trail to the main road, 250, which passed through the Monongahela National Forest.

A short time later, he was home hugging his kids tight. Later that night, he made frantic passionate love to his wife. Afterwards, she looked at him questioningly. It had been a long time since he had shown her this much affection. Usually his job got in the way and made him grumpy. He only pulled her against him. They held

each other all night.

Mark never went hunting again. The events of what happened in the woods never were discussed. The wife did not pry. She was happy. They were a family once more. That was enough.

The man parked in the farthest spot from the building, just in case the woman in the trunk started making noises. He walked to the library and entered the air-conditioned lobby. He smiled. Computers sat off to the right. Students doing research, or whatever they were doing, occupied several stations. The man didn't care. He was only interested in what he came for. He moved toward one that was unoccupied.

He pulled the chair under him and brought the mouse closer. He focused on the screen. He clicked on the spot for the internet. The screen came alive. Typing in the name of a search site, he waited for it to come up. When it did, he clicked on the tab for searching names. The curser blinked. It waited for him to type. He hesitated. He could not remember her last name. He sat back, thinking.

He knew her first name was Nature. He remembered it because it was an appropriate name for the One. The last name...that was something he needed to ponder on. He thought about the men in the gas station. He thought about their conversation. He thought about how they had defiled her with their talk. He smoldered with anger but kept it hidden. He remembered how he wanted to teach the guy in the suit a lesson. He remembered the mouth moving and how he wanted to shut it permanently. As he pictured this, he watched the lips.

Suddenly, it came to him. Kranderson. Her last name was Kranderson. Nature Kranderson. The words flowed as if they belonged in heaven. His fingers flowed across the keyboard in the same manner. He looked at the screen. His hand hovered above the enter button. His heart raced. He held his breath in anticipation. He hit it.

The screen changed. Some squares raced across the monitor. It was searching multiple data banks for the name. It stopped. One name was on the screen. It was hers. He guided the arrow onto it and watched as it turned into a hand. He clicked the

mouse.

The information on the screen made his heart soar. He now had her full information. He now knew how to find the One, the one to complete him, the one who would end his hunting forever. He exited the program and stood. He left the building, keeping his pace casual. He did not want to draw unnecessary attention to himself. The woman was still quiet when he returned to the car. He wondered if she was dead. He would stop later to see. Right now, he had to get on the road. He had to go a long way. He had to go north. He had to go to Montana.

Nature relaxed into her seat. An arm hung out the open window, the fingers waving in the wind caused by the moving vehicle. Her other hand was across the seat. It held onto one belonging to Web. The kidnapped girls were temporarily forgotten. It felt good to be going home. She missed her bed. She missed the calming quiet. She missed Sandy.

Web glanced her way. "Whatcha thinking about over there?"

"Home. I miss Sandy."

"I never thought I'd say this but I miss my job. It's quiet. No mass murderers, no girls missing, only little squabbles between people over fence lines, dogs crapping in yards and stupid shit like that." He caressed her hand.

She no longer wore gloves around him. She felt his emotions as they ebbed through her. She smiled. He meant what he said about his job. It was nice to hear. Moreover, he truly loved her but had yet to say so. To her that was okay, she had yet to say so too.

The mention of mass murderers brought the girls to the forethought of her mind. She shivered. She was glad to be away from so much pain, even if only for a little while. It would be wonderful to finally rest in a place she trusted, with people she cared for around her.

The hand in hers froze. She looked at Web. His eyes were focused on the side mirror. She glanced out hers. She groaned. Behind them was a police car. The lights on top were on. A short blast from the siren informed them to pull over. Web looked at her. He squeezed her hand. She squeezed his in return.

"Maybe it's nothing," she said, hope in her eyes.

"Maybe."

Web pulled the camper to the side of the highway. They were about three and a half hours beyond Savannah. They were close to Atlanta. The police car pulled in behind them. The door opened and a trooper got out. He made his way to the driver door. He peeked inside before coming into full view of the occupants.

"Mrs. Kranderson? Mrs. Nature Kranderson?"

Nature leaned forward in her seat. "That's me. What can I do for you officer?"

"Please step out of the vehicle and come with me."

"What's going on?"

"Please…just do as I ask."

"Can you at least answer her question?" Web said.

"All questions will be answered when we get to our destination. Please come with me."

The officer moved around the camper and opened her door. She glanced at Web nervously before getting out.

"What do you want me to do?" He asked the officer when the door was closed.

"Stay behind me."

"You bet I will," he muttered as he watched Nature and the cop get into the car.

It pulled out onto I-75 with the lights still on and slowed to allow Westerly to catch up. The motor in the camper was good, but not as good as the one in the cruiser. The lights flicked off when he fell in behind it. Nature turned around and waved. He could barely make her out through the darkened windows. He waved back. He followed the car for just over an hour before the turn signal came on. They were exiting into Atlanta.

The cruiser turned right. Web turned. It went several blocks before turning left. He saw a square sign with a white H surrounded by a blue background. He wondered what was going on. They were heading for a hospital. The cruiser turned again. Web followed onto a street appropriate for the state. It was called Peachtree. When they stopped at another intersection, he could see the building. It was older but well maintained. It looked to be a small hospital, maybe 150 beds. Web was intrigued now. He wondered how Nature was holding out. She hated riding in police

cars.

Web turned into the parking lot behind the cop. The car pulled into a spot marked for police. He didn't have that luxury. He had to go to the farthest corner before he found a spot. He opened the door and noticed a pair of gloves on the dash. He grabbed them. Nature would need them, especially here. He grimaced at the thought of her touching anything here.

He hurried back to the cruiser. Nature and the officer were waiting for him. Her arms were crossed in front of her. She gave him a look of gratitude when he handed her the gloves.

"I knew you'd need these."

She gave his hand a squeeze before inserting them inside the soft leather. "Thanks."

The trio started for the entrance. The nametag on the cop's shirt read North. He led the way.

"Have you found out anything?" Web asked.

"No. He was quiet during the entire ride. It was creepy."

"Hey North, what's going on?"

The officer glanced back. "Please, just follow me. You'll understand soon enough."

The automatic doors slid open before them. They entered the air-conditioned lobby filled with seating for those waiting to register for tests. An older woman with a pink jacket sat at the information desk. She glanced up from her paper and smiled. When the trio walked past without stopping, she turned in her chair and watched them go. By the time they reached the elevators, she had returned her attention to the paper.

They rode up to the third floor. When the doors opened, the hall beyond glowed bright. Officer North stepped out first. He guided the other two toward the nurse's station. Another officer sat at the desk. He stood when they approached.

"Everything okay?" North asked.

"Nothing out of the ordinary. No visitors. All new staff checked out."

"Good." He continued past the station. "This way please."

Nature followed the officer down the hall, Web right behind her. She felt a tingling in the air. It scared her. She hated hospitals. She avoided them with a passion. Too much death occurred in them. They were worse than any mode of public transportation.

She kept her arms crossed in front. Even though she had the gloves on, she did not want to touch anything as she walked to their destination.

"You'll be all right. I'll see to that."

Web whispered encouragement after he watched her shoulders bunch. He knew she was frightened. He wanted to enfold her in his arms and protect her but this was not the place. He needed to be professional here. She relaxed but only a tiny bit.

As they made their way down the hall, they noticed yet another officer sitting in front of a room. No other rooms around it were occupied. Both glanced at each other. Questions ran through their minds. It showed in their eyes, but they expressed none aloud. They knew the answers would come as soon as they walked through that door.

North stopped in front of the door. After a brief exchange with the officer guarding it, he said, "This way please." He rapped on the wood and opened it for the pair following.

They walked into a dimly lit room. The officer inside rose to his feet. Another man in a suit moved away from the bed. He met Nature at the door. He did not extend a hand in greeting, even though he saw she had gloves on. He was aware of the woman's special abilities.

"Mrs. Kranderson, it's a pleasure to finally meet you."

She nodded her head in return. Her attention was drawn to the occupant of the bed. Darkness shrouded the person in it. The closed drapes for the windows blocked the brightness from outside, and any prying eyes.

"Detective Franklin." The man extended a hand to Web.

"Web Westerly, sheriff of Garfield County, Montana." He shook the outstretched hand.

"Montana huh, long way from home. Glad to have you working with us."

"If you call not knowing a damn thing about what's going on working with you, then, I guess I'm doing a great job." The sarcasm in his voice was thick.

Franklin arched an eyebrow at North. "You haven't told them anything?"

"I thought it best to discuss it here. No outside sources overhearing that way."

"Good thinking." Returning his attention to the newcomers, he continued. "I'm sorry about the secrecy. Had to keep a tight lid on this one. Don't want the press getting involved and ruining any chance we have. That's why we used this smaller hospital instead of one of the bigger ones.

While the men talked, Nature ventured closer to the bed. She saw a slight form under the covers. The face was turned away from her, shrouded. When she was at the foot, she could make out the features of a girl in the darkness. Her heart raced. She felt her stomach roll. She did not want to go any closer, but knew she had to. The room went silent, all discussions stopped. They were watching her. She wasn't aware. She was focused on the person in the bed.

She inched her way forward. She grabbed the siderail to steady herself. When she reached the head, she took in a deep breath and held it, releasing it slowly. She steeled herself for what came next. Cupping the girls chin with her gloved hand, she turned the face toward her. She gasped. The face was one she never thought she'd see again, not alive at least. It was a face from a dream. More like a nightmare than a dream. She let go. She stumbled away from the bed. She whispered one word.

"Patricia."

Twelve

It was the girl from Texas. The one taken from the beach. The one the man had tricked into getting inside his van. Somehow she had survived, had gotten away.

Nature looked at the detective, "How?"

"Not here. Let's go out."

Nature peered at the girl again. There had been no response when her face was touched. No movement of her arms, nothing that a person aware of their surroundings would do. She turned away and followed the men into the hallway.

When they were out of the room she asked, "What happened to her? How did she get away?"

The detective waved his hand for silence. The hallway had too many hospital staff in it going about their business of caring for the patients. They eyed the trio with keen interest, trying to find out what was going on inside the room. Only a handful was allowed to enter the room, and they were not talking. Mostly due to the fact that if they did, they would lose their job and be arrested on the spot. Because of the lack of tangible information, there was enough gossip flying around to satisfy the best of the busybody society members. He did not need to fuel the talk with anything that was discussed by the trio. He led them into an empty room located next to the occupied one, where the hospital staff could not overhear. He shut the door.

"What do you know of this girl?"

"Only that her name is Patricia and that she disappeared from Florida. She was taken by a man driving a brown van."

"What can you tell me about this man?"

"Nothing. He stays shrouded. I can't see him." Her shoulder fell.

Web moved closer, his presence a comfort. She smiled at him. "We have the van."

Nature and Web jerked their heads toward the man speaking. They stared at him as if he had just threatened to strip naked and run down the hall. Both started talking at the same time.

"How did you..."

"What about..."

Web held up a hand, silencing Nature. "Is that where the girl was found?"

"It was. That van was full of things," Franklin hesitated. He shuddered. "Things used to torture that girl. I have two daughters. The oldest is only ten." He stopped, unable to continue, the pictures going through his head unnerving.

"Is that why she doesn't respond?" Nature asked.

"That's what the doctors say. They say she escaped the cruelty by disappearing into a safe world. A world where the man who took her doesn't exist. Now we have to find a way to let her know she can come back." He looked at Nature, "I don't suppose you can do that?"

"I'm sorry. I can only see what happened by touching something."

"Damn, I was hoping she would come around with your help and identify her attacker." Franklin brightened. "Maybe you can see the guy who did this. Maybe by touching the girl, she can be a better conduit, allowing you to see a better picture. Are you willing to try?"

It was Natures turn to shudder. She folded her arms across her chest, rubbing her upper arms as if she was trying to warm them. She looked at the detective. She looked at Web. She wanted to say no, to run out of the room, to not have to endure the feeling of the man as it went through her every fiber, but knew deep inside she couldn't. She had to see if she could help Patricia...and any other girl for that matter, by catching the killer. With a voice edged with dread, she said, "I'll try."

The three of them moved back to the girl's room. Franklin told the officer outside to allow no one in under any circumstances. He

told the officer in the room to take a coffee break. When only the three remained, he turned to Nature.

"Anything you find out will be useful. Anything."

She nodded at the detective then moved to the side of the bed. Web placed a chair next to it. He had already lowered the side rail. He stood back a pace, refusing to move too far away. She gave him a slight smile of thanks before sitting down.

The girl had not moved. Her eyes remained void. A hand rested on the blanket, placed there by one of the staff when they repositioned her. Nature stared at it. She dreaded what would follow with her touch. Taking in a deep breath to steel herself, she removed her glove and cupped the cold lifeless hand.

At first, she felt Patricia's love for her family. She saw them in Texas. She saw them on camping trips. The scenes moved from the family to the boyfriend. She and Randy wanted to marry. They would have, but the move slowed things down. They were planning to elope when she turned 18. Nature smiled.

Web watched the expressions roll across Natures face. He saw her smile. She was unaware of anything in the room. He glanced at Franklin. The detective leaned a shoulder against the wall, his gaze intent. It was hard enough to watch a session. It was that much worse for those doing so for the first time. He felt sorry for Franklin. Web heard a sudden intake of breath. Franklin straightened. He started for the bed. Web held up a hand.

"Not yet. Wait."

Franklin stayed where he was. Web had to give the man credit. He knew how to listen. He knew how to wait; it was a part of the job. Web returned his gaze to Nature.

Nature saw how the man had lured the girl into the van. She saw the girl go unconscious when her head hit the drum. The next vision she saw was the girl naked, her extremities restrained, hanging apart for easy access. She saw the curtain separate and the man appear. He remained shrouded. Nature grew frustrated at the lack of sight for the one causing so much pain.

Nature's body flopped back in the chair. Her hand held onto the girls like a vise grip. Her legs separated, her mouth hung open. She started to gag. Web waited. It wasn't time to intervene yet. When it was, he'd know.

Nature felt the man's penis go down her throat. She felt his

joy when she gagged. Patricia was not there any more. She was the one in the restraints. She felt the metal rod as it was shoved in. She felt all parts of her body violated. She wished it would stop, but knew it wouldn't. The man was too enthralled in the pleasure he felt. She tried to scream. The penis reached deep into her throat, preventing it. She tried to buck him off. He laid his full weight on top of her. Finally, she felt him ejaculate inside her mouth. He pulled out. She tossed her head back and screamed as loud as possible.

Web jumped to her side when the screaming started. Franklin started toward them. He stopped when the door to the room opened. The officer from the hallway was there, hand gripping the handle of his weapon. The sound of running feet echoed down the hall.

"Shut that door, mister! NOW!"

The officer grabbed the handle and yanked it shut just as a couple of staff members came into view, craning their necks, trying to see inside. Franklin turned back to the bed. The screaming had stopped.

Web hugged Nature against his body. He had pried her fingers off the girls hand and now held it tight. He rocked her back and forth like a baby. She was crying.

"Oh my god...oh my god...oh my god," Nature repeated over and over.

"Shhh, it's okay. You're safe now. I've got you. He can't hurt you any more."

"It took several minutes before Web's words sank in. When she realized she was in the hospital room and not the van, she threw her arms around his neck.

"It was so awful. He did horrible things." Her words were wracked with sobs.

"You're safe now. I'll protect you."

Nature felt the strong emotion coming from Web. She felt certain the man could not get her now and relaxed.

Web felt the tension leave her body. When she fell asleep a little while later, he gently lifted her up in his arms. "Where can I lay her down?"

"Back in the other room. I'll clear the way first." Franklin ducked out the door. A moment later, he peered in. "Come on."

Web carried Nature to the adjacent room and laid her on the bed. He pulled the covers up over her and sat next to her, assuming his watchful post again. He wasn't going anywhere. He was going to protect her as he said he would.

"What do we do now?" Franklin asked.

"The only thing we can do. We wait."

The man crossed the state line just after dark. He had not stopped since he found the needed information about the One. He was so wrapped up in getting to her house that he almost forgot about what he was driving, and through which city he had to pass. He thanked the state of Georgia for putting up a sign showing how far it was to Atlanta to remind him.

He left Interstate 75 and went toward a town called Clyattville. It was just off the highway. When he found another vehicle, he could be on his way within minutes. He pulled into a rural wooded area and parked. He turned everything off, got out and walked around to the trunk. He inserted the key and opened it.

The woman stared at him with wide eyes. They were red rimmed from crying. He smiled at her. She cringed. He reached in and grabbed a handful of hair, dragging her out of the trunk. A whimper escaped from her taped mouth. The man slapped her bare ass to remind her of the need for silence. She quieted.

He guided her deeper into the trees until he found one with a smaller base. He untied one wrist and used the rope to pull it around the trunk. When her hands met, he retied the rope. The woman was forced to hunch over and hug it like a lover. The sight of her, with her dark brown hair, touched with a bit of gray, reminded him of Nature. He felt his pants tighten. He unzipped them and stepped up behind her.

With unleashed passion, he lifted her hips and inserted his penis into her anus. She arched her back in pain. He pumped as hard as he could. He held nothing back.

Visions of Nature rolled past his closed eyes. He imagined her silent expressions of joy at him taking her. He imagined her meeting his pushes with her own. He felt his heart race with untold pleasure. He felt his breath shorten with the effort of matching her love. The woman finally cried out, bringing the man back to his

present surroundings.

He lay over her back and wrapped his hands around her throat, squeezing tighter with every push. The woman started to buck. She tried to twist her body away from him. She fought like a rodeo bull trying to throw him off. He gripped her throat harder and pumped her like a sex-deprived teenager. He felt his groin heat up with energy. This was the best ride he had had in a while. He savored every movement the woman made. He ejaculated at the same time she became unconscious.

The man continued to squeeze her throat while his penis rippled like waves rolling across a lake during a light breeze. He released her and spread his arms wide when her breath left her forever. He smiled like a Cheshire cat, his penis still deep inside, savoring the rush of pleasure flowing through him. He pulled free as it ebbed. The woman's body hung from the tree, her head rolled to one side, her eyes wide with pain and sorrow. He pulled his pants up and returned to the car. He started it, pulled it into drive, and returned to the road.

A few miles out of town, he saw a pickup with a camper shell covering the bed parked in a dirt driveway. It was in front of an old farmhouse. He pulled the Ford into another driveway in front of an abandoned house a short distance away. He walked back to the truck. The keys were in the ignition. He got in and eased the door shut.

Because it was only nine thirty at night, lights should have been on in the house. They were not. Maybe an older couple lived here. Maybe they would not notice the vehicle missing until morning. If he were truly to meet the One, it would happen. By then, he would be well on his way.

The truck was a newer one. The man hoped the engine was quiet when he started it. He smiled with relief after he turned the key. He backed onto the road and returned to I-75. In just over an hour, he had experienced a great ride in a tight ass, changed vehicles, and was back on track for reaching the one he sought. The eternal happiness that had eluded him for so long was finally within his grasp.

On the road he just vacated, a sheriff's vehicle drove past the Ford, making its nightly patrol of the area. The brake lights came on. White lights replaced them as it backed up. A spotlight lit the

area around the abandoned car. The sound of a door opening and shutting echoed across the open field. The sound of boots crunching on gravel followed. That same sound, this time faster, returned as the deputy ran back to his car.

He alerted his dispatcher, who in turn alerted the state police. In just over an hour, two police cars sat near the Ford. Across the way, a short distance from the site of increased activity, an old farmhouse remained dark, its occupants unaware of what was happening just outside their door.

Nature felt the terror rise in her chest. It reached her throat, threatening to cut off her air. She tried to struggle, but the restraints held her tight. The shrouded man drew near. Before he reached her, the restraints fell away. She was able to move, to run, to escape the evil before it consumed her.

The man suddenly appeared in front of her, as if materializing from thin air. She turned and ran in another direction. At each turn, the man was there. She could feel his smile even though she could not see it. The last time she turned to run, she felt his hands grab her from behind. She was naked.

The man's hands cupped her breasts. The fingers massaged the sensitive flesh, sending waves of tingling through her body. She savored the feeling, yet felt disgusted at the same time. She trembled when his hot breath touched her neck. She was afraid of her reaction; she wanted more.

One moment she had her eyes shut, savoring the touch of his body close to hers, the next, she felt herself shoved over and a metal rod crammed inside. The man's rod followed. She thrashed. She fought. She tried to get him out. Nothing worked. The man covered her mouth with his hand. He pumped her harder and faster. She heard him grunting with each push. Pain wracked her body. The hands moved to her throat. They squeezed.

Nature sat bolt upright in the bed, clutching at the sheets, a scream locked deep inside, the feeling of hands around her throat still present. Her breath was rapid, her heart the same. Perspiration covered her brow. Tears covered her face. Web sat beside her, his head resting on his chest. He was asleep. Her sudden movements had not awakened him.

She saw no other person in the room when she glanced around. The sky outside the window was dark. She assumed it was the middle of the night. Slipping out of the bed, she moved to the door and exited as quietly as possible. Web remained asleep.

She made her way back to Patricia's room. The officer outside nodded at her when she approached but did not stop her. He was aware of who she was. In fact, he held the door open for her, clearing the way with the officer seated in the room.

Nature walked to the bed. She sat in the chair used earlier for the session. She reached out and cupped the girl's cold hand. Her gloves were in the other room. She wasn't concerned. She knew what to expect now. Again, the feel of the man filled her every fiber. She leaned close to Patricia and whispered in her ear. The girl remained unaware.

The officer leaned against the wall with his arms crossed before him. He watched for only a moment before becoming bored. He focused his attention on his inner thoughts instead. He missed his wife. These night shifts were murder on his home life. Lately, she had started acting strange. He assumed it was because she was seeing another man. He hoped not. He loved her dearly and the thought of her asking for a divorce sickened him.

He looked back at the woman sitting beside the girl's bed. He had heard some strange things about her, but to actually see her, he didn't see what the big deal was. If he passed her on the street, he would not even give her a second glance. When she continued to whisper words he could not hear, he returned to brooding about his job and marriage.

Web slowly came awake. Something felt different; something was out of place, causing him leave the dream he was having, a dream filled with Nature. He stretched before opening his eyes. Where Nature should be, the bed was empty.

He shot to his feet. The scraping sound of chair legs rubbing across the floor echoed in the room. He ignored it, frantically looking in all directions, trying to locate the missing woman. She was nowhere in sight. He moved to the bathroom to make sure she was not inside. It was also empty.

He had an idea where she might be. Moving with speed, he crossed the room, opened the door, and exited. The officer outside the girl's room jumped away from the wall. He looked tired.

Web could sympathize. He remembered the midnight shift with its long hours. He didn't miss them.

"Did you see the woman from this room?"

"She went in here." He pointed a thumb at the door next to him.

"Thanks."

Web walked past him and pushed the door open. The other officer inside glanced at him but did not straighten; he remained against the wall. An air of negativity came off him. Web frowned.

The frown disappeared when he saw Nature sitting close to the girl. He saw her holding the smaller hand without a glove. He saw the lost look on her face, her eyes open, staring. Her lips moved but he did not think she was aware of what she said. She gave no indication of knowing that he or the other man was in the room.

He reached her side in a few steps. She remained lost, unaware of him, like the girl. He touched her shoulder. She never moved. He shook her gently. Again, no response. Her lips moved, paused, and moved again. Web heard no sound; the words were silent. Grabbing her hand, he forced Nature to release the girl.

The moment the contact with the girl was broken, Nature's eyelids fluttered. She filled her lungs with a deep breath and closed her eyes. Her head turned away from the bed before she opened them again. Web saw the longing in them. He saw the need to talk. He helped her to her feet and guided her to the exit. She came willingly. As the door slid closed behind them, Web saw the officer inside still leaned against the wall. He had not moved; a look of utter boredom locked firmly into place.

The officer outside the room was not of the same character. He moved with Web and held the door open to their room. He nodded once in departure as he pulled the door shut behind him. Web would be happy to have that officer on his department anytime.

Gently, he led Nature to the bed. Her step was strong and steady by the time they reached it. It felt nice to hold her, though. She leaned against him for mental support more than physical. She sat on the side instead of lying down. He tugged the same chair he used earlier next to her. Once seated, he cupped her hands in his and waited.

Nature was reassured by Web's touch. It felt safe. It allowed

her to be free to talk about the new experience she just had. A new experience that was nice, yet scary.

"Do you believe in another world...another place?"

"What do you mean?"

"A place of beauty, a place where everyone is happy."

Thinking about his lost daughter, he said, "I hope one is out there, but, I'm not sure."

Focusing her brown eyes on his, she said, "It exists. I've been there."

He remained silent, waiting for her to continue.

"It's in each of us. A world so peaceful that you don't want to leave. It's in Patricia. I found a way to reach where she was. I was with her. I tried to convince her to leave; she couldn't hear me. She had her parents there, her boyfriend, and no pain. She didn't see any need to return to the land filled with so much suffering when she had everything she needed with her."

"Web, it made sense. Why leave? Pain is on this side. Nothing but love and happiness is on the other." She averted her eyes. "The only thing that brought me back ...was you." She met his gaze. "Even if you were in my make-believe world, I would know you weren't really there." She laced her fingers in his before continuing. "Web...I love you."

Inside, his heart soared. He whispered, "I love you too."

It was the first time either of them had said those words aloud. It thrilled him to know Nature felt the same as he did. But to have her actually say it, that was better than anything else. He wanted her to say it again.

As if sensing what he desired, she said, "I love you, I love you, I love you."

He leaned forward and kissed her, brushing her lips with his. She pulled him onto the bed next to her. She snuggled against him, burying her head into the crook of his arm. He folded his arms around her. Both knew this was not the time or place for sex; they respected the facility they were in and cuddled instead. They fell asleep that way, enjoying the peace of the moment.

Thirteen

It was almost 10:30 in the morning when they pulled into the impound area. The state patrol vehicle led the way. Cars of all types covered the lot. A shiny black BMW sat near the back, a flashy red Mercedes next to it. Even though the camper was a newer model, it looked old and grimy in comparison.

Web drove the camper around the building to a garage. Its large metal door was closed, blocking any view of what lay inside. He parked next to the cop car and got out. Nature opened her door and looked at the garage. Her shoulders shook as a shiver ran up her spine. She dreaded the coming event. She knew what was behind the concrete walls.

Both walked up to the door leading to the interior. North held it open for them, allowing Nature to go in first. All three stopped just inside to allow their eyes to adjust to the gloom. When they did, a plain brown van sat in the farthest work bay. It was the only automobile in the building.

Several technicians were buzzing around it like busy little ants. Nature sighed. Though latex gloves covered their hands, their imprints would be everywhere, possibly covering whatever the man had left. She knew what she was about to do was going to be hard, now that job was made all the more difficult by too many people trying to do their job.

"I'm sorry about all the people. By the time I heard about the van, the damage was already done. I hope you can still get a bead on the driver," Detective Franklin said.

"So do I Detective. This killer has no heart; he kills just for the

pleasure of it, at those poor girls' expense. I want him stopped before he does it again."

"Amen," Web said beside her.

Both his and Officer North's expressions were hard. Nature was sure they wanted to see an end to the killings as badly as she did. Their shoes echoed across the hollow building as they walked to the van. When they reached it, the detective informed the technicians to leave. He may not have been able to reduce their influence before, but he could now. Nature hoped their touching of everything did not mar her reading of its secrets.

The area was cleared quickly. When the four of them remained, Franklin indicated for Nature to move closer. The heart in her chest raced. Her fingers went cold inside the gloves. She forced her breathing to stay regular. None of the men were aware of her discomfort; she kept herself under control. The only one who might see anything was Web. She glanced at him and gave him a slight smile. He nodded his head in return, keeping his face blank.

The van doors were open, revealing the straps used for restraining its victims. Nature remembered the feel of them on her extremities. She rubbed her wrists, unaware of doing so. Her attention was focused. She was building her inner strength for the visions, visions she knew were going to be extreme.

She stepped up onto the bumper and went inside. She was thankful for the clothing covering her legs. It blocked any feelings that emanated from the flooring. Reaching the center of the van, she sat and crossed her legs. She stared at the straps hanging from the roof. They were tattered and worn, as if used far too many times.

A curtain hung behind her, hiding the driver's seat. She remembered the image of the man as he opened them and came at her. She could imagine what the girls went through every time they parted. Again, shudders caused her shoulders to shake. Turning her attention back to the straps, she caught the outline of a toolbox sitting next to the wall. She crawled to it. Tools used to repair an engine were visible upon opening. She saw a long metal rod. She knew what it was used for; she had felt it in her dream. She reached in and brought it out, thankful for the gloves covering her hand.

Detective Franklin watched her intently. He saw the flash of terror on her face as she withdrew a metal rod from the toolbox. It was gone before she looked at him. He remained silent. He knew when it was time; she would tell him what caused her to fear the object in her hand so much. He thought he had an idea but would wait for her to confirm it.

He had taken the time to research the woman in the van before her arrival. He knew of her special abilities and how she had solved so many cases; thus helping law enforcement with their job. Because of this, he knew what she needed and how to act when around her. The time in the hospital was his first experience watching her in action. He learned that it was one thing to read about it and another to actually see it in use. He knew what to expect now.

Nature set the rod on the floor. She reached up with her left hand and started tugging at the fingers of the glove on her right one. It was as if it did not want to come off. It did after several hard tugs. She put it in a pocket, refusing to set it down. Picking up the rod again, she hesitated before touching it with her exposed hand.

Franklin saw her posture stiffen. He saw her eyes become unfocused, rolling back until only the whites showed. He kept his attention on the woman as he heard Web step up beside him. He felt the hairs on the back of his neck rise when he saw several expressions flow across Nature's face. He was glad he did not see what she was enduring. He took a quick glance at the man beside him. His face spoke volumes of his feeling for the woman in the van. Franklin was a bit surprised...though not really.

The sound of metal hitting the floor echoed in the small space. Franklin jerked his attention to the woman. She sat there with tears running down her cheeks, her hand empty, the rod lying next to her leg. As he watched, she opened her eyes. They were clear, no longer lost in the vision. When Web moved to enter, she held up her hand, stopping him.

"No, Web, I have to continue."

Web stayed out, but Franklin could tell he wasn't happy. Nature turned to face the curtain. She made her way to the driver's seat. She disappeared from view. Both men moved so they could keep an eye on her. She was behind the steering wheel when they

saw her again. The window was rolled up and the lock engaged. Franklin devised that she must have done this to keep them from interfering with her reading.

She grasped the wheel. Again, her eyes became unfocused. Her head leaned forward then slammed back against the soft head support. Web started toward the back of the van but Franklin grabbed him. The sheriff whirled on him, trying to shake him off. The detective saw the concern, the fear, and the love in his expression.

"We need to let her finish. She wanted to, remember?"

"She needs to stop. She might hurt herself. She hasn't had enough time between sessions." Web struggled to get the detectives hands off his arms. "Too much happened in there. She might slip away like Patricia did. I have to make her stop. I have to."

"I said let her finish." The words were hard, like his hold on the arms. The detective's expression was the same. He knew this man loved the woman inside the van but he was not about to let that love interfere with his case. A killer was loose and he wanted him stopped. He needed the information only Nature could obtain.

Web ignored the man restraining him. Subconsciously, he understood what Franklin was doing. But, this was Nature. He wasn't going to lose her, not after finally allowing himself to love again. He had to save her; he had to protect her. There had to be another way to find the killer, there had to be.

Franklin sympathized with Web. He knew the older man was not thinking right now. He knew emotions drove him to react as he was. However, he was not about to let a lovesick sheriff from Timbuktu, Montana ruin everything just because of a woman. This case was far too important to him.

Web thrashed his upper body back and forth, trying to dislodge the hands holding him. The younger man held on. In the blink of an eye, he found himself flat on the ground, his arm forced up his back. He felt cold steel clasp around his wrist. The other wrist followed suit. He was now handcuffed like a criminal. He flung his feet up, trying to kick Franklin off.

"If you don't stop, I'll handcuff your legs also." To back up his threat, he pulled out another set and showed them to Web. He quieted down.

The older man had never felt so embarrassed in all his life. To

be subdued so easily was a huge blow to his pride. How could he be any good to Nature now? How was he supposed to protect her if he could not even fight off this punk? The more he thought about it, the madder he became. The madder he became, the more his brain connived. Who did this brat barely out of diapers think he was? He waited until Franklin had his full attention focused on what was going on inside before he moved.

He rose to his feet and quietly inched his way toward the back of the van, keeping an eye on the other man. He made it all the way to the back before he bumped into the open door, causing it to slam shut. He was so focused on watching what was going on by the driver's door that he forgot to look where he was going.

Franklin spun around and saw where he was. He snarled, "Goddamn it! I told you not to interfere."

Web tried to get around the van. Before he could, Franklin was on him. He was thrown; face first, to the floor with Franklin on top of him. Unable to catch himself due to the handcuffs holding his arms behind his back, his breath left him in a whoosh. Pain shot through him when his nose bounced off the concrete. Blood poured from it. He lay there, trying to recover his breath, when he felt his legs lifted one at a time. He tried to resist but his efforts were more attuned to the return of air to his lungs than to the actual struggle. The sound of metal grinding against metal echoed throughout the garage. He was effectively restrained now.

"I warned you, but you wouldn't listen. Now look at you."

"When I get out of these, I'm going to kick the shit out of you," Web managed to say after gaining control of his breathing.

"Not likely, old man." Franklin towered over Web. "I didn't even break into a sweat. You were so focused on getting to your lady that you forgot how to defend yourself. You forgot what was important here."

"Shut the fuck up you mealy-mouthed weasel."

Franklin ignored the comment. He returned to the driver's window to check on Nature. She wasn't there. The seat was empty. Making his way toward the back, he saw Nature crouched next to Web. She was wiping the blood off his face.

"What did you do?"

"He tried to prevent you from completing your reading. I had to stop him."

"With handcuffs?"

"To keep him from interfering, yes."

Nature stood up. Her weary eyes flashed with anger. Everything in her stance said she was pissed. "Detective, if you ever want me to tell you what I saw, I would advise you to release Web...now."

Franklin glared back. "And if you ever want me to release him, I'd advise you to tell me what you know. If you don't, I'll lock you both up until you do."

Nature crossed her arms in front of her and clamped her mouth shut in defiance. She leaned back, supporting her weight on one leg. A foot tapped with impatience. Normally she was reserved and quiet. This time, she was ready to go the distance with this, as she heard Web call him...mealy-mouthed weasel.

Sensing her determination, Franklin rolled his eyes skyward. "Why do you have to be so difficult? All I want to do is solve this case. All I want to do is prevent other girls from falling victim to that sick bastard."

Nature remained silent, not moving, watching him with steely eyes.

"Oh all right, I'll let him go. Will that satisfy you?"

She cocked an eyebrow, waiting for him to do so.

Franklin squatted down and released the cuffs. He stepped away from the now loosened man. "Happy?" he said to Nature. Looking at Web, he added, "Look man. I'm sorry. I just want this bastard caught before he kills again, that's all."

Web sat up, rubbing his wrists. He rose slowly to his feet. Before anything else was said, he closed the gap dividing the two men and slammed his fist into the detectives jaw, causing the younger man to spin around 360 degrees before dropping to the ground.

"I told you I'd kick the shit out of you when I got free. Pretty fast for an old man, huh."

Franklin sat up on an elbow, rubbing his jaw. He stayed down due to the man towering over him, fists held ready to deliver another blow.

Nature walked up to Web and placed a hand on his shoulder. "Let's go get something to eat. I'm starved." She glanced at Franklin, "Join us when you can Detective, we'll be at the diner I

saw down the street."

"You really shouldn't leave. I can have you arrested." The man flinched when Web moved to hit him again.

"You won't do that. You need what I have." She tapped her head. "We'll see you there."

She hooked her arm through Webs and guided him to the exit. He kept looking back at the detective who remained on the ground. After they were outside, away from Franklin's line of sight, he flipped his hand back and forth. It hurt like hell.

"Awww, poor baby. Let me kiss it and make it all better."

He stopped and brought his hand up for her. She smiled and kissed it in several places, as promised. He lowered it and, without hesitation, pulled her against him, touching his lips to hers. He kiss was full of passion. They continued to the camper, his arm over her shoulder, her arm around his waist. He no longer cared who saw them. It felt good to be in love again.

The man drove all night. He was exhausted. In just over eight hours, he had made it past Nashville. No cops with their flashing lights glared behind him. In fact, the cops paid no attention to him at all. It was as if he did not exist. He liked it that way.

The pink rays of sunrise flowed across the brightening sky, chasing away the darkness of the night. He admired the beauty of it as he drove. The sound of a blaring horn brought him out of his reverie; he had almost fallen asleep behind the wheel. He straightened and waved at the driver of the other vehicle as it passed. He pulled the truck to the side of the road. Within minutes, the other car's rear lights were nothing but specks on the horizon.

To leave the truck where it was for too long was to invite disaster. The owners may have already reported it stolen. The cops may already be on the lookout for it. As tired as he was, he knew he had to keep going. Pulling the gear into drive, he merged back onto the highway.

After driving another fifteen minutes, he was almost to the point of finding a spot to park when one of the blue highway signs flew past. Several emblems showing which food places were off this exit caught his attention. He sighed with relief. Some strong

black coffee would help revive him. He exited and followed the signs. When he parked, it took some effort to get his legs to answer.

The coolness of air conditioning hit him when he entered the building. He shivered. Walking up to the counter, he smiled at the older woman standing there. He was saddened that one of the pretty teenagers weren't there; they were probably getting ready for school. Placing his order, he glanced around the sitting area.

An elderly couple sat at one table, a man in a suit at another. Tucked in a corner was a woman who appeared to be in her twenties. She had long straight dirty blonde hair pulled back into a ponytail. Her figure was thin, almost too thin, but her eyes were beautiful. He had to have her. Her attention was focused on the paper in her hand, she was not aware of him watching her.

The crinkling of a bag being set on the counter drew his attention back. He smiled as he paid for the food. Moving to the side so other could order, he opened the drinking area of the lid and took a sip. As predicted, the contents were strong and hot. With a final glance at the woman, he left.

He sat in the truck eating his breakfast and watched the door leading out He knew the woman had to leave sometime. He only hoped she would exit on this side of the building. As the last bite of his sandwich disappeared, she walked out and started toward an SUV parked near by. He washed down the food with a gulp of coffee and started the engine. She got in, took a second to reposition herself, started the engine and backed out. She was still oblivious to the man interested in her. Her mind was on the things she wanted to accomplish today, not on her surroundings.

Clouds had moved in while he was inside the building. They grew dark and ominous. A bright flash of light caused him to close his eyes. He opened them when a loud clap of thunder rattled the truck's windows. It was going to rain. The man hoped it would wait.

The woman turned right and went under the bridge for the highway above. The man kept a discrete distance between them. He did not want her to notice him yet. At a stop light, she again turned right. She was heading away from the small town, away from all the traffic and unwanted attention. She was heading home.

For Miranda, the daily trip to the local fast food restaurant was a way to get out of the house and mingle with people. She lived alone, with a dog and a cat to keep her company. Even though she went out each morning, she seldom spoke to anyone. She was severely shy. It was something she had never outgrown. Working from home was a way to pay the bills, and avoid all the crowds.

She was about a mile from home, braking for the stop sign at the corner, when her SUV lurched forward. She was shocked by its suddenness. She glanced into the rear view mirror. A truck with a camper shell on it was behind her. It was so close; she had a hard time seeing the hood in the mirror. The driver was getting out of the vehicle. He walked up to her, a look of embarrassment etched on his face. He tried to talk through the closed window. She couldn't hear him very well. She cracked the window open.

"I'm so sorry. I wasn't paying attention. Are you okay?"

She nodded her head yes. She was afraid to talk to him; he was so good looking. His dark eyes were mesmerizing. They held her gaze. She felt as if they were seeing into her soul. She turned away. It was her turn to be embarrassed.

"I'm afraid I did a small amount of damage to you bumper. I'll pay for it. It was my fault after all."

When she felt she could look at him again, she turned back. He smiled. She melted. He stepped back, waiting for her to get out and inspect the bumper. She hesitated, aware that the world was full of sickos who would love to get their hands on a woman like her. Taking another look at him: his innocent smile, his polite manners, and the fact that they were out in the open for others to see; she decided it was okay to get out.

Several flashes blinked above. Thunder rolled across the area, seeming to answer the light. Miranda looked up at the increasingly darkening sky. She liked thunderstorms, but in the safety of her own home, not on the side of the road, exposed to the elements, next to a strange man He indicated for her to lead the way to the bumper, something she wasn't used to. She always followed, never led. She bowed her head and moved to the back of the SUV.

A dent was on either side of the silver bumper about a third of the way in from the edges. She saw they were caused by the

pieces sticking out of the trucks bumper to prevent it from becoming damaged. They worked. The trucks bumper was smooth.

A flash, followed immediately by a loud clap of thunder that sounded like it was directly overhead, almost made her jump out of her skin. She let out a little squeal. The man was beside her. He did not touch her, for which she was grateful. She did not think she could handle it. A few fat drops of rain began to pelt them. They were soon joined by many more.

"I think we should sit in you vehicle to exchange information, don't you?"

Again, she could only nod her head. She cursed her shyness. If only she was like the rest of the family, she would give this guy her phone number. She would invite him to her place for lunch and hope things progressed from there. As it was, she remained silent.

She returned to the driver's seat and unlocked the passenger door. The man got in and shook himself. He ran his fingers through his dark wet hair. The muscles in his arms rippled with the movement. She watched at a sideways glance, too embarrassed to do anything else. He smiled at her. She smiled back. Shifting slightly in the seat, he reached for his back pocket and pulled out his wallet.

"I don't have a pen. I hope you won't mind writing all the information down."

"S...s..sure." She grimaced at the stutter that came out of her mouth.

"You live close?"

"Just up the road." She was finally able to make her voice work.

"I have family out here somewhere. I was trying to find their house on my map and wasn't paying attention to the road, hence the reason why we met. You're family live with you?"

"Only Ralph and Mr. Cuddles."

"Ralph and...Mr. Cuddles?"

"Yea, my dog and cat. The rest of my family lives up north. I moved here to get away from them."

"Sometimes it's nice to get away from family." He became distant, as if remembering something from his past. Realizing the woman was watching him, concern in her eyes, he flashed her one

of his wonderful smiles. "Oh well, back to business."

He pulled out a card and extended it to her. Her hand shook as she reached for it. Never in her life had she remembered anyone letting her decide what to do, or even asking her how she was doing. Her family had always made her decisions for her. She never had a voice in anything. It felt weird to have a say now. She wasn't sure if she liked it.

The moment her hand touched the paper, his hand flew up and hit her across the face. Her head bounced off the window. Spots of light juggled around before her eyes. They mingled with the lightening outside, making the world a little too bright. She looked at the man, shocked. Before she had time to react, he hit her with his fist. The lights dimmed and the world outside disappeared.

The man hugged Miranda close when she slumped over. He smelled her hair, it smelled like strawberries. He pulled her slight body onto his and shifted her enough so that he sat behind the wheel while she remained in the passenger seat. It was still early. No one drove past during the altercation. No one saw what happened. The desire to leave crept into his being but he had to make sure the woman was restrained before doing so. If she awoke while he was driving, she might fight him or try to escape.

Reaching over the seat, he rummaged around the back area until he found some rope in a small storage compartment. He used it to bind the woman's extremities. He leaned her back, her head resting on the support behind it, and groped her small chest. Unsatisfied, he unzipped her jeans and pulled them down slightly. He pulled her panties away from her body and saw the bush of blonde hair. He pushed the soft cloth down next to the jeans and ran his fingers through it. A rush of excitement surged through his groin when he touched her vaginal lips. He let go, leaving the pants open so he could see the hair while he drove. He would have time later to give her immeasurable pleasure.

The windows fogged due to their body heat filling the small, enclosed area. The man clicked her seatbelt into place and started the engine. He turned on the defogger. Pulling a u-turn, he made his way back to the highway. The newer model SUV responded smoothly and with power when he pressed the gas pedal down.

He left the truck sitting in the middle of the road. He didn't

care. He had something better; he had a vehicle no one would be looking for. He also had a way to reduce the pent up pleasure that was inside. As if responding to his thoughts, the area around his crotch grew. He released his swollen penis and stroked it lovingly, matching the up and down motion with the rhythm of the wipers. The dark tinted windows prevented any drivers from seeing what he did.

The man knew his intended love would not mind if he had sex with other women. If he remained too pent up, as he was now, he would not be able to perform at his best. He wanted to be ready. He wanted to make her happy. He wanted to spend the rest of his natural born days with the woman from the television, with the One, with the woman who called herself Nature Kranderson.

The mere mention of her name caused him to soar with happiness. His search was almost over. Finally, he could have a life free of unrealistic expectations, free of bothersome people. He and Nature would live in his cabin, without the need for clothes, without interference from the rest of the world. He would make love to her often. He would make sure she remained filled with pleasure. And, he would never have to worry about hunting again, unless she said it was okay. That last thought was the one that kept him going, kept him driving through the exhaustion. He would stop soon to rest...and release. Until then, he would close the distance between them.

Behind them, in a little home, a cat and dog waited for their owner to return.

Fourteen

Nature and Web sipped on their cups of coffee when Franklin entered. Making his way through the diner, they could see the frustration in his step and the frown covering his face. He grabbed a chair from another table and brought it to theirs. He refused to sit next to either occupant in the corner booth. The tired waitress came up and took his order for coffee. The detective wasn't interested in food. After she left, he crossed his arms in front and glared at them.

"Well...are you willing to talk now?"

"In due time Detective. In due time," Nature said.

"Have a piece of the pie, Franklin. It's pretty good." Web scooped another chunk of apple pie onto his fork and shoved it into his mouth.

"While you're pulling this bullshit, another girl could be tortured and killed." His words came out in a harsh whisper. He did not want the other patrons to hear what he said.

Web swallowed the food and said, "Maybe you should have thought of that yourself, Detective, when you were pulling your...as you called it...bullshit with me."

"I told you not to interfere but you wouldn't listen."

"Listen to what...your ignorance?"

"Sheriff Westerly, if you don't stop..." Franklin shut his mouth when the waitress returned with his coffee.

The waitress arched an eyebrow as she set the cup down in front of Franklin. She glanced at each person before stepping away, returning to the counter for the tray of food waiting to be delivered.

Nature watched her pick the tray up with ease. She carried it to another table and set the plates before each of the occupants

seated there. When the woman shot a quick glance at their table, she smiled.

Nature only half listened to the men as they argued. She reflected on what the detective had said, about another girl being tortured and killed. He was right; they were being an ass. Interrupting the men before blows happened; she cleared her throat to get their attention.

"Gentlemen, if you don't mind, I'd like to get back to the subject." She set her cup down, but kept both hands wrapped around it. "About the van...the man who drove it was dark in nature."

Franklin sat forward, his argument with Web forgotten, eager to hear what Nature had to say. "Dark. As in how?"

Web kept a close eye on the woman across the table. If he saw one iota of distress, he would end this. He didn't care if it meant causing a scene in the diner.

"Dark as in his soul." She shivered. "I think his outer appearance matches his inner self."

"What leads you to that conclusion?" The detective knew about the inability to see the kidnapper. He tried to guide her into noticing something that would help.

"The haze, where his head appears, is darker than the rest of him. I don't know if it's because of dark hair or because he is so evil." She shrugged her shoulders. "He seems to be of average build. I can't make out much because he is so shrouded." She looked at Franklin, "I do get a sense of searching. As if he is looking for something, something he has not been able to locate for a long time." Taking a sip of the luke-warm liquid still cupped in her hands, she added, "Detective, I haven't mentioned this before but..." She hesitated, "he has killed many times, at least eight times that I know of."

The words smacked him like a ton of bricks. "Why have you not mentioned this rather important fact to me earlier?" Both his daughter's faces swam into view. He was glad they were safe at home with their mother.

"She didn't want to panic the public or alert the kidnapper to our presence," Webb said. "If word got out, he might go under and we'd never track him down."

Franklin was angry. "How do you expect me to help if you're not up front with me?"

"I'm just an advisor on the case. I was asked to find lost girls. In doing so, I found out about this man, and the girls he took. You yourself asked me to read a van and the girl taken from it. You didn't ask me about the others." She sighed, "Detective Franklin...I'm tired. I need to decompress. If I don't, I will be of no use in the future."

During the silent tension that followed, the waitress returned and refilled their cups. She left just as quickly.

Nature kept her eyes on the stained white cup until after the waitress left. She raised her eyes to meet Franklins. "I want to go home. I need to be free of outside influences so I can...so to speak...clear the channels. Once I've done that, I can return."

"And what about in between? Do you expect this kidnapper to disappear, to wait until you are ready to start again?"

"No." Nature's gaze fell to the cup once more. "He will continue."

"So another girl has to pay the price so you can hide away.

Her head shot upward, anger filled her eyes. "That's not fair. You know nothing about me, about what I've had to endure over the years."

"But I have a perfect example of what those girls endured. She's at the hospital." He waved his arm in the general direction of the medical facility's location.

"That's enough." Web slammed a fist down onto the table. The loud sound caused the patrons of the diner to stop what they were doing and look their way. He kept his attention on Franklin, ignoring the stares.

The detective glared at Web, then at Nature. His gazed stayed on the woman. "So how much time do you need?'

"Two or three days."

"That many huh." Franklin slid the chair back and rose to his feet. "I only hope nothing happens during your recovery."

"Please sit down."

"Why? I don't want to strain you any further."

"Franklin...sit down," Web emphasized.

Nature pleaded with her eyes. She did not want to alienate this officer of the law. "Please...I need to give you more information, information that may help you find the kidnapper."

Franklin paused. The images of his daughters, and the girl in

the hospital, were the only things that made him not walk out the door and leave these pains in the asses where they sat. He brought the chair back under him and resumed his crossed arm position, waiting.

Nature sighed deeply before beginning. She told Franklin about everything she had depicted from her reading of Rew. She told him about how the kidnapper had lured Patricia into his van. From her reading of the van, she told him about the other girls: girls named Vicki, Heather, Katherine, Connie, Gail, Janice, Sarah, and Mindy. She did not know their last names; she only knew how they were treated. She also knew from her session involving Rew, that these other girls were dead, buried somewhere in a heavily wooded area. What she kept from them was her dream, the dream where the man had raped her and tried to kill her.

Both men listened as the information flowed from her. Both faces looked like they were made of granite. Both knew what the implications were, and what was yet to come. Both knew this killer was not done.

"I didn't realize..." Franklin managed to stutter after the stunned silence that followed.

"Why didn't you tell me? God...the burden..." Web had heard part of the story before, but this, this was beyond belief. His concern for her grew.

Nature reached across the table and covered Web's hands with hers. "There wasn't time or an opportunity to tell you, not since we left the van." She turned to the detective, "Now do you understand why I have to go home?"

Franklin nodded his head. Reaching into his suit, he pulled out a notepad and began writing down the names of the girls. When he finished, he pulled out a card and handed it to her.

"If you remember anything else while you're driving home, please, do not hesitate to call me." She gave him a smile of gratitude.

Web jotted something down on a napkin. "Here's my cell phone number. If you have any questions, call."

It was the first time Nature remembered him giving the number to anyone. That said volumes about the trust he held for this man. She waved to the waitress, indicating she wanted the check. She came over, tallied everything up, and gave it to her. Web

frowned. He expected to pay, not her. Sliding out from the booth, she walked to the cash register and paid for everything, including Franklins. Both men frowned.

"You should have let me get that. I am on duty, after all, and it would have come out of the departments expenses."

"Detective Franklin, I know how strapped law enforcement is for funds. I can afford it. Besides, I'm on duty too and can take it out of my work expenses just as easily."

For the first time since he arrived at the diner, Franklin smiled. "If I find anything out, I'll get in touch." He patted his suit where the notepad rested.

"We'll do the same." Web extended a hand. Franklin shook it. Nature gave him a hug before they went their separate ways.

Three quarters of an hour later, they were back on I-75, heading north, toward home. Nature hoped they would make it this time and not have to detour for something else. She snuggled up to Web. He wrapped a protective arm around her and kissed the top of her head. It was going to be wonderful to see Sandy again. As she watched the miles disappeared under the tires, their steady singing lulled her to sleep.

The man drove the SUV past the town of Brockway shortly after three in the afternoon. It had taken him the better part of the day to reach this far. He was forced to stop during the night to release some of his pent up energy, and to sleep. The woman who owned the vehicle lay in the back under a blanket. A large piece of tape covered her mouth; she was naked. He enjoyed the ride she gave when he showed her his pleasures. He fell asleep on her after he ejaculated in her anus, leaving his penis deep inside. When he awoke, he rode her again. He wanted to be free of any unwanted thoughts while he scouted out where the One lived.

Jordan, the town closest to the One's home, was an hour away. He pondered about how he was going to get her during the drive. He knew what her address was, but didn't know anything about the area. He would have to find a way to remedy that once he arrived.

The woman shifted her position, coming partway out from under the blanket. The man was not concerned. He had stopped at a

store some time back and bought window film. It was the reflective kind, allowing the interior of the vehicle to stay cool and hidden, yet did not block the view of those within. That, and the factory-tinted windows, hid her entirely. It also allowed him the freedom to take her anytime without worry of prying eyes. He smiled at the memory of her squirming under him.

He did not stop. He continued toward Jordan. He had to find out information before she arrived home. Even if she was already there, he needed the information anyway. He wanted to be ready in case an opportunity came a knock'n. He hummed a homemade song about knock, knock, knock'n while he thrummed his fingers on the steering wheel.

MT-200 ran through the middle of town, making it easy to find a place to stop for something to eat. The man parked the SUV in the back. He made sure the woman knew better than to draw attention to the vehicle before he got out. He locked the door and listened. She behaved.

He entered the eatery through the front door and stopped just inside to allow his eyes to adjust to the darker interior. Sunlight shined in the windows, but the shades were dropped to reduce its intensity.

An older woman with curly gray hair approached. "Just one?"

"Yes ma'am."

She smiled as she led him to a table against the far wall. The restaurant wasn't crowded yet. He was glad. It allowed him the time to question the woman without interruption. He slid into the chair and took the offered menu. Glancing through it, he selected an ice tea to start. When she returned with it, he gave her one of his winning smiles.

"Thank you," he squinted as he read her nametag, "Mindra."

"Call me Minny."

"Pleasure to meet you, Minny."

"Traveling through our little town?"

"I'm on my way to Great Falls. I wanted to stop for a decent meal instead of the stuff served in those fast food chains." He picked up the glass and sipped at the contents.

"I hear you. The food in this place is the best. I should know; I help make it."

"Then you can help me choose." He leaned over to allow her

to see the menu. She didn't need it.

"The country fried steak with mashed potatoes and a vegetable is the specialty of the house. I recommend it. And it comes with my guarantee. If you're not satisfied, I won't charge you. Deal?"

"Deal."

Minny took the order to the kitchen. The man glanced around the room. It was quaint, in a country kind of way. Pictures of horses, rodeos, and western paraphernalia hung throughout the room. He noticed a picture of a woman, standing beside another person, hanging a couple of tables away. He rose to get a closer look.

The woman in the picture caused his heart to race. It was her. It was the One. He recognized her from the news. He was still looking at it when Minny emerged from the kitchen, his food in hand.

"I see you found our local celebrity."

"Local? You mean she lives close by?"

"Yup." The woman beamed with pride.

"Who's the guy?"

"Oh, that's Senator Enesco. She helped find his kidnapped son a while back. Since then, she's become a hot commodity."

"Does she come here often?" The man kept his face blank. He gave no indication of the turmoil going on inside.

"Once in a while. We see Sandy mostly."

"Sandy?"

"Her secretary."

"Wow. Does she live in town? Can I drive past her place so I can brag about it?"

"She lives down 341, close to the end. It's way out of your way, young man. Besides, thanks to the nosy news people, she put in a humdinger of a security system."

"Oh, well, maybe next time." He returned to his table.

Minny realized she still had the plate of food in her hand. She moved to the table, muttering, "Minny, you ole chatter box, now look what you did."

"Are you okay?" The man feigned concern for her.

"Yea, but I let your food get cold."

"I bet it's just fine." He reached up and took the plate from her

hands. Setting it down, he picked up the fork and scooped up a pile of potatoes. They still had some warmth to them when they hit his tongue. He picked up the knife and sliced off a piece of the steak. It followed the potatoes. "Wonderful," he said after swallowing. He smacked his lips to emphasize his point.

Minny relaxed. "Just for that, you get a piece of my special cherry pie." She moved back toward the kitchen, "along with some vanilla ice cream on the side. My compliments."

During her absence, the man thought about what Minny had said, about the security system. His knowledge of them was zilch. How was he going to get past it? How was he going to get the One away from her fortress? The only thing he could think of doing was watch the place and see if an opportunity presented itself. He finished the meal with thoughts of Nature dancing before his eyes: her flowing brown hair, her creamy skin, her deep brown eyes, him piercing her many times, and her loving every ounce of it. His reverie was interrupted with the return of Minny.

"Here you go, young man, enjoy."

"Thanks Minny."

He watched the older woman walk away. Her slightly plump hips caused her mid calf length skirt to swing to and fro. If she had been a touch younger, he would have been tempted to sample her, to show her his pleasures. Since he had the other woman, he didn't need to. He scooped a small bit of the pie onto the spoon. Putting it into his mouth, he savored the tartness of the cherries, mingled with the sweetness of sugar. Minny was right; the pie was special. Smiling, he dipped the spoon into the ice cream and ate every bit of it, along with the rest of the pie.

The man paid the tab and waved to Minny as he left. He rounded the building and got into the SUV. He glanced back at the woman. Her face was uncovered. She had tear tracks on her cheeks. She watched him with dread. He smiled, Soon he would have everything he wanted. Soon he would be free of the need driving him. Until then, he had Miranda.

He started the engine and pulling the lever into drive. He returned to MT-200 and drove back the way he came instead of towards Great Falls as mentioned. The exit for 341 came into sight. He put the turn signal on. Within minutes, he was on his way to the address of his intended love.

The dirt road kicked up a dust cloud. He watched it with fascination in the side mirror. It reminded him of a huge billowy marshmallow half cooked by an open fire. Memories of his childhood rushed in. The man gasped at the sudden intrusion, causing the SUV to fishtail several times. He pulled over to prevent wrecking the vehicle. He gripped the steering wheel with white knuckles while he tried to get himself under control. Several trees stood nearby. He decided to hide the truck. He had to release. He had to gain control once more. There was only one way to do that.

Turning the wheel, he drove across the open area until he could not see the road, only the trees. He pulled the lever into park and turned off the engine. Silence filled the cab. Sweat covered his forehead. He shifted his position so he could see the woman in the back. He no longer saw Miranda; he saw another, another from his past.

He crawled into the rear area and tugged the blanket off her naked body. He ignored her whimpering. Unzipping his pants, he yanked them down to expose the erect penis hidden inside. He flipped her over and lifted her hips. He spread her cheeks. He shoved himself into her anus as hard and deep as he could. He pumped her unmercifully. He dug his fingers into her skin, pulling her against him.

While the man rocked his hips, he cried out, "I promise to be a good boy! Please mommie, please! Please..." He felt the level of pleasure inside rise. "Okay mommie, I promise to please you. I promise."

His grip on her hips lessened, and his brutal behavior reduced. He rotated his hips in a circular pattern, savoring the feel on his cock. He withdrew and gently helped Miranda onto her back. He spread her legs and guided his penis toward her vagina. Her tied arms got in the way so he pulled them up over her head. The tape on her mouth prevented him from inserting his tongue when he kissed her. No matter. He kissed her anyways.

Her erect nipples brushed against his. He felt her intake of breath as he pushed inside her.
He cupped her breasts, thumbing the tips. He nibbled on her ear, whispering, "Love you mommie, love you; love making love to you mommie."

A moan escaped from Miranda. She couldn't help it; he was so

gentle. It felt good. He did not seem to notice the sound. She was glad. Whenever she made too much noise, he made her shut up with blows.

"Am I making you happy mommie?" He glided in and out smoothly. The glide took on a faster tempo. He hugged her against him. His sweat ran onto her body. His eyes were closed. "Happy mommie...making mommie happy with love."

The man arched his back, supporting his upper body with his arms, and yelled, "Here we come mommie; here we come." He gritted his teeth and ejaculated. A howl of sheer joy echoed in the small space. When the surge of pleasure washed through him, he lay down on her.

Suddenly, he began to hide his head with his hands, almost as if he was being hit. "I'm sorry mommie, I'm sorry! I didn't mean to yell. I won't do it again. I promise. Daddy won't find out! I love you mommie; I love you! Please don't hit me anymore. I'll be quiet."

For the first time since he kidnapped her, Miranda felt sorry for the man. She understood what it was to be dominated by family. She had experienced it many times before she left. Hesitantly, she moved her arms down. She brushed his sweaty hair with her fingers. She wanted to tell him it was okay, that he didn't need to fear being hit, but the tape stopped her.

The man kept his eyes squeezed shut. The fingers going through his hair soothed him. He relaxed. The arms circled him, holding him against the body underneath. He slid down until his face was level with her chest. He suckled on a breast, as if it was a pacifier. The arms held him, keeping him warm and secure. He fell asleep, dreaming of the pleasure, and the person who gave it to him at such an early age.

fifteen

Sandy drove down 341 toward MT-200 and Jordan. The Chevy's radio blared. It was not the typical country music listened to by many in the area but a head banging heavy metal kind. When she first met Nature, she listened to classic rock. The Rolling Stones, The Beatles, Kansas, and many others adorned her collection. Now Korn, Nightwish, Metallica, and Marilyn Manson sat next to them.

She was on her way to the store for supplies. Nature called the previous night to inform her she would be home either today or tomorrow. She wanted to make sure there was enough bread, lunchmeat, and easily prepared meals available. After such a long and difficult session, like this one had been, her boss would not feel like eating any heavy meals.

A dust cloud hung in the air when she neared the highway. It was the kind caused by a vehicle driving on the dirt road. Having not seen one between the house and here, she shrugged it off. Maybe it was another lost tourist trying to find Great falls, or the wildlife refuge. Many used the road as a turnaround point. At the stop sign, she turned right. Rocking her upper body with the tempo of the music, she pushed the gas pedal toward the floor.

The man woke to the feel of warmth under him. He opened his eyes. The woman taken from the fast food place was cuddled against him. He was confused for a moment, until he remembered losing control. It had been a long time since that happened. He

hated it. It showed him as being vulnerable, something he never allowed to show.

Miranda felt the change when the man woke. She held still. She wasn't sure how he would react to her holding him. When he raised his head and looked at her, she lowered her eyes in submission. She felt his eyes on her for what seemed like an eternity. Finally, he shifted his position. He reached up and cupped her chin. She was elated, yet scared.

The man bent over and kissed her on her lips. He sat up and backhanded her. Her head twisted to the side. To her credit, she remained silent. He smiled. This one was worth taking to the cabin. He would enjoy giving her much pleasure. It was obvious to him that she had not had any before; therefore, it was up to him to give it to her. With both her and the One, his needs would be fulfilled for many years to come.

Thinking of the One brought his mind to the present. The sun was three quarters of the way across the sky. Night would soon be upon him. He was not sure if Nature was home yet. He needed to find out; he needed to find where she lived before dark.

He pulled his pants up and zipped them before moving back to the driver seat. He turned the ignition and started the SUV into motion. He didn't bother covering the woman. Who would see her out here?

The road disappeared over the horizon. Nothing but open plains was visible for as far as the eye could see. An occasional clump of trees spattered the vast openness but no houses dotted it. He followed the road until a gate crossed it. He stopped and got out. Walking up to it, he put a hand over his eyes to reduce the glare blinding him. He saw what appeared to be a house in the distance. Minny's words about a security system flashed into his mind. He turned back to the truck.

About half a mile away from the gate, a thick growth of trees followed a small stream. It led toward the house. The man got in and started for them. He smiled when he discovered a dip in the ground large enough to hide the vehicle. Getting out, he backtracked a short distance. The SUV was not visible when he turned around.

He heard a low grumble in the distance. It sounded like something was on the road, coming near. He ran for the cover of the

nearby trees. He just made it before the cause of the noise appeared. It was a sheriff's car. He ducked lower.

A lanky tall man in uniform got out and walked up to the gate. He did not look around. Reaching up, he unlatched it and swung it wide. No alarms went off; no voice echoed out of a security device, no camera whirled as it turned to focus on the intruder. He returned to his car, pulled it forward, closed the gate then drove toward the house. About ten minutes later, the car returned. Again, no alarms went off when he opened the gate. The man stood once it was out of sight. He processed the information just witnessed. A smile slowly etched across his face. He was excited. He now knew of a way to get to the One. He returned to the SUV to plan.

Getting in, he moved to the back and brutally attacked the woman in his possession. He dreamed of Nature during the entire time. He used the rods, both his and the metal one. He remembered thinking that if Nature were truly the One...they would get together. It seemed that all the pieces were falling into place. Now he knew, without fail, that he was going to have her...that she was going to be with him in the cabin, away from all the annoyances, the two of them forever side by side.

Nightwish blared from the CD player, disturbing the person trying to sleep in the passenger seat. He pulled his hat lower and flipped toward the window. He scrunched his shoulders in an attempt to find a comfortable position. The intense heavy metal, complimented by the sounds of an orchestra, helped Nature to reduce the stress flowing through her, almost as good as a hot shower did. The hot shower was something she looked forward to when they reached home. For now, she had to settle for the noise.

They drove straight through, stopping only for food, the bathroom, or to trade drivers. Plus, one stop to get some music from a Wal-Mart in Fargo. Nature insisted on the music. Web fretted about wasting too much time while they were in the store, but he bought snacks and drinks, in addition to a couple of CD's of his own once they were there.

Nature tapped the steering wheel with the beat of the drum. She was tired. The haunting dreams of the killer and the alternat-

ing of drivers wore her down. The music kept her awake. Web finally gave up on sleeping. He straightened his hat and sat up.

"How can you listen to that crap?"

"It's art...not crap."

"If it's not done by Alabama, Loretta Lynn, George Strait, Hank Williams Jr, or singers like them...then it's crap."

"I always knew you were a county bumpkin."

"Why...thank you ma'am." He raised a hand and tipped his hat. "Mighty fine of you to say so."

She shook her head. "Maybe that's the reason I like you so much...always went for the hard luck bumpkin cases."

"I aim to please." He slid across the seat and draped an arm over her shoulder.

Her only answer was a yawn.

"Why don't you let me drive? We won't reach your house until after seven this evening and you need to rest. Besides, it's my turn to take over the CD player."

"I hope you're not this dominant when it comes to the covers."

"Watch me woman! I'm the biggest blanket hogger in Montana...especially after the cold winter sets in." He winked at her and raised his eyebrows a couple of times.

Nature smiled. It was amazing to see the change in him. When they first set out, he was cold and aloof. The outer shell melted when he discovered her own shell was nothing more than a cover for the vulnerable scared woman inside. She felt safe with him. She felt able to let her guard down, knowing he would be there. "I love you."

He leaned over and kissed the top of her head, "Love you too."

"What are you going to do when we get back?" She hated to ask the question, yet, knew it had to be said.

"I have to go back to work. I was elected sheriff and I need to fulfill those duties."

"Will I see you?"

"Of course. Just because I go back to work doesn't mean I'll stop seeing you." He looked at her in disbelief. "Did you think that once we got back, I would not want to be seen with you? I don't care what people think."

She sighed. "I'm sorry."

"Don't be...I love you, nothing will cause that to change." His

expression softened. "Now pull over and let me drive. You're exhausted."

She shoved the turn signal upward and slowed. Veering off to the side of the road, she stopped and got out, making her way to the passenger door. Web slid across the seat. Once she was seated, he indicated for her to slide against him. She tucked herself under his arm.

The turn signal came on, warning traffic of their reentry. He glided smoothly onto the road. Five miles from the exchange point, the sound of *Alabama* blared from the open windows.

They made it to the gate at almost 8:30 at night. Nature got out and pushed it wide enough for the camper to get through. She closed it before climbing in again. Neither saw the SUV hidden a half mile away, the man watching, his heart racing at the sight of Nature standing in the glow of headlights.

They pulled up to the house minutes later. As Nature opened her door, Sandy flew outside. She raced up to her and threw her arms around the older woman.

"Man, did I miss you! This house is boring without you here."

"Glad to see you too." The grin covering her face showed the sincerity of her words.

"I bet you're pooped."

"Naw, Web drove most of the time."

Right on cue, Web opened his door and got out with a groan. Sandy rounded the camper and met him with a hug. "My you've grown." In actuality, he was still the same 6'2", but she loved to kid him about it.

"Nice to see you again, Sandy."

"My...those clothes do look good on you." She stood back to admire him. Web rolled his eyes. Sandy glanced at Nature, inquiring with her eyes.

"We'll talk later. Right now I want a hot shower and a good nights sleep in my own bed." She started toward the back to retrieve her suitcase.

"Me too." Web turned toward and met her at the door.

Sandy followed. She saw the way their hands touched when they reached inside the camper, the way they looked at each

other. She crossed her arms in front and whispered under her breath, "Well...I'll be damned."

"What did you say?" Nature asked.

"Nothing."

Nature glanced at her secretary as she lugged the suitcase onto the porch. She could tell from the expression on her face that she was going to be grilled once they were alone.

"I've got to be heading home," Web said after he set his luggage inside. His eyes lingered in Nature's direction before he left. Her eyes followed him.

She moved to the doorway when he was out of her line of sight. Sandy was right behind her, peering over her shoulder. Both women watched him drive back toward town. When his truck was gone, she spun around.

"What?'

"I always knew there was hope for you. I'm just glad I was here to see it." A smirk covered the younger woman's face. "Was he as wonderful as I predicted?"

"Sandy! That's none of your business."

"Aha! So he was!" Sandy threw up an arm; the way a preacher did during a sermon. "God, I'm glad to see you finally happy."

Nature grinned, "Me too. Now let's go in so we can talk. I know you won't let me get an ounce of peace until we do." She guided her inside, closing the door behind them and engaging the lock.

It was late. Unfortunately, Web couldn't sleep. He was too wound up from the long drive to relax. He decided to go to the office instead. His hand strayed to his lips. He could still feel Nature's touch. He looked forward to touching her again. Tomorrow he would check with Frewerson about how things fared while he was gone. Afterwards, he would call her. Turning right on MT-200, his thought returned to the daunting job of running the county.

Nature and Sandy talked well into the night. They discussed the cases, the girls, and finally, Web. They were in the room with

the fireplace. A pot of tea sat between them. Nature held her cup close to her lips and sipped. Sandy did the same. Neither wanted to break the quiet that ensued after their lengthy discussion. The crackling of the fire was the only sound disturbing it.

Finally, Nature yawned. It was around two in the morning. She was tired. Getting to her feet, she set the cup down. The shower she wanted so badly would wait until the morning. "I'll see you sometime tomorrow. Wake me if you go somewhere, I'll go with you."

"If I go anywhere I'll get you up."

"Thanks Sandy."

"For what?"

"For being you. I owe you a lot."

"Are you kidding? My life would be a complete dullsville without you." She brought the cup to her lips and took a swallow. "Even when you leave me here to do nothing but tend house." Sandy saw the woman staring at her and gulped down another mouthful. She smiled to show she was kidding.

Nature rolled her eyes toward the ceiling, smiling, as she left the room. She went upstairs to her room. At the doorway, she stopped and took in the sight of her bed. It looked so inviting, especially after so many nights in either a motel or the camper. Changing into her pajamas, she slid under the covers and exhaled a breath of complete ecstasy. The sheets felt like a cloud, the mattress seemed to envelope her in its welcoming pads.

Curling onto her side, she snuggled into her pillow. She wondered what Web was doing. Was he lying in his bed thinking of her? She remembered the feel of his body against hers and longed to be against it again. Sleep embraced her with its comforting arms while she dreamt of the man who finally caused her to love once more.

Web leaned back in the creaky wooden chair. He placed a boot up on the desk while he read through the faxes. Several dealt with local problems involving cattle and the need for police assistance at a rodeo. Of course, the ever-present missing person's bulletins were there. He read them quickly. The ones involving men went into one pile, while the women went into another. The door to the

building opened. Web looked up to see Deputy Frewerson step in.

"Saw the light on and came to check it out. Good to see you back Sheriff."

"Good to be back. Anything happen while I was gone?"

"Nothing much." The deputy gave his superior a full report. "By the way, why are you here so late?"

"Couldn't sleep. You?"

"Couldn't sleep."

Both men grinned. The deputy poured stuff that looked like mud into a cup and handed it to Web. "Here, this should hold you until you're through that mess." He nodded his head at the pile in front of Westerly.

Web took the cup with the logo that read *cops know how to holster their weapons best* stenciled on it. It was new. "Where did you get this?"

"Great Falls. Went there for a new hat and saw it. Knew I had to have it. Has a lot of meaning to it don't you think?" The deputy winked.

"If you go there again, would you pick me up one?"

Frewerson moved toward the exit, "Sure thing, Sheriff. Anyone in particular you want to holster?"

"Frewerson..."

"Hey...just asking...what with you taking that long trip and all." He threw his hands into the air before grabbing the handle to open the door.

"Frewerson..."

"All right, all right, I get the hint, get the heck out, I have work to do."

"You got it."

"See ya later Sheriff. Don't stay here all night...okay?"

"Yes mother...now get!"

Frewerson tipped his hat in departure before he pulled the door shut. With a sigh, Web returned to the papers piled in front. He went through the routine stuff pretty quick, making schedules to accommodate the needs. When that was finished, he picked up the missing reports involving the men. Most were from other states. A few were from the Great Falls and Billings areas. None required immediate attention.

The stack involving the women was saved for last. He wanted

to see if there were any similarities to the ones being worked on, the ones involving Rew and Patricia, along with the other girls Nature saw in her reading of the van.

One was about a woman and her daughter who had not returned from a shopping trip. Another was about a young teenager who took off after an argument with her parents, presumed to be a runaway. Many more dealt with similar situations. Near the bottom, one gave information about a dead girl found in West Virginia. He brushed it off as probably a hiker that took a wrong step and fell.

He sipped at the mud and grimaced. It tasted worse than it smelled. Getting up, he moved to the bathroom and poured the contents down the drain. He rinsed the cup, dried it, and returned it to the peg where Frewerson had grabbed it. Looking at the remaining pile, he decided to go home instead of finishing. More would be waiting for him anyway by the time he showed up tomorrow. Picking up his hat, he turned off the lights and locked the door. He got into his truck, backed out of his parking spot, and drove to his empty house. The emptiness helped his decide on visiting Nature sometime tomorrow, as soon as he finished letting the county know he was back.

In a clump of trees near a small stream, a man watched the house in the distance. He was patient. He knew the One was there. He knew a sign would be given when it was time to go in. Until then, he would give the girl in the SUV all the pleasure she could take. Until then, he would dream.

Sixteen

Sandy decided to go to Great Falls instead of Jordan. She wanted to get something special for Nature to say welcome home. The stores in Jordan were good but there were more options in the bigger city. She left the house shortly after eight in the morning. Nature was still asleep. She did not wake her; the woman needed sleep more than she needed shopping.

Great Falls was about 230 miles from the house. It was at least a four-hour drive. If she put her foot down, she could make it sooner. Turning up the radio, she grooved to the beat blaring from the speakers.

Fifteen miles past Jordan, lights glinted in her mirror. She looked up to see a sheriff's car behind her, the lights on the roof twirling brightly. She glanced at her speedometer. It read ninety-five. Cursing, she pulled off the road and turned the radio down. The car slid in behind her. She watched as a tall lanky officer got out and approached.

"Morning Lem"

"Sandy. Where you going in such a hurry?"

"Great Falls. I'm going to get Nature something, and I wanted to get back before it gets too late. Wish you were off so you could go with me."

"Me too. Can we get together later on?"

"You asking me out?" Sandy leaned out the window, resting her chin on her arms. She liked Lem and wondered why he had not asked her out before.

Frewerson's face turned a faint red and his gaze fell to the

ground. He shuffles a foot before looking up. "Well, yea, if you don't mind."

"Why Lem, you're positively cute when you blush. Of course, I'd love to go out with you. What time do I need to be ready?"

A grin, filled with relief, covered his long face. "Say about seven?" That was a late time for this area, but he knew how long it took to do a roundtrip excursion to Great Falls.

Sandy sat up, "Consider it a date then. I'll see you at seven." She pulled the truck onto the road after Frewerson stepped back to his vehicle. She waved her arm out the open window as she sped toward her destination. He waved back.

After watching her leave, he got in and pulled a u-turn. He decided to check out the road leading to the Kranderson place. He wanted to check out the area near the wildlife refuge. Kids who skipped school hung out there to smoke pot. If he caught any, he would hang them by their buster browns then hand them over to their parents. He smiled as he remembered the same thing happening to him when he was a teenager. Old man Random was sheriff at the time. He was the one who found the hiding spot and busted them. He treated them with respect, even though he didn't have to. He let the boys off with only a warning. It was at that point that Lem knew he wanted to be a deputy. When Random retired, Westerly became Sheriff. The dream became a reality shortly after that.

The turn off for 341 came into sight. He started down the road. When he reached the Kranderson place, a glint of sunlight bounced off something hidden in the trees about a half mile from the gate. It was still early so he knew it wasn't Nature. It was probably some kids. He drove his car toward the glint.

The man heard the car long before it came into view. He saw the sheriff's car drive up. He watched as it braked to a stop then turn toward him. He frowned. If the cop discovered him, he would stop him from getting to the One. That was not an option. He had to get to her; he had to take her to the cabin so he could finally be happy. He ducked under an overhang etched out by the stream over time. He peering out to see what happened.

Miranda heard the vehicle pull up. She heard the squeal of the

brakes and wondered who was here. It couldn't be the man who took her. He had been there moments before. If it were the police, they would take her away from him. She wasn't sure if that was something she wanted. She was in love with her kidnapper and wanted to stay. Yet at the same time, she wanted him to stop hurting her. She was confused about her feelings. With dread, she waited.

Lem parked near the SUV hidden by a dip in the ground. He watched it for several seconds before grabbing the handle and opening the door. Nothing moved. No kids frantically squirmed inside, trying to hide stuff from him. In fact, he didn't see anyone inside. The dark tinted windows made it difficult to see. He walked up to it cautiously. The front seat was unoccupied. The keys dangled from the ignition. He turned his eyes to the surrounding area. Again, nothing moved.

He noticed something lying in the back. Moving to the rear, he gripped the handle and pulled. The door opened to reveal a woman. Tape covered her mouth and her hands were tied together. Her upper body was naked; a blanket covered the rest. Lem gawked in surprise. A noise sounded behind him. He tried to turn, but it was too late. The world disappeared as an intense pain shot through his head.

The man watched the officer walk up to the SUV, his hand resting on his weapon. He looked around his hiding spot and discovered a large rock amongst some smaller ones. He grabbed it and returned his gaze to the officer. Now he had a weapon too. When the intruder made his way to the back, the man moved. He was directly behind him when the woman was discovered. The man brought the rock down hard on the back of the head, near the neck. The officer crumpled.

Blood flowed from a large gash. It pooled underneath the head. The man bent over. He felt for a pulse. It was absent. He stood and looked at the woman. Her eyes were wide. They returned to their normal size within seconds. While gazing at her, an idea popped into his mind. He remembered when the deputy had

gone to the house without difficulty. He looked down at the body. The blood started toward the uniform. He pulled it away from the red puddle.

Using the blanket, he soaked the mess off the neck. Small blotches decorated the collar, otherwise, the shirt was clean He stripped the dead man quickly to prevent the oozing stuff from ruining his plans. Once the deputy was undressed, the man rolled him into the stream. The upper half of the body lay in the water. It blocked the steady current enough to cause a detour. A thread of redness intertwined with the clear water. The man watched, fascinated.

Walking to the police car, he held up the uniform; it would fit. He put it on and admired himself. It was perfect, like it was made for him, instead of the previous owner. He reached up and removed the nametag. If the One knew the deputy, it would alert her and he might not get her. Bending over, he picked up the hat and placed it on his head.

The woman saw the deputy fall when the man hit him. She could tell by the way he acted that the officer was dead. After a brief passing of time, he put the uniform on. The transformation to his character was amazing. She felt her heart skip. He was gorgeous. She wanted him to take her. Maybe if she made too much noise, he would. Attempting to talk, she watched for his reaction. He ignored her. All he did was glance to the left. She quieted.

The man shut the door, enclosing her in her prison once more. She heard him reach in and grab the keys to the SUV. A second later, an engine started. She wondered where he was going and if he would return. She lay still, afraid to try anything. If he returned and found her trying to escape, he might kill her. She did not want that, she wanted to have more sex.

Nature turned over in her bed. The angle of the light shining through the windows told her it was still morning. The house was quiet. Sandy must have slept in too. She tossed the covers back and placed her feet into the slippers located next to the bed. She went down the hall to Sandy's room. It was empty, the bed neat and tidy. Shrugging her shoulders, she went downstairs to the kitchen.

A note sat on the breakfast bar. It was from Sandy. Nature sighed. Instead of waking her, as promised, her secretary had let her sleep when she left. She crumpled the note and tossed it at the trash bin. It missed. She started across the room to pick it up when a knock sounded at the front door. She retreated to the hall, leaving the ball where it landed.

Nature glanced out the window to see a Garfield County sheriff's car in the driveway. Thinking it was Web, she opened the door. It was someone else. A tall man with dark hair stood on the porch. She didn't recognize him, but there was something about him that nagged at her, something she could not place.

"Can I help you?"

"Nature? Nature Kranderson?"

"Yes."

"Can I come in please?"

"Is something wrong? Did something happen to Web...I mean Sheriff Westerly?"

"I'm afraid so. May I come in?"

Stepping out of the way, she said, "Of course, please, come in."

The deputy moved past her, into the hall. He stopped and faced her. Nature shut the door. She was turning around when the nagging feeling returned. She brushed it off, concerned to hear what had happened to Web.

"What happened? Is he hurt?"

"He was involved in an accident this morning and is in the hospital. If you will come with me, I can take you to him."

Nature looked at the man standing before her. Something was amiss. The officers under Web knew she did not travel in a police car, unless forced to. There were too many unwelcome feelings inside. They always suggested she follow them in her own vehicle. She glanced at his shirt. Where a nametag should be resting, there was none. Her inner voice screamed at her. She looked up at the eyes watching her.

The man saw the suspicion enter her eyes. He knew it was time, time to move. As quick as a striking snake, he attacked. He grabbed her arm and threw her around, slamming her into the door while wrenching her arm up her back, thus stunning her. He pressed up against her, holding her against the wood. He pulled

the handcuffs clipped on the deputies belt out and wrapped them around both her wrists before she had time to recover from the sudden move.

She started to struggle. He hit her. She tried to kick him. He drew back and slugged her across her jaw, hard. This time, she went limp. He had knocked her out. Catching her, he lowered her gently to the floor. The arms under her caused her chest to arch upward. He admired her breasts. He cupped each one, feeling the nipples under the clothing. Feeling himself rise to the occasion, he quit. He did not know how much time he had before the other woman came home. He wanted to be far from here when she did.

The man picked up the One and tossed her over his shoulder. He made sure nothing looked out of place as he turned to leave. Nothing was. He carried her to the police car and placed her in the passenger seat. Getting in, he drove to where the SUV sat. He transferred Nature to it. He backed it out of the dip and parked the cop car in its place. Satisfied, he changed out of the uniform. It had served it purpose. He tossed it into the open window, along with the hat and gun belt. He kept the handcuff key.

With eager anticipation, he drove the SUV back to MT-200. He was going home; he was going to the cabin. He rubbed his crotch. Soon he would do the same thing to the One. Until then, he had to give himself pleasure. Until then, he had to put as much distance between the ones who thought they loved her, and the one who loved her now. The clock on the dash read 9:20 a.m.

Seventeen

Web stretched after the long meeting. The other members of the committee had left after accomplishing almost nothing to help with the manpower shortage the department suffered. He yawned and he glanced at his watch. It was 5:35 in the afternoon. He stood and made his way to the phone. He wanted to call Nature. He wanted to take her out to eat. As he reached for the receiver, the door to the conference room opened. It was Deputy Sandpiper.

"Sheriff, glad I caught you."

Web saw the concern on his face. "What is it?"

"It's Frewerson. He didn't report in this afternoon."

"Maybe he left without doing so. He's done it before." Web stayed where he was. He intended to call Nature after Sandpiper left.

"We thought of that, so we called his house. There was no answer. Harrison went over to check. No one was home." The deputy hesitated. "We tried calling him on the radio. He still didn't answer."

"When did you hear from him last?"

"This morning."

"Nothing since?"

"Nothing."

Web sighed. "Let's go find him." He knew dinner was out. He had a missing deputy, which took precedence over food. He grabbed his hat off the table and exited the room, Sandpiper right behind him.

"When we find him, you'd better keep him away from me, because if I get a hold of him, I'm going to slap the dog shit out of him."

"Sheriff...if we find him goofing off, you won't be the only one."

Sandy made it home by six. She had an hour before Frewerson showed up for their date. Carrying the heavy packages inside, she shouted for Nature. "Hey! A little help here!" No reply came.

She moved into the kitchen and set the bundles on the bar. She saw the ball by the bin and picked it up. It was her note. She smiled. She knew her employer was probably fuming at her for leaving without her, but...oh well. She needed the sleep.

Going upstairs, she looked into Nature's room. The bedcovers were still down, something Nature didn't usually do. Sandy made the bed as a favor. She figured Web had called and the two were out. She moved to her own room and took a quick shower. After the long drive, the hot water relaxed her tired muscles.

With towels wrapped around her body and her hair, she walked to the oversized closet and picked out a sleek black dress. She returned to the bathroom and sat at the vanity table. The sound of a hairdryer filled the room. It was 6:30 p.m.

Web drove all over the county looking for his deputy. He was still missing. None of the other officers reported seeing him either. The sheriff was worried. It wasn't like Lem to up and disappear like this. He shined his spotlight at the trees next to road 543. It lit up the area around them, leaving the rest draped in darkness. So far, all he saw were eye shines bouncing off animals hidden in the growth. He kept the cruisers speed slow in case something showed up.

His cell phone started ringing. He flipped it open and saw Natures number on the screen. Putting it to his ear, he said, "Hey."

"Hey."

"Sandy?"

"Who else. Can I speak with Nature?"

"She's not here."

No sound followed. He thought he had lost the connection.

"Sandy?"

"Web...have you seen her today?"

"No, I've been in meetings all day, then hunting for my missing deputy."

"Missing deputy...is it Frewerson?"

"How did you know?" His stomach began to turn, leaving a bad taste in his mouth.

"He was supposed to meet me at seven. He didn't show. I was mad and wanted to talk to someone about it. After what you just told me, I put two and two together."

"When was the last time you saw Nature?"

"This morning, before I went to Grand Falls. I peeked in on her while she slept. Why?"

"Sandy...I'll be right over." He flipped the phone shut, tossed it into the passenger seat, and slammed the gas pedal to the floor, making the gravel under the wheels shoot out like bullets. He almost fish tailed out of control when the tires met solid pavement. When the sign for 341 came into sight, he slowed before turning. He floored it again once he hit a straightaway.

The gate for Nature's place was up ahead. He was about plow through it when his headlights reflected off something to the right. He slammed on the brakes and lit the area up with the spotlight. The reflection bounced back. He spun the wheel toward a clump of trees. As he skidded to a stop, a sheriff's cruiser sat before him. He could tell it belonged to Frewerson.

He exited his car with caution. He didn't know if anyone was still inside, waiting to ambush him. With his weapon in hand, he crept up to the back. Taking a quick look in with his flashlight, he found it empty. The front seat was another matter. A uniform lay crumpled on the seat, a hat on top of it, a gun belt next to it on the floorboard. He put his gun away and grabbed the mike hanging on the dash.

"Sandpiper...do you read me?"

"Yea, Sheriff."

"I found Frewerson's cruiser. But I don't see him."

"Where are you?"

"Near the Kranderson place."

"On my way. Be there in a few." As the mike cut off, Web heard a siren wailing in the background.

He searched the area around the car. A dark pool of something was under the trunk. He knelt down and touched it. His fingers glowed red when he trained the light on them. The bad feeling he had when talking with Sandy grew. He knew Frewerson never left anything in his vehicle, much less his uniform and prized hat. He straightened and directed the light farther out.

The rainbow effect of water bounced off the trees. Web moved closer. At the edge of the embankment, he carefully looked over. Frewerson lay half in, half out of the stream. He wore only his underwear. Web leaped down the short drop. He raced to the fallen man. Congealed blood, partially washed away, covered the back of his head. His eyes were open, forced that way by the water. Web felt the side of the neck. He knew he wouldn't find anything. He didn't.

His thoughts returned to his earlier conversation with Sandy. Nature was missing. He bolted up to his car. Slamming it into gear, he plowed across the open ground toward the gate. He drove right through it, leaving a mangled mess of metal in his wake. The distance to the house was covered in seconds.

As he slid to a sideways stop, Sandy flew out the door. "What's the matter...did you find her?"

Web leaped to the porch and ran inside. He ignored the questions tossed at him. He searched every part of the expansive house, hoping Sandy was wrong, that Nature was in a room, missed by the previous search.

Sandy ran behind him, shouting, "I've already done that. She's not here."

He stopped by the front door to catch his breath. Sandy grabbed his shoulders, "Web...what's wrong? Tell me."

He locked his eyes onto hers. "Lem is dead. I found him near the gate."

"Oh..." She let go and stepped back, her eyes wide with shock. That's when her foot bumped into something sticking out from under the stand near the door. She looked down to discover a slipper. Sandy had missed it when she came home, due to the packages in her arms blocking her view. "That's Natures." She bent over and picked it up. "Wonder why it's here? She always leaves them by her bed when she's not wearing them."

Fear gripped Web's gut like a vice and twisted it several times.

"What do you think happened?" Sandy asked. She set the slipper on the stand.

He didn't answer. His mind was racing. Grabbing her hand, he pulled Sandy out the door.

"Let's go. I have to get to the office."

"Why?'

"I think Nature's in some really deep shit. I need to make some phone calls so I can try and track down where she was taken."

"Web, what are you thinking? Where is Nature?" Her voice filled with the same fear he felt deep inside.

"I think she's in the hands of a killer...the same killer who did the Mosby girl."

Web threw himself into the car. Sandy did the same. He floored it into a spin and started out the way he came. Sandy noticed the gate when they flew past. She knew then the seriousness of the situation. While Westerly raced to the office, Sandy prayed they would find her employer, her friend, before it was too late.

Nature woke to light shining in through tinted windows. She had no idea where she was. The last thing she remembered was the deputy at her door, telling her Web was hurt. That was before he attacked, knocking her out.

She knew she was in a moving vehicle. The steady rocking motion informed her of that. She tried to shift her position but found her arms restrained behind her and her feet tied together. Tape covered her mouth. A chill ran up her spine as she realized she was naked. The only thing keeping the cold air at bay was a thin blanket covering her. Glancing around, she saw the other woman.

The woman stared at her with blue eyes speckled with dots of green. Her blonde hair was a mess. Some of it was still in a ponytail, but the rest was free...unlike them. Tape covered her mouth as well. Bruises were on her face. Nature's eyes took in everything; she saw the bruises covering the rest of the exposed naked body. Her legs were not restrained. She wondered why the woman had not tried to escape. Because of the tape, she couldn't

ask.

Nature rolled her head upward. She looked toward the driver's seat. A man with short dark hair sat behind the wheel. His attention was focused on the road. As if sensing her watching him, he briefly glanced back at her. A smile was on his face. She saw it was the same man who impersonated the deputy this morning.

"Don't worry love, we'll be home soon."

He turned his head forward. Nature felt her heart beat faster. She knew who he was now. To confirm her thoughts, she let her senses take in what her hands felt, the carpeting beneath her. The zing of the man: the man who killed Rew, the man who kidnapped and tortured Patricia, the man who killed so many before them, coursed through her. She was more afraid now than at any other time in her life. She knew what he did to his captives; she had seen it in her dreams. She hoped she would not have to experience it first hand. She hoped Web would find her before then.

The sun progressed across the sky toward night. Darkness now enveloped everything. They had been on the road since this morning and, except for gas, the man had not stopped. She knew he must be tired, and hungry. She was. She was surprised he had not taken her yet. The visions told her he usually raped the girls early on. Why he waited was beyond her. The only thing she knew was that when he finally did; her dreams...or rather nightmares...were going to become a reality.

Web sat behind his desk, the phone against his ear. He immediately called Detective Franklin when they arrived. Sandy paced back and forth. She was frustrated. She wanted to go find Nature, but didn't know which way to go. The ticking noise from the clock hanging on the wall drove her nuts. It read 2200, or 10 p.m. in regular time. The sound of a phone being set back on its cradle brought her attention back.

"Well? What did he say?"

"It looks like the girls listed by Nature were all from a central location. He picked up a piece of paper and showed it to Sandy. "See? Patricia was from Florida, Katherine from Georgia, and Connie was from North Caroline. The rest were from one of those three states or Virginia or South Carolina. He moved some papers

covering a map. Using the paper as a guide, he poked thumbtacks into each spot where a girl was abducted.

He leaned back when he finished. "Do you see a trend?"

"They appear to follow a line, kind of up I-95, right?"

"Correct."

"But what about these three?" She pointed to the pins for Rew, Vicki and Sarah. "Vicki was taken from Tennessee, Rew from the northern part of Virginia, and Sarah from near Charlottesville. They don't seem to fit the pattern."

"I haven't figured that out yet." He stood and started to pace in the same spot where Sandy had moments earlier. His frustration grew with each pass. The longer it took...the more likelihood of not finding Nature alive. He had finally found someone worth loving and he was not going to lose her. Not like the last time.

Suddenly, he stopped in his tracks. "Shit. Why didn't I think of this before?"

He flew to the map and glared at the pins. He traced each one north. The ones by I-95 stopped at Charlottesville. He looked at the three strays. Starting with the pin for Vicki, he traced it up I-81 to where Sarah disappeared in Virginia. The ending points were close. He found the one for Rew and followed it. It also met at the same spot as the one from Vicki, at Staunton. Looking to the east of his finger, he saw I-64 met with I-81. He looked up at Sandy. It was her turn to swear.

Web's phone rang, causing the two to jump. He picked it up. On the other end was Franklin. "It's late but I knew you were still there. I just read a report of a young woman who disappeared a few days back."

"Go on."

"The woman used to eat every morning for the last six months at a McDonalds a short distance past Nashville. Suddenly she doesn't show. They were not worried at first. By the third day, they knew something was wrong and called the police."

Web put a finger on Nashville as Franklin talked. It wasn't on either road leading to Staunton. He failed to see the connection. He said so.

"At the same time, close to the woman's home, a stolen truck was found sitting in the middle of the road. We traced it back to an elderly couple living outside Clyattville, Georgia. Close to their

home was an abandoned older model Ford. It belonged to a woman and her daughter who disappeared from the Atlanta area at about the same time Patricia was found." He paused. "Are you following me on this one now?"

Sandy saw the scowl work its way across Web's face and the way he held the phone in a death grip. She knew the information was not good. She hoped it was not about Nature, though had a feeling it was tied in somehow.

"We asked what kind of vehicle Miranda, the fast food lady, drove. They told us it was a Dodge Durango. It was dark blue in color. An all points bulletin went out the moment I got the info." He stopped, letting Web absorb the information. "Web...I think it's the guy we're looking for. I think, by all indications that he's on his way there." Silence filled the airways. "Web, you there? Did you hear me?"

"I heard you." The words were spoken with calm force. "But you're too late. He's already been here. He's got Nature."

This time it was Franklins turn to fill the gap with silence. He managed to say, "Shit. Are you sure?"

"I'm sure, buddy." Web told him about his dead deputy and that Nature was last seen this morning, and not since. His voice cracked when he spoke of Nature. He also told the fellow officer of law about his conclusions concerning the girls, and where they led him. "I think he's close to that area. This kind of person always goes home."

"That's a huge area. He could be anywhere."

Web stared at the map of Virginia. He leaned forward quickly, cradling the phone against his shoulder. "Hold on, I have an idea."

He traced the road from Charlottesville, toward Staunton, as he had prior to the call. He used his other hand to trace the path from Tennessee toward the same area. Close to where he stopped were the Appalachian Mountains. He looked at Sandy. "Didn't Nature say Rew was near some mountains, in a forest?"

"I think so...yea...come to think of it, she did." She leaned over the desk, as excited as Web. Her eyes scanned the area. "The area is so vast. How can we narrow it down?"

Web heard Franklin speaking. Straightening the phone, he said, "Say again? I didn't hear what you said."

"I said...leave that to me. I'll start looking into reports from the

area. I have a hunting buddy up there on the local force. You start your ass that way. I'll call you when I get anything."

The gratitude in Web's voice said mountains. "Thanks Franklin, I owe you."

"Shut up and get moving. It's a long drive or flight, whichever you do."

Web hung up and immediately dialed another number. After the person announced who they were, he said, "I need to book the earliest possible flight for two to Richmond. It's a police emergency." He paused while the speaker gave him the information. "Is that the earliest?" Pause. "I'll get back with you." He tried several other numbers and got the same, or worse, information. He slammed the phone down in frustration.

"Not good huh?"

"The earliest flight I can book is 9 a.m. There's others, but they take too long. A lot can happen in that much time." Web leaned back in his chair and laced his fingers behind his head.

"Is it quicker to drive?"

"No. It takes anywhere from 24 to 30 hours. I go fishing there sometimes when I want to get away."

"Then it will take him that much time too. Maybe we can figure out where he's going and beat him there."

Web looked at the secretary with renewed hope. He brought his arms down and picked up the phone again. "Delta? I want to book two for your 9 a.m. flight to Richmond." He gave their names and the necessary information so the charges went to the department. "Great. We'll be there."

He set the phone down and grabbed his hat. Starting toward the door, he indicated for Sandy to lead the way. "Did anyone ever tell you you're pretty smart for a blonde?" He grinned for the first time in a while. She spun around and socked him in the arm. He rubbed the spot, "You know I could arrest you for battery on an officer of the law?"

"Try it bud and I'll kick the shit out of you," she said as she walked to the passenger door and got in.

He got in behind the wheel and turned the keys. "I bet you would."

"I hope Nature kicks the shit out of her kidnapper." Sandy faced the window. She did not look at Web.

His smile fell. Backing out of the parking spot, he drove toward Great Falls. The flashing lights on the roof of the cruiser announced the urgency of their mission to anyone on the road at this time of night. He remembered the look on Nature's face at the diner as she told him and Franklin about the girls. He also remembered what was done to them and felt a shiver of dread run through his body.

Reluctantly, he glanced at the clock built into the dash. The time of 12:27 glared back at him. To him, it was too long. At least 16 hours had passed since she was last seen. The kidnapper could have done any number of horrible things in that much time. Grinding his teeth together, he mashed the gas pedal to the floor.

Eighteen

The SUV pulled off the highway well after dark. Nature saw the man look both ways before turning left. She could tell he was trying to find a place to park. She had witnessed his head jerk a couple of times prior to their slowing and knew he was not able to go much farther, not without risking an accident.

She had no idea what time it was or where they were, she just knew stopping was not a good thing for the unknown woman or herself. When he stopped, pain followed. She glanced at the other woman's face. It was mostly hidden by shadows. Nature thought she saw anticipation written on it. She again wondered about the lack of restraints on her legs and the reason for not escaping. Suddenly, she began to understand. This woman loved him.

She was horrified at the thought of anyone loving what he did to them. As she continued to look at her, the woman looked back. Her eyes reflected the hunger in them. Something else surfaced. Nature was shocked to see jealousy in them. Before she could think about it any longer, the SUV stopped.

Crickets chirped all around the vehicle. The sound of distant trucks hauling their payloads to their destinations echoed faintly. They weren't far from the highway. Keys jungles as something brushed against them. She saw the man stretch his arms up over his head. She heard him yawn. Instead of curling up in the front seat, he rolled over into the back.

He crawled up to Nature. She cringed back as far as she could. He smiled and reached out with a hand, grabbing a fistful of hair, tugging her toward him. He bent over and kissed her taped lips.

His lips traveled down her body to her breasts. He licked the nipples into a perky point before sucking on each one. Nature was disgusted. She wanted to throw up. She wanted to smack the shit out of him but knew he would only enjoy it. He reveled in causing pain. It seemed to give him pleasure.

His hand rubbed his crotch while he ran his tongue over her skin. She saw it bulge. A movement beside her drew her attention away from the man. The other woman shifted her position so that she was within easy reach. The man responded by moving a hand to her breast. He cupped it before giving the nipple a wicked twist. The woman inhaled with pain, but remained silent. Nature was shocked to see the pleasure on her face.

The man moved away from her and toward the woman. She watched as he unzipped his pants and pulled them off, thus freeing his erect penis. In horror, she saw him yank the tape off and cram it into her waiting mouth. Averting her eyes, she was unable to block the sound.

With her eyes closed, she waited. The slurping seemed to go on forever. She hoped that when he finished, he would be too tired to use her. She peeked when she heard movement. The man had the woman on her knees, her ass high in the air. She squeezed them shut when she saw him slam his cock into her anus. He grunted when he pushed. Nature tried to block the noise with a nursery rhyme repeated over and over in her head. It worked until she felt his hands on her body again.

The man saw the One with her eyes squeezed shut. He thought it was adorable. It made him want to please her more than ever. He withdrew from Miranda and flipped Nature over before she knew what was happening. He lifted her hips and admired her ass. He circled the opening with a finger. He inserted two fingers inside. She stiffened. He withdrew and inserted them again. He was ecstatic. He was finally going to experience the ultimate pleasure. He was going to sample the One.

Nature felt herself flipped over. Her hips lifted. She whimpered softly. She felt his fingers as they went inside and wiggled back and forth. She tried to squeeze her ass shut. It didn't help. He was going to take her, just like in her dreams; and there was nothing she could do about it. Her head was turned toward the other woman. Hatred filled her eyes. She would have gladly traded

places.

Suddenly, the worse pain imaginable rushed through her. The man was leaned over her back, lying on her handcuffed arms, pumping her ass with his cock. She tried to fight; the restraints and the confined space would not allow it. She arched herself to one side, to no avail. He held her tight and pumped as hard and fast as he could.

The next thing she knew, she was on her back and the tape was gone. It was replaced by him. He shoved his penis in as far as it would go. Nature gagged. She couldn't help it. She knew he like it from Patricia. She felt her knees separate as she struggled to maintain control of herself. His mouth touched her vagina. It sent a shiver up her spine. The dream where she enjoyed his touch returned. She had no idea how she thought it was nice. She hated it.

The man loved the tight feel of her ass, but he wanted more. He wanted her silky tongue around him. He had her on her back and the tape off in an instant. Flipping around, he pushed his cock inside. He felt the tip hit the back of her throat. It was wonderful. She gagged. He ignored it. He was too enthralled by her to care. He had to see if she tasted as good as she felt. Pulling her knees as far apart as the restraints allowed, he snuggled into her groin.

Her juices flowed, showing him she was thrilled as well. He licked them up like a kitten with a bowl of cream. When he finished, he guided his tongue inside. It was warm and soft. He lay down, lifting his hips and rotating them to get the full effect of her mouth on his penis. As he worked her, he felt his insides swell with pleasure.

Nature could not believe what was happening. It was one thing to experience it through a session. It was another thing to experience it in real life. Thinking about the sessions brought Web to her mind. Where was he? Did he know she was missing? Did he have any idea where to look for her? Was she going to wind up like the others before he found her? With what was happening to her right now, she wasn't sure if she cared. At least then it would stop.

The man on top of her arched his upper body upward when the pressure to release grew almost too intense to handle. He whispered, "Love you mommie, love making love to you mom-

mie," repeatedly.

A warm sticky substance filled her mouth as he ejaculated. She wanted to spit it out, but his penis remained in the way. She was forced to swallow it. He withdrew after a few seconds. Getting off her, he lay next to the other woman. He latched onto one of her breasts like a wee babe. She smiled and put her arms around him, holding him against her. He fell asleep in the protection of her arms. The jealous hatred returned to the woman's eyes when her gaze fell on Nature.

Nature ignored it. She hurt too much to be concerned with petty jealousy. She felt dirty; she felt used...she felt the other girls, the ones already dead, touching her with their sympathy. She managed to keep the tears from flowing while the man raped her. They flowed freely now that he was asleep. While she silently wept, she wondered if Web would ever want her again, especially after what happened tonight. She hoped she saw him again so she could find out.

Web fidgeted in his seat. Sandy sympathized. She was as tired of the plane as he was. "We're landing."

"I know." The words came out a bit too harsh. A moment later, he said, "Sorry...I didn't mean it that way."

"Don't worry about it. I understand." She gripped his hand. He squeezed hers in return.

"She's been with him since yesterday morning. God knows what he's done to her by now."

"Web...don't think about it."

"Goddammit Sandy...it's all I can do. I love her. I want her back, safe and sound." He kept his voice down. He did not want to draw the attention of the other people on the plane to their conversation.

"Have you heard from Detective Franklin?'

"No. I don't know what the hold up is. He knows how important this is."

"He's working as fast as he can, you can count on it."

The Captains voice came over the loudspeaker, "Hope you have enjoyed your flight with Delta. Please make sure to check out the sights in Richmond, they're fabulous. We'll be landing in a

few minutes so please do not walk around until the plane has come to a complete stop. Once again, thank you for flying Delta."

"Wish he'd stop yapping and land this son of a bitch already. I want to get off."

Sandy smiled. She pat the hand in hers, "Web...you're a wonderful man. I want you to take good care of Nature when we get her back...hear me?"

He looked at the woman seated next to him. "You can bet your sweet ass I will."

Ten minutes later, the wheels touched down on the runway and at 5:02 in the afternoon, thanks to the time differences, the passengers disembarked into Richmond. Most walked toward the luggage claims area. Web went straight to the rental car counter. He rented a Mustang, one of the newer kinds with a powerful motor. Sandy raised an eyebrow but said nothing. Minutes after checking out the vehicle, they were heading for the highway.

The drive to Staunton normally took about three to three and a half hours. However, this was Richmond, and it was rush hour. Time crawled as slow as the car. It did nothing to help the mood of the man behind the wheel. The fact that the cell phone had not rung, didn't help either. Sandy stared at the miles of cars. She normally loved motorized vehicles. This was one of the times where she wished there weren't so many of them. She kept quiet while Web fumed. He hit the horn several times out of frustration. The noise was met with obscene gestures on some occasions, bored bland faces on others.

An hour and fifty minutes later, they were past the huge city and up to speed. The other cars sharing the road flew past in a blur. Sandy was glad Web was driving. He was a cop of many years and knew how to handle the speed. She saw that his hunched shoulders had relaxed, his manner calm, his full attention focused on the road ahead. She thought about Nature. If they found her, she would need that calm to help her.

"Now I know why I hate big cities."

Sandy jumped. Web's sudden words caught her by surprise. "This your first time in one?"

He hesitated, "No."

"Where were you before?"

"New York."

"Wow, that's a big city. How long were you there?"

"Seventeen years. I moved there to see the sights and try my hand at Broadway." He smirked, "Can you see me in tights, dancing around and loving it?"

Sandy smiled, "Not really."

"One day, I was on my way to the studio when a child was hit by a stray bullet. A couple of gang members were trying to take each other out and a little girl got in the way. A police officer was in the area. He killed one of the shooters. The other guy got away. Instead of chasing after him, he comforted the girl while waiting for the ambulance." He shuttered. Keeping his eyes straight, he continued. "She died before it arrived. I was so impressed with how the cop handled everything that I decided to become one. That was 30 years ago."

"I always knew you were old...but ancient...damn you look good for your age."

Web glanced at Sandy. A faint smile worked its way onto his face. It disappeared when he returned his attention to the road.

"What brought you to Montana? New York has so much to offer: what with the theaters, stores, and such." Sandy always wanted to go there but had yet to make it.

"Death."

She stared at him, shocked. She waited. She knew he would continue.

"I was on the force for 16 years. I only had four more to go before I could retire. I was looking forward to it. I was tired of seeing the sick side of people, of seeing people whacked out on drugs, people killed."

"I was undercover, trying to bust a car theft ring. It was late by the time I made it home. The house was dark." The Mustang slowed. Web had taken his foot off the gas pedal. "I thought that a bit odd. Lights should be on. The next day was a school day and Megan always hated to go to bed too early. When I opened the door, the smell hit me, the smell of death."

"I pulled my weapon and advanced inside. I didn't see anything in the first few rooms. I reached the kitchen and saw my wife sprawled across the floor. Blood was everywhere. Her clothes were torn and her skirt was hiked up. I could tell she had been raped. Blood covered her face where the attacker hit her repeat-

edly." Web's breathe faltered. He couldn't stop. He needed to get it out.

"I checked her and found a thready pulse. Ugly stab wounds were all over her arms where she tried to fend off her attacker. The one to her belly was the worse. That was where all the blood came from. I ran to the phone and called for an ambulance. As I kneeled by her, I remembered Megan. I ran up the stairs to find her. She was in her room, on the bed, blood everywhere."

His breathe raced. "I lost it then. I barely remember rushing up to her and scooping her up into my arms. Cuts marred her beautiful face. Her clothes lay in a heap across the room. Her belly lay open, cut from the middle of her chest to just below her belly-button. She was dead. My baby girl was dead." He paused, unable to continue for a moment. "Everything was a blur after that. The ambulance, the flash of the cameras, the questions, all of it. That was until we caught wind of who did it. That was when everything became crystal-clear. It was a drug dealer I busted several months prior. He bragged about paying me back for ruining his business. After that, anger took over."

Sandy wished she could hug Web. She couldn't because they were still moving at a high rate of speed. She reached a hand over and placed it on his shoulder instead. His grip on the steering wheel tightened.

"Wanda survived, but it was never the same. We caught the bastard, and a month after he was convicted, she filed for divorce. I couldn't stay in the house, too many memories filled it. I saw Wanda several times; she always looked away. When I saw the sheriff position for Garfield County, I tried for it. I had nothing to lose and everything to gain. I got the position and have been there ever since."

"I was an asshole to begin with, never giving the deputies a break, even if it was stupid shit. After a couple of them threatened to leave, I learned to handle the anger. Then I met Nature. At first, I didn't know what to make of her. I thought she was a shyster. After her success with the Senator, I knew she was the real thing."

The faint smile returned. "I grew to love her but wouldn't allow myself to admit it. If I did, she might become like Wanda...or Megan. She helped by being aloof." He glanced at Sandy again.

"Your coming into the scene kept her distracted. It allowed me to keep my feelings hidden. The trip south brought them to the surface."

Sandy remembered all the times Web had been there, distant, always professional, never smiling. Now she understood why.

"I finally allowed myself to love again. By doing so, I placed her in jeopardy. She was taken because of me, taken because I let my guard down."

She listened to him and felt the anger inside swell. She let him have it when the self-wallowing talk started. "Now look, you self pitying asshole...because of you, she's happy. For the first time since her husband was killed, I might add. Because of you, she finally felt free enough to love again. She told me so the night you both returned."

"Because of me, she went to Florida! Because of me, the media focused on her and the killer found out about her!"

"It wasn't because of you, you stupid shit! Remember...the Mosbys contacted her first. They brought her into the case! All you did was give her hope...hope to continue...hope to love again!"

Web looked at the angry woman seated next to him. Her eyes glared and her nostril flared. He started to chuckle. "God, you're a terror when you're angry, do you know that."

"You betcha, mister. And don't you forget it." A horn honked behind them, reminding Web of the fact that he was traveling below the speed limit in the left lane. "Now, put your foot against the floor and get this damn thing to Staunton, instead of wallowing in that self pity shit." She crossed her arms and faced forward. When he hesitated, she turned her head toward him. "Well?"

"Wow." It was Web's turn to be surprised. Complying with her order, he lowered his foot. The Mustang leaped forward, leaving the annoyed driver behind them in its wake.

Staunton came into view three hours later. Both were tired. Both wanted to continue on but had no idea which way to go. They were deciding where to stop for the night when the area was lit by flashing lights. A police car pulled up behind them, its spotlight blinding them. Web frowned. He wasn't speeding or doing anything out of the ordinary. Someone got out of the passenger

side of the car once they stopped. The person cut behind the Mustang and walked up to the window. Web could not make out who it was due to the spotlight.

"About time you got here."

"Franklin?"

"None other." He stepped back, allowing Web to open his door.

Web faced the Detective. Reaching up to shake his hand, he said, "What are you doing here? Didn't think you were able to get away."

"I'm on vacation. My superiors know the real reason I'm here but gave me the time off anyway." He grinned, "They were happy to get me out of their hair. Haven't taken a vacation in five years. I was driving them nuts."

"Great to have you with us."

A man in uniform walked up behind Franklin. "Hank, let me introduced you to Sheriff Westerly. He's from Montana." The officer tipped his hat. "Hank is a deputy in Pocahontas County in West Virginia. He met me here as a favor. We'll be staying at his place."

Web shook the other man's hand. "Thanks for helping in this matter."

"My pleasure. Joe filled me in by phone. My department agreed to give you any assistance you required. We want to see Mrs. Kranderson found quickly and this jackass brought to justice."

Web saw the men straighten. Their faces betrayed their approval of the sight before them. "Gentlemen, may I introduce you to Mrs. Kranderson's secretary and friend..." He indicated for Sandy to stand next to him. "Sandy, this is Detective Franklin and Deputy...Deputy..."

"Boone, ma'am. Hank Boone." The deputy jerked his hat off his head and twirled it in his hands.

"Pleasure to meet you Mrs...." Franklin extended his hand toward her.

She gripped it firmly, "Miss...Miss Nemoy. Glad to meet you too."

"Pleasure to meet you, Miss Nemoy." He held her hand a bit longer than necessary.

She flashed Franklin and the deputy one of her award winning smiles before letting go. Her stance remained professional though, letting both know she was here for business only. Web had to admit it; she was a pro at working men.

Bringing the focus back, Web asked Hank, "Where's your place?"

"Just outside Thornwood...about an hour drive from here."

"Since it's already after ten, don't you think we should get there?"

That brought the man out of his puppy love haze. "Yes sir. Follow me." He returned to the cruiser and got in. He turned off the bright spotlight.

Franklin looked seriously at Web once his eyes adjusted to the darkness. "I found some information out. We'll talk about it when we get to Hank's. You might find it interesting."

Web stared at the man as he walked back to the car. He hated it when people did that. He should know...he'd done it enough times himself. Starting the engine after they got in, he pulled back onto the road and followed the cruiser.

Nineteen

The two vehicles traveled up a dirt road to a quaint log cabin tucked underneath some tall pines. Boone pulled his cruiser to the right side. Web pulled the Mustang along side him. The four occupants got out and walked up the steps to the front porch. Sandy rubbed her arms. Even though she wore a long sleeve sweater, the cool October night air managed to make them inadequate. In their haste to get here, she had forgotten to grab a coat. Boone took his jacket off and draped it over her shoulders. Snuggling into its warmth, she gave him a grateful smile. Franklin grabbed the handle and opened the front door. He held it for Sandy so she could enter first. Boone followed. Web brought up the rear, shaking his head.

The inside was as quaint as the outside. The kitchen and living room were one room. A small breakfast bar was the only thing separating them. Two doors led from the room. A bed showed through one of the open doors, a bathroom in the other. Everything was neat and clean. Sandy moved to the couch and sat down. The men were a step behind her. Several folders littered the coffee table in front of the couch. Web sat next to Sandy while Franklin and Boone occupied the chairs across from them.

Remembering his manners, Boone stood. "Does anyone want anything to drink...soda, coffee, beer?"

"Coffee...strong," Web said.

"Me too," added Sandy with a yawn.

"Coming right up."

The sound of running water began, followed shortly by the

smell of fresh coffee. By the time he carried the cups across to them, the folders were open and their contents spread out. Web savored the hot brew. He was exhausted and the caffeine helped him wake up. It had now been over 36 hours since Nature disappeared. He needed sleep but his imagination would not allow it. He had to find her before it was too late.

"You said something about information." He directed his statement toward Franklin. The man leaned forward and grabbed some papers. He handed them to Web.

"Read those...they're interesting." He leaned back, threw a leg onto the other, and picked up his coffee. He watched Web's face while he sipped at the strong brew.

Shock, disgust, and finally, understanding crossed it. He looked up. "When did this happen?"

"It was over a two year span, about nine to eleven years ago. We weren't able to find out who did the killings due to the lack of evidence." He sipped from the cup. "The animals had their genitals maimed or cut off before they were strangled." He put the cup down. "They stopped for a while but then things escalated. A young girl's body was found in the Monongahela National Forest. She was tied up, raped, tortured, and then strangled. Her vagina had been ripped open, as if something too large was forced into it. The coroner found tree bark inside." He looked at Boone for confirmation.

"That's right. The incident happened about eight years ago. Her case remained unsolved. The girl wasn't a local, so, given time, the incident was forgotten. After helping Joe with his latest case, I remembered it. It struck me as similar."

Web set the papers down and steepled his fingertips together in front of his face. He thought about both reports. At the same time, he tried to remember something he had read recently, something dealing with the death of a girl. Suddenly, it came to him.

He started shifting through the papers. "Is there anything in these about a dead girl found in this state? I received a fax about it at my office while I was away."

"I remember that one," Boone said. "I worked it and sent out the fax. We got a hit from Florida. It turns out her name was Mindy, Mindy Stax. Her parents reported her missing."

Web didn't hear what else Boone said. The words "Mindy" and "Florida" caused everything in the room to fade. He recalled the names given by Nature. One of them was Mindy.

"What's the matter?" Sandy touched him, bringing him back.

"How was she found?"

"A hunter found her."

"No...*how* was she found."

"I'm not following you," Franklin said. "What are you driving at?"

Web ignored the detective. He kept his focus on the deputy, waiting for an answer. His heart threatened to beat out of his chest and his palms felt like they were becoming lakes.

"Her arms were tied together and she was naked. It looked like she fell from the cliff above. Hard to tell anything else, animals helped themselves before the hunter found her, if you know what I mean."

Sandy blanched. Boone gave her an apologetic look.

"Was she anywhere near the spot where the girl was found eight years ago?"

Franklin and Boone turned their faces toward at each other then at Web. It was Boone who spoke. "Now that you mention it...yea, she was close to the same spot."

"Show me on the map."

Boone slid the map book around to face it toward Web. His pointer fell on a spot north of their present location. "Here." The area he pointed to was free of any roads. It was inside the National Forest. It was close to several mountain ranges, the Allegheny and the Appalachian.

"That's it! That's where he's got her. It fits." He jumped to his feet. "It fits the location where Nature said the other girls were buried." He glared at Boone, "Come on man, pick up the phone and start calling. We have to get a search team together." Looking at Franklin, he said, "Get off your ass. Let's go find her."

Boone and Franklin looked at the excited man. They remained seated. Web stared at them, unable to believe they were not moving. His anger flared. "Goddammit! Get off your asses and move!"

"Web...it's dark outside, we won't be able to see a thing. We might miss a clue, something that would lead us to her," Boone

stated.

"Besides, you don't know the area. In the dark, you might walk past her and not know it. But the killer would," Franklin threw in.

"Web, you've only had a couple hours of sleep since you arrived back in Montana," Sandy said. "You need sleep. We'll leave at first light."

"Shit!"

Franklin moved next to Web. "Come on, let's go sit down. We have a good idea of where to look, thanks to you, but we need to be fully rested when we start hiking in those woods."

"Go to hell. If you lazy shits want to sit on your thumbs and do nothing...then go ahead. I'm looking for her now."

Web turned to leave. Suddenly, the floor met his face. He felt his arm forced up his back and heard the rasping sound of handcuffs as they closed on his wrist. He tried to push up with his free hand. A knee in the middle of his back ended that. Another knee pressed on the side of his face. The free arm was forced back. The rasping sounded again. He found himself in the same situation he was in at the killers van, when he tried to stop Nature from pushing herself too far—handcuffed and helpless.

Sandy was screaming in the background. She yelled for the men to leave him alone, that he didn't deserve this kind of treatment, that he only wanted to help Nature. The knee on his back left. He heard several hits land on flesh as she fought to get to him. Just as quickly as the shouting began, it ended.

"What did you bastards do to her?" He shouted. He wasn't able to turn his head due to the knee pinning it to the floor.

"I stopped her from tearing me apart." Franklin's words came from the other side of the room. Web heard more rasping and the sound of someone being dragged across the hardwood floors. He watched Sandy's limp form land next to him. Her arms were handcuffed behind her.

"You're such a big shit, beating up a woman. Does it boost your ego...huh...does it?'

The knee shifted off him. Franklin kicked him over and grabbed the front of his shirt, lifting him off the floor. "You dumb fuck. All you see is one person. All you see is your latest fuck toy. I see the whole picture. I see the faces of those girls before my

eyes every day I go home to my daughters. I want this sick son of a bitch found before he can kill anyone else." He flung Web back onto the floor. "And I don't need a dumb shit sheriff in my way."

"When I get loose, Franklin, I'm gonna kill you."

"You have to wake up first. Say good night, Sheriff."

Franklin brought his leg up and kicked Web in the face. The sheriff flipped over, partway onto his side. He didn't move. Standing nearby, Boone watched. He followed Franklin's movements to the coffee table, then to the door. He followed him outside. Boone knew the area well. He knew where to look, because he had been there not too long ago, helping to investigate the discovery made by the hunter.

"He's going to be pissed off when he wakes up."

"So? I hope we'll have the killer in custody by the time he gets free."

The engine for the police car roared to life. It backed out and rolled toward Thornwood. At the interchange, it turned north onto Route 28. About 11 miles from the turnoff, it passed a lone holly bush. Its berries shined bright red in the headlights. Neither man paid attention. Their thoughts were focused on what lay ahead, and how they were going to find the needle in the haystack disguised as a man.

The cabin came into sight. Nature did not remember much about the trip to it. She was cold, hungry, and thirsty. Additionally, her body hurt in more ways than she thought possible. She did remember the man taking her one more time before he made her and the other woman hike up the mountain. The Man...that's what she called him since she did not know his name. He barely spoke.

The collar around her neck chafed her skin raw. She couldn't move it because her hands were still cuffed behind her. The other captive wore one also. The difference was her extremities weren't tied. She moved freely. She followed the man like a puppy, always trying to get his attention, always trying to get him to hit her and use her badly. It made Nature sick to watch.

A shiver up her back caused her shoulders to shake. She wasn't sure if it was because of the cold or the dread emanating

off the building where so much suffering happened, making the air around it heavy with grief.

The man saw the shiver and tugged on Nature's leash. He had to get the One inside before she came down sick. The sudden action made her stumble. His hands caught her, preventing her from falling. They lingered on her breasts. Nature closed her eyes. She didn't want him to see the revulsion in them. Another tug forced her eyes open.

Rage filled Miranda. She wanted the man for herself. He had no need for this interfering slut. She gave him everything he desired, and more. Why was he so infatuated with her? Her gaze landed on the woman in front of her. Thoughts of how she could get rid of her flowed through her mind.

The man brought both women into the cabin. He held onto Nature's leash while attaching Miranda's to the end of the bed. When he was finished, he guided Nature to the mattress. He laid her down and secured her legs in the swinging straps. Her arms remained under her. The man admired the way it forced her breasts upward. He wanted to hold them. An arm circled around him, distracting him.

Miranda wrapped her arm around the man's waist. She knew he would be mad, but at least it drew his attention away from the slut. He spun around; she ducked her head, waiting for the blows to begin. They didn't. She peeked upward to see why.

The man looked at her through slits. He appeared to be thinking. She waited. He turned back toward Nature, ignoring her. Miranda was shocked. She couldn't understand why he didn't hit her. He had before and it always caused him to get excited, thus causing him to take her. She had come to enjoy the beatings and the sex that followed.

The man cupped Natures breasts and squeezed them. Miranda saw his crotch grow. She wanted it. She didn't want him to give it to the slut. Determined to get it, she grew bolder. She stepped up to him and ran her fingers over his chest. She tried to bring them to his pants so she could unbutton and unzip them but he grabbed her wrists, preventing it. He threw her backwards, making her fall onto her ass. She stayed down, legs sprawled. This time she knew he would come to her, she knew he would take her like she so badly wanted.

Again, he turned back to Nature. Miranda saw him move his hand toward the swinging legs. She saw his hand disappear between them. She saw Nature stiffen. It was too much. She couldn't take it. This man was hers, she was not about to watch him share his cock with some interfering bitch. She jumped to her feet and forced her way against him. She ran her hand over his bulging crotch. She ripped at his pants, trying to get them out of the way.

The man jerked Miranda away. He backhanded her several times. Miranda responded by jumping on him. He was not expecting it and fell. He felt her hands clawing at him. He felt his shirt rip open. He felt her nails rake down his chest toward his abdomen. He felt his pants fly open and his penis jerk out. The tape covering her mouth fluttered into the air. Lips closed around his erection and her tongue moved over his skin. He became enraged. He was the one in control, not this bitch.

He hit her across the head with his fist. She scrapped his penis with her teeth. He bellowed with rage. Grabbing handfuls of her hair, he jerked upward. She sank her teeth in. The man lost control; he hit her with his fists again and again. He kept hitting her even after she had released him.

Nature watched in horror as she saw Miranda attack the man, attempting to get him to have sex with her. Her horror over the situation grew when she saw the man retaliate. He wouldn't stop hitting her. Miranda started to cry, but the tears only infuriated him more. His hands moved to her neck. He tightened them under the collar encircling it. Miranda's eyes widened. Her lips turned blue. She struggled to get his hands off. They were clamped on her like a vice grip. She sank her fingernails into his arms. Blood trickled from the wounds. The man didn't appear to notice, that, or else he was too angry to care.

Her hands fell to the floor when Miranda became unconscious. The man continued to choke her, though not for long. He let go and hiked up her hips, spreading her legs for easy access. With unleashed furry, he shoved his penis deep inside her vagina, finally giving her what she wanted all along. He jerked her body against his, not caring if he hurt her in any way. Pulling free, he threw her over onto her belly and crawled onto her back, cramming him erection deep into her anus. Grabbing her breasts, he

twisted the nipples viciously. He bit one of her shoulders and shook it like a dog while he pumped her ass.

Nature watched the scene unfold, unable to tear her eyes away, her breath matching the speed of the man's hips. She saw him flip the woman over and shove himself into her ass. He was so furious. It showed in his actions. She saw him grab Miranda's arms and pull them back, using them as he would the reins on a horse. The woman's body tried to shift away. The man released the arms, letting the head hit the floor with a thud. Nature winched. He grabbed the legs, near the groin, and began to ride her again, pulling on her as hard as he could.

His face was hidden, something Nature was glad for. The pumping action resumed. Sympathy pains echoed throughout her body. Not that long ago, she had endured the same treatment, but not to this vicious level. A noise caught her attention, pulling her away from the awful memory.

The woman's hips felt like they were welded against his skin, he held her so tight. He leaned back, letting a roar of achievement escape from his throat when his cum shot out. He had conquered the bitch. He had conquered the one who tried to take what was not hers to take. His heart raced, his breath matched it. He remained in that position for what seemed like an eternity. The feeling was powerful. He didn't want to give it up yet. Finally, when all his energy drained from him, he fell onto the body, panting.

When his heart and breath slowed, he got up. He stared at the bruised and battered body. A sense of loss flowed through him. The experience was so full of pleasure that he regretted its end. The remembrance of her attack brought the anger back. He kicked the body in the ribs several times before bending over and lifting it to his shoulder. He walked out the door, pulling it closed behind him.

Nature saw the red stain on the throw carpet. She stared at it, hoping the same thing wasn't going to happen to her. She knew better, though. She saw the crazed look in his eyes, before he left. Unless Web found her soon, she was doomed to endure what many before her had endured.

After what felt like forever, the man returned. His manner was calm. He stiffened when he saw the stain. He strolled to a stack of old rags and picked one up. An hour of scrubbing with water and

the stain was gone, like the woman who put it there. He threw the bloody rag into the fireplace and placed several logs on top of it. Lighting a match, he tossed it inside. The dry wood and the kindling under it lit quickly. Within minutes, a fire warmed the inside of the cabin, thus removing any sign of the outburst that had occurred earlier.

Nature saw him turn toward her. She held her breath as he moved toward her. The angry crazed look was gone; something far worse replaced it. A yearning hunger was there. She saw him remove his clothes and advance. She knew she was going to suffer horribly at his hands, far worse than previous. To her shock, he crawled onto the bed and lay beside her. He moved his mouth to her breast and latched onto it. One of his hands gently cupped her other breast as he started to suckle. He fell asleep.

Having her arms restrained behind her made the man's weight on her uncomfortable. She put up with it. If she moved or shifted in any way, it might wake him and set him off. She wanted to see Web and Sandy again. The thought of the two most important people in her life sustained her through the long night. The man changed his position a couple of times. His mouth always returned to her breast. By morning, after he was up and outside, she wished she could wipe the feeling of wet slobber off.

Web's face throbbed. It felt like a 300-pound gorilla had used it for a basketball. He flexed his jaw and opened his eyes. Sandy lay next to him; her hair sprawled in different directions. He watched her eyes open.

"What happened?"

"Franklin decided we were in the way. He put us out of commission temporarily."

"You look like shit. You're going to have a nasty bruise later."

"What else is new? Help me out here. We have to get free so we can find Nature. Roll over and put your back against mine, let's try sitting up."

Sandy did as instructed and they were sitting up a second later. His head swam. It took a moment for the world to stabilize. Once it did, he glanced at the coffee table. The folders were still there. An envelope sat among the papers. Getting up onto his

knees, he stumbled his way to it. Writing was on the front. It was from Franklin.

"Sandy, the asshole left us a present. I have a guess at what it contains." He bent over and picked it up with his teeth. Shaking his head, he heard the sound of something solid sliding inside. He worked back to her and dropped it in her waiting hands. She tore it open. A key fell out. "Yup, it's what I thought. It's the key to the handcuffs."

He backed up to her and grabbed it. Feeling around, he inserted it into the opening located on the metal. The cuff fell off with a twist of the wrist. She brought her arms forward and rubbed circulation back into them. Web waited patiently. She freed her other wrist then released his. Rising to his feet, he returned to the table. His eyes fell on the place on the map where he thought Nature was. Sandy joined him. Her eyes followed his line of sight.

"Web, what if the area where the girl was found eleven years ago, and the more recent one, were not the right spots. What if it was more south of that?"

"But Nature said it was near a mountain, in a little used forest area. It fits the profile."

"Think about it." She looked at Web. "If you were killing girls, would you bury their bodies in your backyard? Or would you take them a short distance away, somewhere still close enough for you to visit when the need arose."

"Web stared at the map, "You know…it makes sense. It makes more sense than mine." Glancing up at her, he said, "Where do you propose we look?"

Her slender manicured finger touched directly north of their present location. The one Web had pointed to was more in line with the road, more east of where she pointed.

"We better get rolling. Nature has been with that shit for three days now. That's three days longer than I like."

Outside, they were glad to see all four tires on the Mustang remained loaded with air. The departing men had not punctured them. Web started the powerful engine and guided the vehicle down the dirt road, back onto the paved one. He turned right, heading the way they came last night. The sign for Route 28 showed where to turn. Once they were on the road, both kept a

sharp eye out for any indications of where a vehicle might have pulled off. The sign for Cherry Grove welcomed them 17 miles later. Pulling the Mustang over, Web blew out a frustrated breath.

"I didn't see anything."

"That doesn't mean it's not there. We just missed it."

"What if we're looking in the wrong area? Damn!"

Sandy reached over and laid her hand on his. "We'll find her."

He gripped the hand with his free one. "I hope you're right Sandy. I don't think I could stand to lose someone I love again."

She kept her voice level. "Let's drive the road, again and again if we have to, until we find what we're looking for." She gave him a warm smile, which he returned.

"Okay."

He pulled a u-turn and pushed the gas pedal downward. They met Route 250 without seeing anything. Web grew more frustrated with every passing mile. He was smoldering by the time he pulled the car to the side of the road.

"Web, I need you to do another pass."

"Why!" He barked the word out. "So we can waste more time and allow that dick to kill Nature?"

"No...so we can save her." Her voice remained level, her words soft. "Web...please."

He said nothing as he slammed his foot down, causing the Mustang to whip around. Smoke rose up and long black stripes showed where they recently sat.

They were about eleven miles from the interchange when Sandy shouted, "There!"

Web slammed on the brakes. Thankfully, both were wearing seatbelts, preventing them from being hurled into the windshield by the sudden stop. Web glanced where she pointed. He didn't see what she was so interested in. The only thing he saw was a lone holly bush. That wasn't unusual. They grew wild in this area.

"That bush. Do you see it?"

"Yea. So what. They grow here."

"Yea. But do you see any other holly bushes around here?"

He twisted his head around. Not another one was in sight. "No. But I wasn't paying attention to bushes. There's probably more farther along."

"There aren't. I watched. This is the only one."

He focused his attention on her. "So what are you thinking?"

"I think the killer planted it to mark a pathway." Her features showed her excitement. It was infectious. "If we check it out, I think we'll find what we're looking for."

The tires spun. Again, black stripes showed on the road. Web pulled up next to the bush and put the Mustang into park. Both got out and walked closer. As they approached, tire prints became evident in the dirt. They led deeper into the forest. Web followed them. He saw the path. He looked at Sandy standing next to him. She looked back, a grin of satisfaction planted on her face.

"Has anyone ever told you your pretty smart for a blonde?"

The grin broadened. "All the time."

Turning around, Web said, "Let's follow this and see where it leads."

After the engine roared to life, Web backed up so the car pointed toward the path. Stepping on the gas pedal, the back tires, which were the only ones on the pavement, spun. He gave Sandy a sheepish look. "Guess I'm more anxious than I thought."

"Me too."

The bush disappeared and a path wide enough for the car appeared. They followed if for a couple of miles, both hoping it was not a wrong move. Before long, an abnormal thick wall of vines hung in their way. Web stopped and got out. He walked up to it and pulled a section back. A SUV came into view. It was a blue Dodge. He peered in the windows; it was empty. Excitedly, he waved for Sandy to join him.

"Is that it?"

"It sure is." He walked the perimeter and found what he was looking for near the back. "Sandy, look here, boot prints go this way." He pointed up a narrow trail leading into the trees. "And look, two sets of bare footprints follow." He started up a narrow trail, anxious to find Nature.

Sandy hesitated. "Web, do we need to call someone and let them know about this?"

"Who am I going to call? Franklin?"

"As a matter of fact, yes. I don't like the idea of going after a killer without someone knowing it."

"Fuck 'em. That asshole can go to hell." He spun around and continued up the trail. He yelled over a shoulder, "You coming?"

Sandy sighed and ran after him, catching up in a few strides. "I hope we won't regret your stubbornness."

"We won't."

Twenty

The man paced around the inside of the cabin. Something was bothering him. Something felt out of sorts. He didn't know what it was or why. He just knew. He fiddled with the fire then moved to the window before returning to the fire. He fingered his penis while he walked. It was a nervous habit he had acquired over the years.

Nature gripped the straps holding her arms. The man had released the handcuffs and spread her extremities so he could lay on her more comfortably. The feel of the other girls ran through her. It helped her to remain quiet. It helped her to plot a way to get free. While the man slept last night, she became angry. Angry at what he had done, angry at how he took life so easily, as if it wasn't important. The angrier she became, the more determined she was to end his destructive spree.

The man walked over and sat beside her on the bed. His free hand reached up to finger her breast. Nature felt his evil ebb into her. Each time, it washed deeper into her soul, threatening to consume her. She still had a problem seeing his face when the visions of the girls overtook her. She wished it were the case now as he sat next to her, touching her with his soft caress. His outer appearance was handsome, by today's standard. The darkness inside made him ugly. Unable to stop herself, she flinched in disgust.

Sadness filled the man's eyes. He had felt her resistance the first time he showed her his pleasures, but hoped the One would come around. Unlike the other girls, she remained distant. Unlike

the others, his patience was growing thin. He wanted peace. He wanted the inner turmoil to go away. Her eyes were vacant when he tried to please her. They filled with hatred during the interims. He saw it, even if she didn't realize what she was doing. Maybe she was not the One after all. His finger circled her nipple while he thought. With a sigh, he crawled on top of her.

He kissed her taped lips. Wanting to savor her taste, he jerked the silver strip off. Her eyes widened and her breath rushed in as the shock of removal hit her. She recovered immediately. The man knew he was going to miss her. She was calm, unlike the others. She helped ease the restlessness for a short time. Unfortunately, it wasn't long enough. He felt it pacing in the background, ever-present. The restless beast always found a way back. He kissed her lips softly, inserting his tongue into her mouth. As gently as he kissed her, he inserted his erect penis into her.

Nature felt his body against hers as he disappeared deep within. The evil permeated into every pore. She arched her head sideways when the man moved his lips down to her neck. She gritted her teeth, forcing herself to not cry out with disgust. He started gliding in and out. The feeling was sickening. His hands roamed over her body. She wished he would die. But, then, so would she. Because of the remote location of the cabin, the likelihood of anyone finding her was zilch. Thus, she suffered through his gentle assault until he ejaculated in her.

The man lay there, kissing her, the muscles of his penis expanding and contracting as the semen exited. He wondered if he should keep her, but decided he did not want to waste any more time. He had to hunt for the One. He had to find her so the beast would go away. The decision made, he got up and started releasing her.

Nature saw him stand and undo the restraints holding her legs. She wondered what he was up to. While she watched, he moved to her arms. He helped her sit before retying her hands together, this time in front, not behind as before. Nature had been in the bed for two solid days, her extremities unable to move. The ability to do so now, was therefore reduced. When he helped her to her feet, she collapsed back onto the bed. Her legs tingled with the return of circulation. Her arms too. The man began to rub

them.

After a couple minutes of brisk rubbing, he assisted her to her feet once more. This time she managed to stay up. He slipped the collar back in place. It was removed when she lay restrained on the bed. Picking up the leash, he pulled her outside. He guided her to the left, onto a worn path. The sun was high in the sky; it gave no warmth to those beneath it. The air had a chill of the coming winter to it. It blanketed Nature's exposed skin, making goose bumps rise. She shivered. The man had his back toward her. He missed the shiver.

They walked into an open area. Nature stopped, causing the leash to go taunt between them. The man halted. He glanced over a shoulder. He saw the look of horror on Nature's face. He gave her a faint smile and tugged on the leash. She resisted. He tugged harder. She reached up with her hands and grabbed the leash while planting her heels in the soft ground. She wasn't concerned about whether it made the man angry or not, not with where he had taken her. Beyond the struggle lay an open pit. The man had brought her to meet the others.

His face became a mask of rage. He pulled on the leash so hard that Nature wasn't able to stay upright. She flipped over, landing hard on her left shoulder before rolling onto her back. In an instant, the man was on her. He straddled her, pinning her with the weight of his body. Nature twisted and tried to pivot under him. His fist hit her face with full force. She tried to block him with her arms but he grabbed them and held them out of the way. He hit her over and over. When he stopped, blood ran from her nose and split lip. Her eye started to swell. It matched the swelling on her cheeks and jaw.

The brutal attack seemed to excite the man. He was erect by the time he had her subdued. He moved backwards so he could lift her legs, making access to her easy, allowing one last ride before he set out. As he guided his penis toward her ass, he heard a scream.

Miranda leaped onto his back, wrapping her arm around his throat, pulling it tight with the other. The man fell away from Nature, struggling to get the surprisingly alive woman off. He grabbed at her arms, her face, at any part he managed to reach. She clung to him like a leech. Nature barely made out the com-

batants. Her head swam and the swelling made it difficult to see. Her ears worked fine, though.

"You only needed me! You had to ruin everything by bringing that bitch here. I could have satisfied you for years, but noooo; you had to ignore what you had and dip your wick elsewhere." Her loud words echoed across the area. "If I can't have you then no one can, especially some worthless slut who doesn't appreciate what you have to give!" She wrapped her legs around his waist and pulled her arm tighter around his neck.

The man brought his arm forward and slammed the elbow into Miranda's ribs. The woman let out a cry of pain. Her grip loosened. The man felt the change. He grabbed her wrist and gave it a wicked twist. Even through the numbing haze, Nature heard the pop. That pop seemed to energize her. It enabled her to get to her feet and run. She stumbled and fell many times because of the reduced vision caused by the swollen eye. The screams, which followed her down the path, ended abruptly. Nature knew Miranda had not cheated death this time. She picked up as much speed as her battered body would give.

The man released his grip on Miranda's head. He had managed to work his way behind her and, with a quick twist, broke her neck. This time, he made sure a pulse was absent. Nothing beat under his finger. Rising to his feet, he saw the other woman was gone. He wasn't concerned; he would find her quickly. Her trail was easy to see. He walked in a calm determined fashion after her.

Nature stumbled past the cabin. She turned her head in all directions, trying to locate the way out. Before she could find it, she heard a male voice echo through the trees.

"I'm coming for you. It's only a matter of time before I find you. You can't delay me from finding the One. Why not give in and embrace what you truly want."

The silence that followed was unnerving. She gave up on the path and ran into the trees. She could hide in their cover.

The man stood at the edge of the clearing and watched as the False One disappeared from view. He casually made his way across the open area and followed her. He smiled. The hunt and the final ride would be glorious.

Sandy and Web had been on the path for more than four hours. Others had branched from it but they remained on the main one, certain it would lead them to their destination. As the fifth hour was coming to a close, the trees parted to reveal a cabin. It was quaint. Both halted in their tracks. They dropped to the ground and waited. Nothing moved. No sound came from it. Web pulled his gun from its holster and advanced toward it, indicating for Sandy to wait until he checked it out.

He placed his back against the wall and listened. He still heard nothing. Moving toward the door, he slammed it open and darted inside, crouching low just in case. The place was unoccupied. Web saw the straps hanging by the bed, empty. His heart fell. Where were they? They had to be here somewhere. They had to be. Stepping back outside, he indicated for Sandy to come over. She was making her way to the cabin when a shout reached her. It was a male voice. It came from the left.

She faced the forest and listened. The voice sounded again. Web walked toward her. She darted toward the left edge of the small clearing. He ran after her. She pulled up short of the forest, trying to listen for which way to go before entering. Web met her, giving her a quizzical look. He hadn't heard the voice.

"What the he..."

Sandy cut him off with a frantic wave of her hand. He shut up. Off in the distance, he heard, "I'll find you...the others want to you to stay with them; they're lonely."

The hairs on the back of his neck stood. It was the voice of the killer, he was sure of it. He tried to hear more, but the voice never sounded again. Sandy started into the trees. He held her up, letting her know he was going to parallel her a few yards off to her right. She nodded her head. Separating, each stepped into the trees, heading toward where they thought the sound came from.

Nature ran as fast as she could. It seemed as though every tree branch grabbed her bare feet and body. They cut into her, leaving blood trails all over her. She stopped for a breather; the voice followed her. It sounded like it was right behind her. She bolted away from the tree and fell over a root sticking out of the

ground. Her ankle twisted and pain shot up her leg. Rising to her feet, she limped deeper into the forest. She was hopelessly lost.

The man saw Nature go down. He saw her rise and start to limp. He knew she was his, that she would be with the others soon. Then he could get back to finding the One. He was about to move from the protection of the overgrowth when a snap sounded close, on his left side. He lowered himself and waited. A slender woman with blonde hair appeared. She hesitated, glancing around before heading in the same direction as the False One. The man waited. He wanted her. She might be the One, and he wasn't going to lose the opportunity to find out.

Again, he almost moved when another noise sounded, this time on his right. A man appeared. He was carrying a gun. The man froze. He seethed at the intrusion. He had to find the False One and the other woman before they disappeared. He watched the intruder move in the same direction taken by the women. Gliding with the quiet of someone long accustomed to secrecy, he followed.

Web saw Sandy off to his left. She moved carefully, trying not to make too much noise. Occasionally a snap sounded, indicating she had stepped on something. He cringed every time he heard it. If he heard it, then the killer probably did also. He moved deeper into the thick growth, gun held ready.

Sandy kept her vision focused ahead. She thought she heard someone moving several times. Each time she looked, no one was there. As if reading her mind, a crashing noise sounded. Sandy caught a glimpse of movement through the trees. It looked like a person. She picked up speed. It might be Nature.

Web saw Sandy pick up speed, ignoring the fact that she was making a lot of noise. He heard the crashing that drew her attention; he moved faster. He didn't care about the noise either. If it was Nature, she would need them in a hurry, and that wasn't going to happen if they remained silent.

The man watched the others picked up their speed. He heard the False One as she crashed through the forest. He knew what they were following. He trailed them, silent as a snowflake falling from the sky. He kept a discreet distance between them. When the opportunity arose, he would know it. He would use it to end the interfering man's life, thus freeing himself to bring the False One to the others and to sample the other woman; the woman he hoped was the One.

Nature heard the man running after her. It sounded weird, like it was coming from two different directions. She tried to increase the speed her body gave. The wounded ankle reminded her of its displeasure at such an idea. It finally rebelled by buckling out from under her. She sprawled face first onto some leaves. They made her landing less painful. She rolled over, ready to fend off her attacker, knowing she would loose in the end. She braced for the inevitable struggle just as Sandy flew into sight. She practically sobbed with relief.

"Nature! My god, Nature!" The secretary ran up to her friend and folded her arms around the scratched and bruised body. Her skin was so cold, and her face...her face was a battered mess. "Thank god we found you."

Nature hugged Sandy tight, unable to believe the younger woman was really here. It felt too much like a dream, a dream filled with many nightmares. She was afraid that if she let go, her friend would disappear. That was something she couldn't handle under the current circumstances. She bawled like a baby who thought her mother abandoned her. Suddenly, she looked up, frantic. She remembered where they were and who was after her. The man was here, somewhere. He might get Sandy. That was not an option. She would not see her friend used in such a horrible way.

"Sandy, we have to get out of here...*now*. He's still here. He might get you."

"That won't happen. Web won't let it." Sandy pulled Nature's head against her body, trying to sooth the distraught woman.

"Web? He's here?" Nature pulled away again. She looked around, trying to see every direction at once.

At the mention of his name, Web appeared, out of breath from the run. His eyes focused on the woman in Sandy's arms. His heart soared. "Nature."

Nature peered at Web. His concerns, fear, and love for her was evident, even with her diminished eyesight. A look of wonder creased her swollen face, the hope inside her rose to new levels. Maybe he still wanted her, even after what had happened. Maybe he saw her as the woman he loved and not as a soiled thing. The happiness inside showed on her face. One of horror replaced it when she saw the man appear behind him. She struggled to get free of Sandy. She tried to shout out a warning; her throat constricted with fear.

Web saw the change in Nature and started to turn. He was partway around when a man, presumably the killer, jumped at him, knocking the gun out of his hand. With the quickness of a snake, the man threw a fist. It landed on the left side of Web's face. He spun around, but did not fall. He tried to throw himself at the killer, to land a few hits of his own. Each time, the man wasn't there. He was too quick. Web felt another blow land on the same spot as the previous one. A foot kicked him in his stomach. It was followed by a foot in his face He landed hard on his back. Dark circles danced in front of him. He struggled to get up, trying to get to his feet before the killer attacked again. He made it up to his elbows before the shot rang out.

A searing pain hit his shoulder area. Another shot echoed almost immediately afterwards. More pain started close to the original spot. It became hard to breath. He rationalized that he had a collapsed lung. But, rationalization was beyond him at the moment. He main thought was on helping Nature. He tried to see where the man holding the gun stood. He fell back, unable to hold himself upright.

Sandy couldn't believe Web was shot. She watched the spread of blood slowly change the color of his shirt. Anger filled her every fiber. This was the first time that Nature allowed herself to love, since Brad, and she was not about to let that end...not at the hands of this shithead. She bolted across the space and tackled the man before he could fire another round. They landed in a tumble of arms and legs, the gun still gripped in his hand. Even though he was taken by surprise, he recovered quickly, too

quickly for Sandy to take advantage of it. He kicked her off and jumped to his feet before she could get to hers. He trained the gun at her head.

Before he pulled the trigger, a shot rang out from another direction. Sandy saw the man spin around. He somehow stayed on his feet. Another shot sounded. He finally fell. Blood poured from two holes, one in the upper abdomen and the other just to the left of his breastbone, close to where the heart was located. She was shocked to see the man trying to lift the gun. In answer, a third shot rang out. The man's head slammed onto the ground. This time, there was no getting up. This time, a gaping hole opened up his forehead.

Nature watched the man go down. She didn't care; her attention was on Web. Blood covered the left side of his shirt. It spread to the other side before she managed to get to her feet. Her ankle screamed at her for using it. Its swelling matched her face. She ignored it, she had to get to Web; she had to see if he was still alive. She managed to make it to his side before her ankle quit supporting her all together.

She pressed down on the wounds, trying to reduce the flow coming from them. Tears mingled with the red. Web moaned with pain. He opened his eyes and gave her a weak smile. She smiled back. He was alive. She hoped he was stubborn enough to stay that way. He had to. She needed him.

Web tried to speak when he saw Nature next to him: her bruised and battered body, her swollen face, and her tears. He wanted to console her, to let her know it was all right. But the effort needed to speak was too hard, there didn't seem to be enough air. In addition, he felt so weak. All he could give her was a smile. He couldn't even raise his arm to touch her beautiful face.

The smile faded as intense pain wracked through him. She became harder to see through the fog surrounding everything. He heard her whisper in his ear. It caused him to smile again. The words that echoed through his mind as he slipped from the world of consciousness were, "I love you.", "You better not leave me," and "I need you so much."

Twenty-One

When she awoke, Nature lay on her side, under soft sheets, in a warm room. At first, she didn't remember how she had gotten there. Slowly the memories returned. She remembered being kidnapped from her home by the man who had killed so many. She remembered the tortuous ride to his cabin and the events that unfolded there. She remembered him killing Miranda and her getting away. Then she remembered Sandy, and Web, and seeing him collapse, shot by the man. After that, the events were a blur. She rolled onto her back and sat up. The room was empty. She noticed a chair next to her bed.

The door opened and Sandy entered, burdened with a tray overloaded with food. "Hey, good to see you finally awake sleepyhead. I brought lunch. The food here is great, but it's not like the stuff at home. It's passable though." She plopped the tray onto the stand tucked in the corner. Moving the overbed table in front of Nature, she put a cup of tea and a bowl of chicken noodle soup in front of her. "Eat up. It's been a couple of days since you ate and you need to get your strength back."

The smell coming from the soup was nauseating. The tea smelled wonderful, though. She picked it up with shaky hands and brought it to her mouth. She sipped at the dark contents. A stinging inside her mouth caused her to grimace. She reached up and felt the split lip, butterfly strips held it together. She moved her hand to her eye. The swelling was gone but it was tender to the touch. She dropped her hand back to the table. Tears welled in the corners. They ran down to fall onto her hospital gown.

Sandy was about to take a bite of her hamburger when she saw the tears. She lowered it and asked, "Are you in pain? Do you want me to get the nurse?"

Nature shook her head back and forth. Wiping the tears off, she looked up at her secretary. "He's dead, isn't he?"

"Who? The man who took you? You bet your ass he's dead."

"No..." Nature maintained eye contact. "Web."

Sandy returned the burger to the plate and sat on the bed next to Nature. "Aww, honey, he's alive. He's in the ICU." She comforted her, brushing her hair off her face. "He was airvaced to this hospital and given emergency surgery. They managed to patch him up, and, several pints of the red stuff later, he's still with us. He's unconscious though."

Her words slowly sank in. She was glad to hear them, even though she wasn't sure if she believed them. "Who saved us?"

"Would you believe...Franklin."

Nature frowned. "Franklin?"

"The detective from Atlanta. He caused a lot of grief while we were hunting for you, but we managed to find you anyways. In the end, he made up for his bungling. He shot the asshole that kidnapped you."

"I have to see Web." She shoved the covers out of the way. She had to make sure he was really alive.

Sandy stood, blocking her way. "You're not strong enough yet. You need to rest."

"If you don't get out of my way, I'll knock the crap out of you."

"Go ahead...try it."

Nature pushed on Sandy's shoulder while throwing her legs closer to the side of the bed. The woman barely moved. Her left ankle throbbed when it hit the floor. It was wrapped in a soft cast. Nature tried to stand. The effort left her winded. She flopped into Sandy's hovering arms. They were the only things preventing her from going all the way down. Sandy hit the call button.

"Can I help you?" The voice said from the call box located on the wall.

"The patient is overly anxious and needs something to calm her down. She's trying to get out of bed."

Nature pleaded with her, "I need to see Web...I need to see if he's okay."

Sandy held her upright, waiting for assistance. "Not until you're stronger."

"We'll send the nurse right in." The box squelched when the person speaking turned it off.

The door opened and a nurse walked in with several syringes in her hand. The nursing assistant walked in behind her and helped Sandy put Nature back into the bed. She pulled the lower rail up to prevent any further attempts to escape and flicked on the bed exit alarm. Nature did not have the energy to resist. Sweat covered her brow and her muscles shook from her exertion. They felt like they were made of jello.

She watched as the nurse spun the syringe onto the IV site in her arm and pushed the clear liquid into the vein. She glared at everyone in the room. Her eyelids became as heavy as lead weights. They lowered. She snapped them open. The weights exerted their pressure once more, forcing the lids shut. Again, she snapped them open.

"Don't fight it," Sandy said. "I'll keep him safe until you can take over." She grabbed Natures hand.

Nature felt her sincerity through the grip. She knew Sandy would keep her promise. She disappeared into the drug-induced land of slumber, uttering one word before she slept, "Web."

Three days later, she was able to get out of the bed and into a wheelchair with minimal assistance. Sandy pushed her into the hall, toward the elevators. While they waited for its arrival, the secretary hummed a tune under her breath, her foot bouncing to the tempo. Nature smiled up at her, a finger tapping in response. It was a song from her favorite band. She returned her attention to the elevator when a ding sounded. The wheelchair rolled over the track for the doors and Nature pushed the button for the fourth floor. They were heading to the intensive care unit.

Nature squirmed in the seat. She was anxious...anxious to see Web. This was her first visit since they arrived at the hospital six days ago. Sandy warned her that he still had many IV's hooked up to him and that he had a chest tube. At least he was off the ventilator and breathing fine on his own.

Sandy already had clearance to enter. She pushed the auto

door opener and waited until they swung out of the way. She turned to the right after they were past them. Solid walls partitioned the rooms, but glass faced toward the walkway, allowing the staff to watch the patients inside without difficulty. Nature saw an old woman, her eyes closed, her family hovering at her bedside, and a middle-aged man with tubes coming out of every visible opening. Then, a room with the curtains drawn came into view. She heard voices inside. Several females giggled. As they pulled up to the entrance, the curtains opened.

Nature saw a couple of staff walking around. One was pouring out a pan of water. They smiled when they saw her. "We knew you were coming so had to spiff him up a bit." Stepping out of the way, the tech asked, "What do you think?"

Her heart nearly flew out of her chest. Web looked at her with his beautiful hazel eyes. He gave her a weak smile and reached for her. Before Sandy was able to push her in, Nature rolled herself to his side.

"Hey beautiful" The words sounded hoarse because the breathing tube had irritated his vocal cords. They were still adjusting to the fact that the tube was out of the way, that they were allowed to work now.

Tears welled in her eyes. She took his hand in hers and pulled it against her face. "I love you."

"Love you too." He stroked the side of her face with a finger, careful not to rub the bruises too hard. "Never going to leave you again. Hope you can handle that."

"You betcha, mister." She smiled and the tears overflowed onto his hand.

Sandy and the staff discreetly exited, leaving the two alone. No one had dry eyes when they left.

Three and a half weeks later, Nature sat in an easy chair in the study, the one with the fireplace. A blanket covered her lap to ward off the afternoon chill; she held a cup of hot tea in her hands. Glancing beside her, she saw Web tip a cup of coffee toward his lips. Her gaze returned to the dancing flames behind the protective screen. The fire reflected throughout the room, making it feel alive. They were waiting

Sandy poked her head in. "They're here." She disappeared back the way she came.

Nature set the cup down and removed the blanket. She draped it over the back of her chair before moving behind the one holding Web. Grabbing the handles, she wheeled him to the other study, the one for visitors and company. He leaned forward, eager to see the occupants. Web continued to be dependent on the wheelchair, but rigorous physical therapy helped him get stronger every day. He was able to walk from the front door to the kitchen before he had to sit and catch his breath.

The pair entered to find several people inside. The new sheriff for Garfield County rose to his feet. He twirled his hat in his hand. It was Officer Spangle, from Brevard County, now Sheriff Spangle. When he came to ask for Nature's help with a case, several weeks ago, he was so taken by the beauty of the area, he decided to move here. He won the election held after the county discovered the current sheriff could no longer continue at his position. He moved quickly to Web, shaking the extended hand with vigor. He glanced at the woman behind him.

"Mrs. Kranderson...I mean...Mrs. Westerly." He tipped his head instead of shaking her hand.

"Nature, please." She reached for his hand.

He took it, grinning with embarrassment over not calling her by her correct name. "Dan, please call me Dan."

"Dan. Thank you for coming out today. I know how busy you are, getting to know the new job and all."

"Well, I do have to get to know the people I'll be working with. *All* of them." He gave her a crooked smile.

"Dear...we have people waiting." Web nodded toward the man in a pinstriped suit standing patiently near the French doors. They could see men in dark suits walking the perimeter beyond the glass. Dark sunglasses hid their eyes.

Nature nodded her head. "Senator Enesco."

"Mrs. Westerly, Mr. Westerly." The Senator smiled as he said her new name. "I'm glad to see the two of you doing so well." Looking at the woman standing behind the wheelchair and the man in it, he closed the distance between them. The smile faded as he continued. "I want to apologize for what my son, Jonah, did. He wasn't himself."

Nature gripped the handles harder than necessary. The mention of the kidnapped son brought back the memories of him as a child, when he was brutally assaulted, before she found him and returned him to his family. It also resurfaced the memories of him as a man...the man, the one who kidnapped her and almost killed her and Wes in the process. She had not recognized him because of the changes that occurred with healing and aging.

She guided Web next to the couch. Once his chair was situated, she sat down, indicating for the others to do the same. The Senator sat in the chair across from them. Sheriff Spangle moved to the French doors and peered outside. Nature smiled. The way he stood reminded her of a younger Web. Senator Enesco started talking. She forced her attention back onto him.

"I met Francine before I started into politics. She already had Jonah from a previous marriage. He was three. I felt sorry for the lad; he seemed so shy, so withdrawn, even at that age." He leaned forward, resting his elbows on his knees and laced his fingers together.

"I wasn't his father, but I tried to be. Throughout the years I was married to his mother, I took him camping and fishing and did all the things a dad did with his son. But, when my political career took off, our outings became less and less. The kidnapping several years later didn't help matters. When he was returned to us," he gave Nature a half smile, which faded as he continued, "he always clung to his mother.

I thought it was because of the brutal treatment given by the kidnappers." The Senator's voice broke as he remembered the boy's bruised and swollen face, the battered body, the charges of sexual misconduct. "I never suspected it was because of Francine. Little did I know she had already damaged him beyond any chance of recovery, that the kidnapping would have little effect on him. Little did I know she was already too far gone herself. She hid it so well."

He raised his eyes to meet the couple watching him. "When I found out how sick the boy was, I insisted on counseling. For years, we bounced from one psychiatrist to another, with the same results. I kept this fact from the papers. I wanted to spare the boy more public shame. Finally, when nothing seemed to be working, I insisted he be institutionalized. His mother wouldn't

hear of it. She saw nothing wrong with him. Since I hadn't adopted him when we married, I had no say in the matter. I decided it was time to leave. I couldn't stay where I wasn't wanted. Jonah was eleven when I divorced his mother."

"I heard about the mutilation of animals and the case from eight years ago, the one where the girl was raped and killed. I didn't believe it was him. I couldn't," the Senator continued. "But after he moved from the area, the killings stopped. It seemed like too much of a coincidence."

"Why didn't you contact the police?" Web asked. His voice still had some of the hoarseness from the hospital stay. Nature saw his posture stiffen with anger.

Enesco sighed. "I don't know. I guess I couldn't believe that that quiet shy little boy could do those kinds of violent acts." He sat back. "His mother moved a lot and I lost track of them. I occasionally heard about them from other people. But, when I found my current wife, Gene, I quit looking. I had a new family and my political career to worry about. I didn't want something from my past to come back and bite me in the ass."

"How do they feel?"

"What?"

"The bite marks covering your ass."

Standing, the senator clasped his hands behind his back and paced around the chair to the area behind it. "I said I was sorry. If I could make it all go away, I would."

"That doesn't help the ones he killed, or almost killed...now does it." Web was glad he was still dependent on the chair. If he'd been able to, he would have crossed the room and knocked the shit out of him, thus getting himself into deep trouble. He grabbed Nature's hand and held it tight. She squeezed it in understanding.

"No...it doesn't." His eyes diverted toward the floor. "You know," he paused, "I learned his mother died at his hands. He did the very same thing to her; he killed her while having sex, making her suffer a long time before she died. Ironic isn't it?" A tense silence followed his statement.

Nature broke the silence. She rose to her feet and extended a hand toward the older man. "Thank you for coming, Senator. I know how uncomfortable this must be."

Enesco came around the chair and gripped her hand in his.

"I'm sorry for your suffering. If I can ever do anything for you, let me know, okay?" He released her and walked to the glass doors. He halted next to them and added, "If you're ever in California, come by and see us. Gene would love to meet you." He exited before she had a chance to reply.

"Nature. Web. See you soon." Sheriff Spangle put his hat on and followed the senator out.

Web turned on her the moment they were alone. "What did you do that for?"

Nature walked to the side of the wheelchair and squat down. "Web, he's suffered enough. The media's having a field day with this. They're accusing him of knowing about it all along and doing nothing. All because the killer was family at one time."

"Well...he just admitted that."

"No, Web...he said he suspected. One can't be put away for suspicion alone."

"But..."

"But nothing!" She stood and placed her hands on her hips in irritation. "It's over...move on. Don't bring yourself down by dwelling on something you can't do anything about!"

Web stared at her, shocked. He chuckled, "Man, you and Sandy are two peas in a pod. I don't know how I'm going to make it with the both of you giving me verbal whiplash."

Mollified, Nature moved to the back of the chair. She guided Web into the hall and passed through the kitchen, heading outside to the patio. Sandy joined them.

"Feel better?"

"Now that you mention it...yeah." Nature smiled.

Web glanced up at her, "Speak for yourself, woman. I won't feel any better until this cavernous pit called a stomach is filled.

Sandy grinned. She went inside and brought three plates out to the table. Sandwiches and chips covered each. After setting them down, she sat opposite Nature, Web parked between them. All three stared at the rays of the setting sun, admiring the beautiful scenery, eating the food in quiet contentment. No one wanted to disturb the wondrous display with idle chatter. Sandy took the dishes inside to get drinks when everything was gone. The phone rang while she was there. She picked it up, listened, and then began to write information on a notepad next to the phone.

Web looked over his shoulder and groaned. With the Sheriff's department, he knew what he was getting into. With this pair, he had no idea what would happen from one moment to the next. It was okay though, as long as he had Nature at his side, he could put up with anything. He turned his head toward her. "Love you, wife."

"Love you back, husband." The two had married while they were still in the hospital, with Sandy and, of all people, Franklin, as the ones giving them away. They had not wanted to wait until they returned to Montana.

Sandy joined them with the drinks. She sat down to finish watching the sunset, a folded piece of paper clutched in her hand. Nature lifted an eyebrow in question. Her secretary ignored her.

The coming darkness replaced the shades of pink and crickets sang their welcome before Sandy rose to her feet. She slipped her chair under the table and went inside. Nature jumped to her feet. In her haste to go after her secretary, she forgot about pushing him inside. He started to say something but the door slammed shut, cutting him off. He gawked in disbelief.

Within seconds, she returned, her face red with embarrassment. She propped the door open and nearly pitched him out of the chair trying to get him inside quickly. He grabbed the wheels and stopped her forward momentum before she killed him. "It's okay. I'll make it. Go on ahead. I'll be there in a few."

"Are you sure?"

"I'm sure. Now get. Sandy's waiting for you."

She pecked him on his cheek and darted down the hall to the study with the fireplace. He watched as she disappeared with a wave. It was good to see her so alive, especially after looking dead for so long. It also felt good to have a family again, even if it involved being married to an unpredictable psychic and her strong willed secretary.

Web rolled down the hallway and arrived in time to hear Sandy talk about the next case: a case involving a missing man with Alzheimer's, and the family that wanted him back. He shook his head, closing the door behind him with a smile.

About the Author

Janet started writing while trying to help her son find his own words. Since then, the passion for writing has taken over. When not working as a registered nurse, she is pounding on the keyboard to her computer creating new worlds. On the other hand, she could be found sitting on the back porch enjoying the gentle breeze, wreaking havoc on her laptop. Her genre includes sci-fi, horror/thriller, and many others yet to leap off her fingers. Janet resides in the warm state of Florida with her son, furry friends known as cats, and a couple of neurotic dogs. To learn what other books are available from this author check out www.janetdurbin.com.

"I love to entertain the reader. I don't like to drag the story on with a bunch of pondering over lost things, or things not done. Or repeat an idea several times within a few pages. I like to keep the story flowing, to keep the reader wanting to see what's happening next. When I hear people say, 'You're going to go places with this book', 'I loved it', 'When is the sequel coming? I can't wait for the next book,' and so many other nice statements, I feel I've done my job. I've entertained them."